DEATH'S AUTOGRAPH

DEATH'S AUTOGRAPH

Marianne Macdonald

Hodder & Stoughton

First published in Great Britain in 1996
by Hodder and Stoughton
A division of Hodder Headline PLC

10 9 8 7 6 5 4 3 2 1

British Library Cataloguing in Publication Data

Macdonald, Marianne
Death's Autograph
1. English fiction - 20th century
I. Title
823.9'14 [F]

ISBN 0 340 67153 X

Typeset by Avon Dataset Ltd, Bidford-on-Avon, Warks

Printed and bound in Great Britain by
Mackays of Chatham PLC, Chatham, Kent

Hodder and Stoughton
A division of Hodder Headline PLC
338 Euston Road
London NW1 3BH

For
ABSENT FRIENDS
'What thou lov'st well shall not be reft from thee . . .'

ACKNOWLEDGMENTS

I would like to thank Eric Korn (M.E. Korn Books) and Detective Inspector John Crease of Islington Police Station for their kind advice on a number of technical matters of various kinds. The story of William Henry Ireland is recounted in John Mair's book *The Fourth Forger* (1938) and Bernard Grebanier's *The Great Shakespeare Forgery* (1966). Finally, thanks to Alex Wagstaff for reading the proofs and liking the book.

CONTENTS

1

A Wink in the Dark

I have my own personal nightmare. It's dark, of course, and I'm lost in the corridors of a strange building. The walls are lined with doors: all of them are shut. My mother is waiting for me somewhere, and I creep from one door to the next listening for her voice, but all the unseen rooms are silent.

It happened like that once, when I was four or five and went with her to visit a friend. Obviously she opened a door and found me, because here I am, thirty-two years old, complete with my own name and history. But being lost in the dark comes back in nightmares now and then.

I wasn't really lost that April night – I knew that my ancient Volvo estate was heading eastward in the tangle of minor roads between Banbury and Milton Keynes, with the M1 motorway which was my route home somewhere ahead. Nameless villages and invisible hills lurked in rain-swept darkness beyond the headlights, but this unknown secondary road would lead me sooner or later to the motorway, which in due course would bring me down perfectly safely into London. So although I didn't know which stretch of wet and empty road I was following at that moment, I could reassure myself. No problem. Nothing important enough to distract me from the creeping certainty that I'd spent the evening making a fool of myself.

Dido Hoare, the world-famous-soft-touch antiquarian book dealer.

The back of the estate car was crammed to the roof with slightly damp cardboard boxes. They held the collection of books I'd bought that evening, with great difficulty, from the optimistically greedy heirs of a retired Oxford University professor of English literature, recently buried but once known to (and thoroughly disliked by) my father, Barnabas.

In order to clinch this deal I'd had to close the shop early, drive the eighty miles from north London to Banbury through slashing rain, and spend hours persuading the family that the dead man's shelves held no volumes that could possibly be expected to make them rich beyond the dreams of avarice.

There's nothing unusual in this. As I learned several painful years ago, most people believe that any book more than ninety years old is worth hundreds of pounds. Unless of course it happens to be bound in rotting leather, in which case naturally you multiply that figure by ten. Nineteenth-century Bibles printed in their hundreds of thousands, yellowed late editions of Tennyson's collected poems, volumes of sermons by eighteenth-century preachers who on a good Sunday reduced whole congregations to slumber: these are the book dealer's horrors.

There was a time, BD of course, when I used to think that kind of thing myself. The way history is divided into BC and AD, my life is 'BD' – before Davey – and after.

'Who taught me everything I know,' I heard myself say aloud to the smeared windscreen. Even now, the bitterness in my own voice shocked me. There were things about my ex-husband that I couldn't bear to recall.

After the process of persuasion, they (that is, the sorrowing heirs) had announced, 'Now, we'll just pick out a few things for ourselves.' They had seemed injured when I explained that in this case I (the honest purchaser) would actually have to reduce the price I'd offered. After four years in the trade, it still bothers me that people can't accept me as just a fairly successful, reasonably straight, possibly well-meaning antiquarian book dealer – not a feather-brained bimbo or a harpy gnawing the bones of widows and orphans.

Rather a harpy than a fool, damn it.

It had taken three hours and more patience than I knew I had before they condescended to accept my money. Then they wanted cash. The daughter-in-law had counted it slowly. Then they'd left me to do all the packing and loading. Fair enough, but now it was the middle of the night and I was still miles from home, my shoes were soaked (probably ruined), there was an ache in my shoulders, and I was slowly realizing that I couldn't remember one single volume that I really wanted to own. The eyes that stared coldly back at me from the driving mirror told me I'd been a soft touch.

I *know*.

You know? Then why did you do it?

Because I couldn't bear to go all that way for nothing.

So you bought a load of rubbish.

It's not rubbish, it's perfectly good, solid stock. People want that kind of stuff all the time.

You gave them at least a hundred too much – at LEAST.

They were such awful people.

Oh, I see. *That's* all right, then.

Shut it.

And then you missed the turning to the M40.

I was tired.

And couldn't be bothered to turn around. So now you're in the middle of nowhere. What happens if the car breaks down? Because she was due for servicing last month.

I couldn't afford it. Anyway, this car is a lady. She never lets me down.

In my rear-view mirror suddenly there was a pair of dipped headlights about three hundred feet behind. One winked out for a moment, then reappeared. A lecherous wink aimed at my car's stately rear end? When I'm tired, my sense of humour plays tricks. It happened again a few minutes later. I felt for the music tapes and pushed one at random into the stereo. The opening bars of the Trout Quintet flowed gently into the darkness.

The wipers thumped. Beyond them, the Volvo's lights glimmered faintly on hedge and ditch as the road twisted sharply. Some of the boxes behind me whispered and shifted. When I glanced into the mirror again the road was dark, but after a moment the headlights were there again, further back.

You, back there – time you were home and in bed. (Time, more than time, for me too. How long – another hour, with luck?) I was thinking with unusual longing about my flat above the shop. Oh, damn – I'd forgotten to feed Mr Spock before I left. Something else to reproach myself for.

Davey had named him. Why do you call your cat 'Mr Spock'? Because he has pointy ears, of course.

I shook myself.

Feed the cat. Then a drink. Warmth . . . a bath, maybe . . . The books

3

could stay in the car until morning. Not even in Islington would anyone be desperate enough to break into the old Volvo for whatever rubbish could be found in such tattered boxes.

Still, remember to set the car's alarm.

At some point, the music had stopped. I yawned, caught myself, rolled down the window. Wet air slapped my face.

Something flashed in the hedge ahead. My lights picked out a reflecting sign, a name – but the car had passed before I could read it. I was in a dim village street. The dashboard clock hadn't worked for months, but when I snatched a glance at the luminous dial of my watch, it was after two. I let my speed rise and then had to brake when something small ran across the road almost under the wheels.

The winking light was back. The other car was probably heading for the motorway too. It couldn't be far away. And then, as the Volvo reached the summit of a shallow rise, the idea slid into my mind that I was being followed.

Pull yourself together, Dido!

I pulled, but my eyes slid back to the rear-view mirror for a moment too long, and my tyres rumbled on the broken verge. The thought of upending in a wet ditch under a rain of old books made me more careful.

But I wanted to find out. I raised my right foot gradually so that my speed drifted down to a sedate forty . . . thirty-five . . . and the headlights closed in behind me.

Then, after all, fell back.

Perhaps they didn't want to risk overtaking on this narrow road? I shifted down, and the acceleration pressed me against the seat. At fifty-five I changed into top gear. The Volvo hurtled through another unlit village. The headlights kept their distance.

The Volvo was a heavy metal box, solid and strong, safe. So whatever happens, I told myself, I won't stop. Not out here, not alone . . .

But there was light – an unexpected loom of brightness ahead. Perhaps an all-night filling station? Or only some lights left on by mistake? The black bulk of a building masked the source, but at the last moment I saw the lighted sign and a forecourt with a solitary figure in a glass kiosk. I twisted the wheel, swerving too sharply and braking hard between the rows of pumps. I glimpsed a startled face in the kiosk before I turned and looked back at the road in time to see a white car, one of the thousands of little, over-powered hatchbacks that were everywhere that year, flash past.

There had been no tell-tale brake lights. I switched off my engine and sat in the abrupt silence, listening to my heart grow quieter.

It was an effort to open the door and crawl out; I'd stiffened up on my slow journey, and I fumbled the line and splashed fuel as I topped up the Volvo's tank. The cashier, an old man with a white, night face, stopped staring at me when I went to pay. He bent his eyes on his greasy magazine.

I said, 'Is there a telephone?' Of course there was – in some office in the darkened garage building.

He slammed the cash drawer and pointed back west. 'Box half a mile up the road.'

But anyway, who could I phone at two thirty in the morning? Not Barnabas, the way things were now. Or my sister Pat, asleep beside her husband in their St Albans house not so far away. (I could almost hear her big, outraged voice saying, 'For God's sake, Dido, it's the middle of the night and you've woken the boys . . .') The police, to explain, 'There was a car. I thought they were following me. They've gone now . . .'?

Once I would have phoned Davey, just for the pleasure of speaking to him.

I gritted my teeth and shut myself into the Volvo. While I was making sure that the doors were all locked, I wondered why my thoughts were so out of control tonight. Usually I go for days without thinking about Davey. And I hadn't even asked the old man how far it was to the motorway. But then knowing wouldn't bring it any closer.

I looked again at the door catches and caught myself at it. Damn it, what was wrong with me? I was so tired that I wanted to put my head down on the steering wheel and howl. If the Volvo broke down. There was a woman, that last winter, who broke down on a motorway and somebody . . . They hadn't caught him. I listened to the engine's mutter. It seemed normal enough.

I had almost passed it before I noticed the pale shape waiting under a hedge. They must have been sitting with their engine running. In the mirror I saw the headlights come on.

Just playing games. Don't let yourself be scared. Be angry! Two can play games, shit-head . . . I clutched at a feeling of outrage so that it couldn't escape and pressed down the accelerator, waiting and being angry.

Safe in the middle of another of the dead villages with the white car fifty feet behind, I braked. The lights behind jinked and fell back even as I was shifting down and up again, driving now the way Davey had taught me, watching the broken white line in the middle of the road, gluing the offside front wheel to it, holding the heavy car steady on the straight and then braking and skidding and accelerating through the curves.

The other car was lighter and faster. Brightness filled the back of the Volvo and the headlights themselves grew closer and then vanished because they were so close – two or three feet of nerve-wracking space between our bumpers. There was no time or space to be frightened. The white car was light and quick, but the Volvo was a solid old monster, its rear end ballasted by half a ton of books. I stopped thinking, gripped the wheel and braked hard. But after all something in my head didn't believe that I'd decided to do it, and I felt my own flicker of hesitation. Nice girls don't try to smash up other people's cars. Almost before the Volvo's brakes bit, the other car was skidding away and I was changing up through the gears again. At eighty, I looked into the mirror. Now there was only a single headlight, perhaps a quarter of a mile back. The wink had been abolished. It felt almost like a small victory.

The darkness had changed. Not dawn, but something pale stretched across my horizon: the haze of motorway lights.

I didn't notice when the white car came back, and even when I noticed, it was as though I was awake again and could ignore it. The blue motorway signs slid past. A quarter of a mile to the slip road . . .

They pulled out, driving beside me on the wrong side of the road. Not trying to overtake. The road ahead was empty. I dragged my imagination away from the image of crumpling metal. I thought I wouldn't give them the satisfaction of noticing them, but it was impossible not to turn my head. Their dashboard lights touched two shapes, two pale faces turned towards me. My fingers were clamped to the steering wheel.

They cut in, braked insanely close. My own tactics. My body took over, braked, felt the engine jerk and die, heard the boxes shift. The car felt airless and the ignition had frozen. Time stopped.

Five yards away, the white car went dark. In the instant when nothing moved, my eyes had time to see that they had a comic sticker on their back window. In the glow from my headlights I read it as carefully as though it contained essential information: CAUTION – MOTHER-IN-LAW IN BOOT. I wondered through my astonishment that this was really happening, wondered what this strangely independent body of mine would do when they got out of their car.

I'd been trying to turn the ignition key the wrong way. I reversed it and the engine caught and as it did the white car moved. They didn't turn their lights on until they were two hundred yards down the road. It was then of course that I remembered that I ought to have taken their number.

I sat with the engine running until I'd almost stopped shaking. Then I turned the Volvo sedately on to the motorway.

Even at this hour the London-bound traffic was heavy. Safety in numbers, but I couldn't stop looking for the white hatchback, because now that it was over the anger came back: I wanted to see them crash, see them hurtling through the side barriers, crumpling, burning. (Just watch the road, Dido. Steer the car and get a hold of yourself before you do some hurtling of your own.)

It had turned cold. I switched on the heater and filled my lungs with warm, stinking air. By the end of the motorway, I'd stopped shivering.

It was an easy run through the northern suburbs and on down the Holloway Road. At Highbury Corner a white car ahead of me shot off toward Barnsbury, and I was so distracted that the Volvo's wheels banged the kerb.

Even in the early hours, Upper Street is full of people, ordinary people going to the all-night supermarket or walking home. The two from that winking car could easily be there. Anywhere. Any time. You could go crazy thinking about it. I took a grip and told myself that it had been a nasty experience, casual and unlucky. Just somebody having a perverted joke. *Hey, I was coming home last night late and there was this woman driver creeping along the back road at about five em pee aitch* . . . Nothing had happened. I was already beginning to doubt the whole business. They could have been kids out partying, having a laugh, showing off. I'd jumped to conclusions. Anyway, it was over and no real harm done: not as bad as being hit by a drunken driver and left bleeding or dead. It's a dangerous world, but most of the time you just have to live with it because there isn't really any choice.

There was kerb space just in front of my door, and I jammed the Volvo into it with a sigh of relief and exhaustion. At least the unloading wouldn't be too bad. And now I'd give myself a good big cognac, and feed the cat, and sleep. Suddenly every muscle hurt. Even so, I sat for a moment and looked up and down the street before I could make myself get out and cross to my own door. At least the rain had stopped.

2

A Nod in Daylight

Something nearby was cheeping like a demented chicken. I hauled myself out of sleep and managed to summon up enough willpower to open one eye. The noise was coming from beside the bed. I fumbled the alarm clock silent. The effort left me awake but without any immediate desire to move.

A warm weight landed on my chest and head-butted my chin; Mr Spock had arrived to enquire whether I was alive. I can recognize a losing battle as well as anyone; rolling out from under cat and duvet, I prepared to come to terms with Friday. At that point I remembered the boxes waiting in the car.

'If you were worth your kittymunch, you'd unload for me,' I told my ginger tormentor. Ignoring the suggestion, Spock moved briskly to the windowsill and began to comment on the weather.

Coffee first.

My flat is the floor above the bookshop: the top floor of what had once been a small Georgian terraced cottage. The sitting room stretches across the front of the building; my bedroom, and the room that had been divided into a small kitchen and an even smaller bathroom, took up the rest of the floor space. It's what estate agents call 'cosy', meaning small, but it suits me. There's something light and shapely in the proportions of the rooms and the floor-to-ceiling sash windows across the front wall of the sitting room. I'd furnished it – Davey and I had furnished it – with early-nineteenth-century pieces that we'd found cheaply one by one in the little antique shops around Camden Passage, and covered the walls with original prints and a few pretty oil landscapes that we'd come across in the same places, and they also suit me. At least, I haven't changed anything in the past two years, so they must do.

Even in my rough condition, I managed to stagger into the kitchen and grind the last of the coffee beans. While the kettle was boiling, I fed Spock – though as I used the tin opener I was asking myself why I'd ever agreed to act as a servant to an orange-striped tyrant – and pulled on an old jogging suit and trainers. It's a wise fashion choice when you are going to shift stock, because old books are the dirtiest things in polite society. I allowed myself my first coffee of the day, let the cat out the kitchen window on to the flat roof of the ground-floor extension which is the doorway to his back-yard hunting grounds, pocketed my keys, and dragged myself downstairs.

Unfortunately, nobody had stolen either my car or its contents, so I spent the next forty minutes moving heavy boxes from kerb to shop, then through the shop into the back room. Normally when I'm shifting some lot of books I've just bought, I keep stopping to look at things, because there's always the chance of something strange or curious or valuable. It's like a private treasure hunt. Not today. The books were part of the bad feeling that belonged to the night before.

I wasn't going to let myself think about the night before.

The car was empty by ten o'clock, but I was so down that I relocked the shop and went upstairs. If any of my regulars turned up they'd know where to find me. I reckoned that half an hour sitting in another hot bath drinking coffee might even turn me back into a more or less normal human being.

In fact, I'd had about twenty minutes when the phone rang in the sitting room and I had to drip down the passageway to answer it. At that hour of the morning it was usually Barnabas, and I always need to answer his calls now. My father – seventy-two years old, widowed for five years, seven years retired from university teaching, and four months past his heart attack. For the last hundred and twenty days, I'd been afraid of losing him after all. Nowadays, when my telephone rings, I answer it – wet or dry, sober or drunk.

'Good morning, Dido.' It was his voice: measured and precise, with an old actor's clarity which came from his lecturing days. I wound the bath towel more firmly around myself while we exchanged our usual careful questions about one another's state of mind and body.

Barnabas said, 'I've had a letter. Not a letter – I mean a note. Delivered to the door – there's no stamp on the envelope. I wonder whether you can help me?'

'What?' I wiped at the water trickling coldly down my shins and wished I hadn't been trying to save money by turning the heating off at the beginning of the month.

'It's just a sheet of plain paper,' the voice explained in my ear. 'Handwritten. Black ink. All swirls and furbelows. Obviously disguised. The message is entirely incomprehensible.'

There was another trickle of water down my spine. I yelled, 'What message?'

'Three lines. First, there's the registration number of your car . . .'

'*What??!*'

'. . . and then it simply reads, "about two miles south of Milton Keynes, but next time question mark question mark".'

I sat down on the arm of the settee, ignoring the danger of damp stains. Because of course it was impossible. Not possible, that is, at all.

'Dido? Did you hear . . .'

I spoke over his voice. 'Wait. I have to get dressed. I'm coming over. It's . . .' Well, what was it? I tried to hide the panic washing over me, but it made me breathless. 'I need to talk to you.'

'So it does mean something! Just explain . . .'

'Ten minutes,' I said, and hung up.

The sight of my dark and empty shop troubled my conscience enough that I paused to open the door and stick on the handwritten notice that claims I AM OUT ON BUSINESS BACK SOON. I turned the car, bullied my way across Upper Street, and joined the usual traffic jam heading north towards Highbury Corner. An edgy north wind was blowing the rain against my windscreen. The calendar was insisting that spring had arrived a whole week ago, but somebody had forgotten to inform the weather.

Barnabas owns a flat converted from the ground floor of a big mid-Victorian villa halfway up Crouch Hill. I could see him watching at his sitting-room window – a tall, thin old man (obviously I take after my mother), with sharp grey eyes under a shock of white hair, wearing thirty-year-old cords and a sports jacket with leather patches on the elbows. He dresses like a fifties academic, which of course is what he is: it's less a fashion statement than a kind of identity card.

He opened the door for me with the words, 'As a child, you always were pig-headed and abrupt.'

I decided to ignore that. 'Where is it?'

Barnabas nodded me into the chaos that was the sitting room of his flat but looked more like the accessions department of a library. He was still working on his edition of Tudor love poems – four mornings a week in the British Library, five afternoons here – which was the excuse for the paper avalanche on the desk under the window, and the books that had engulfed tables, overwhelmed chair seats, and flooded across the carpet since my mother's death. Until he retired he'd had the luxury of his Oxford rooms for his work. Now he was living like an old bear in a book-lined den.

The note on top of the mound on his desk was exactly as he described: a handwritten flourish in black ink on thin paper, threatening because it was both personal and anonymous. *About two miles south of Milton Keynes* . . . Last night had seemed as distant as a nightmare, and I would rather have kept it that way.

I became aware of Barnabas looming over me, his face all attention. If I'd been able to think of something he would accept, I would have lied. I told him the truth.

He said slowly, 'You should have phoned me. You shouldn't have been on your own.'

'I thought it was just chance – a couple of drunks having a stupid game with a woman driver. There are idiots like that everywhere. You get used to it – or women do. You've led a sheltered life, Barnabas.'

His raised eyebrows said that this was nonsense. 'It seems rather lengthy and elaborate for a couple of drunks having fun. However, that's not the point. It turns out to be anything but random.'

I closed my eyes. I could feel a headache begin to tighten my temples.

'The men in the car knew you, Dido. They even know about me. Are you sure you didn't recognize them?'

'Oh, Barnabas, it was pitch dark! And no, I don't know anybody that runs a newish hot hatchback.'

'What about motive?'

I said weakly, 'What about it?'

He glowered, letting me know I was being slow. 'It's a threat, of course. This note is telling us both what happened last night was not chance, that they know us both, they can find us both. "But next time," he says – a direct threat.'

I said stupidly, 'Why?'

'Ah. You tell me.'

'Which of us is being threatened?'

'That's true. Theoretically this could be aimed at me through you.' Barnabas cleared his throat. He was winding up to being businesslike. 'I presume you didn't take their number.'

'Right at the end, when I remembered about it, they had their lights off.' Obviously to make sure I couldn't do just that. I pulled myself together. Suddenly what worried me most was his worry: not good for a man with a bad heart. I managed a little laugh. 'Barnabas, have you been misbehaving? You haven't gone to some conference to give a paper, and called Professor Tussock a raving idiot in public, have you?'

'Tullett,' he corrected me stiffly. 'And don't be so silly. I am always courteous – poor old emeritus has-been that I am. I'm much more inclined to feel that you are mixed up in something shady. Have you brought the Mafia down on my head in my old age? I am joking. Am I?' He pretended to consider it. 'I am beginning to sound like King Lear.'

I groaned at him.

'Let's take it from the other side. Who could have known about your trip to Banbury?'

'Only the people I was visiting. By the way, you were right – they were a miserable lot.'

'Like the old man. Perhaps they were trying to steal back the books you'd bought.'

So we were back on our usual ground, reassuring one another. I adjusted my tone and said, 'Quite possibly. They were just about the most unpleasant . . .' Then I remembered. 'Oh, hell – anyone, everyone knew about it. After the book fair last Monday we were all having the usual drink, I mean drinks, and somebody suggested that a lot of us might have an evening out. I told them I was going to Banbury last night to look at a library, so we put it off.'

'Who was there?'

'Booksellers. The usual. All people that we know. Nobody who could have any reason to go to such lengths . . . much less involving you.'

He rose to the bait. 'I wish you'd stop thinking that I'm an invalid!'

'Have you taken your aspirin today?'

He said, 'Of course I have!'

He had been taking half an aspirin a day. His doctor had quoted figures

13

that seemed to prove that half an aspirin a day, taken for ever after the first heart attack, prevents others. Barnabas says that the whole thing is mumbo-jumbo designed to prevent more costly demands on the over-stretched and under-funded National Health Service, but he'd been pretty good about remembering.

'Don't change the subject! Just think: did you tell anybody else where you were going?' I hadn't. 'Then, apart from that, how could they find you in Banbury? You didn't mention names and addresses during this unladylike boozing session?'

I looked at him.

He looked back at me triumphantly and pushed his advantage. 'Then how could they find you?'

My heart sank. 'They couldn't.'

He waited.

'Unless they followed me all the way from home.'

'Oh, dear. What a great deal of trouble to take.'

I agreed. Oh dear. 'I left in the afternoon. I didn't notice anything, but then it was a common kind of car. It was only the loose wiring in the headlamp . . . It all seems mad.'

'We'll assume that there's a reason,' he said briskly. 'If there's a reason, then it can be discovered. Let's think . . . Why *now*? Unless we believe you've made a deadly enemy who has waited years to take a terrible revenge, something must have happened recently. Is there something in your private life that I should know about?'

I sighed at him.

'And why drag me in? It's as though somebody needs to apply pressure to us both.'

He stopped so abruptly that it made me watch him. In a long silence he crossed to the window to observe the watery sunlight in the uninteresting street outside. There was nothing to see out there except the occasional passing car – none of them small white hatchbacks, as it happened – but he continued to keep his back to me. After a moment I realized that he was avoiding my eye. I let the silence drag on. We could both be pig-headed, couldn't we?

He said, 'There might of course be hidden criminal depths to you which you have carefully concealed from your doting father. But somehow I think it's Davey. Isn't it? Have you seen him?'

'Don't be silly.'

14

'Let's,' said Barnabas to the window pane, 'accept for the moment that Davey is the one person we both know who is most likely to be connected with some silly game . . .'

I wanted to howl. 'Let's not! Let's not be stupid! All that is finished. He's gone. Leave it!'

'If you wish.' He cleared his throat. 'Then if that's all for the moment, I'm going to get down to work again. I'm not making any progress today.' He half turned and pretended to scrutinize a photocopy of some ancient manuscript scrawl among the papers on his desk. 'This is actually illegible, but it does *not* – I can see this much at least – read "*Quieter of mind and my unquiet heart*", whatever Tullett said in that incompetent version he published eleven years ago.'

I said humbly, 'I'll phone you if I think of anything. Be careful . . .' and crept out, leaving him folding his lanky body into the swivel chair at the desk. It looked as though he had switched from one academic problem to the next. I wished I could too. But we had spoken about Davey, and that wouldn't go away.

There was a space opposite the shop about a foot longer than the Volvo. I let the cars behind me wait until I had edged in delicately. Then I sat with my problem. It made me look hard at the shop: a narrow frontage with the door to my upstairs flat on the side; the plate-glass window with its display of nineteenth-century children's books, some of them opened to chromo-litho illustrations (a good display, but time to change it), the chocolate-brown sign with its gold lettering, new since the divorce had renamed the business: DIDO HOARE ANTIQUARIAN BOOKS AND PRINTS. The dark interior with its shadowy shelves of buckram and leather bindings invited browsers.

The shop had been Barnabas's wedding present to me: the lease of the whole building, the money for the stock, and his own expertise with the older books, where my knowledge faltered. Before that, I'd worked for two years for Barrow and Bates, the big Charing Cross Road specialists in nineteenth- and twentieth-century books. That's where my own knowledge had come from.

And where Davey came in.

Davey had been dealing in colour prints and water-coloured engravings, both the real thing – which gave him genuine pleasure – and the bread-and-butter prints labelled 'Hand-coloured Genuine Antique', which he was running to various central London shops. They were nineteenth-century steel engravings of London scenes torn out of cheap octavos and given a water-colour wash by Davey himself, or by a girl he knew. Tourist-trade prints, they were; we sold them mounted on card as slightly superior souvenirs. After we married, they brought in a useful regular income for our own shop from the mahogany display cabinet by the door.

I unlocked that door, removing the BACK SOON sign. The prints cabinet was beginning to look empty. I'd been putting off a decision. I put it off again and wandered into the office in the rear extension where the Banbury books were still waiting in their boxes. They needed to be unpacked, sorted, collated for completeness, priced. It was going to take me the rest of the day, and probably Sunday too. Saturdays are the busiest day in the shop, the day when the local market and antique shops are full of customers, so I wouldn't get anything done tomorrow.

While I'd been away, the mail had arrived. There were half a dozen orders for things in my last catalogue, out a fortnight now but not yet dead. I ought to sort through those, write invoices, wrap and weigh parcels, take them to the post office – the antiquarian bookseller's routine.

Instead, I sat down at the desk and stared numbly at the blank computer screen.

That was what I was doing – not really thinking, just blanked out – when the little Nepalese bell that hangs on the door jangled. The figure outlined against the light was unmistakable, and I realized that I'd been waiting to see it. My heart slid into my toes.

'Speak of the devil,' I allowed myself to say, making sure he would hear it clearly. I felt quite proud of the steadiness in my voice.

Davey grinned at me the length of the shop. 'Hello, pet! Coming for a drink?'

3

Pet

I heard my voice saying, 'I'll get these,' as though the intervening months had vanished and this was any Friday lunchtime two years ago, when we used to shut the shop for the 'hour' that always turned into two and a half, and walk together round the corner to the Crown just before it got crowded, and stay drinking and talking – me with Davey, Davey with everybody. I was just the person with Davey, whom everybody knew.

The pub had been refurbished after Christmas. It had turned into a Hollywood-Victorian stage pub, all frosted glass, horse brasses and imitation wood panelling. You'd expect Mr Pickwick to walk in. The bar staff were new too. I ordered Davey's pint and my gin from a strange white-faced girl. While I was waiting, I looked back at our table in the curve of the plush bench seating.

He wasn't quite unchanged: older, muscle in the tall body running more to plumpness. His blond hair was longer. He'd caught it in a little ponytail, like the ones you see on trendy advertising men – or the street-market traders, the boys who fancy themselves. It occurred to me that he looked more than ever like the man on the cover of a cheap romantic novel – the one who ambushed the heroine in a sexual diversion from her path of true love, whatever that might be.

Oh, I ought to have known better.

When I turned away, my own reflection stared at me from the mirror behind the bar with a face confusingly framed by the shelved bottles and their reflected doubles. What about that face – was that one changed too? In the mirror's depths beyond my own accusing eyes and wild short hair, I saw Davey again. Davey and Dido, Dido and Davey. His reflection took a cigarette from the pack on the table and flicked the lighter with those tapering, curiously feminine fingers. There was a smudge of green paint on one knuckle.

I carried the glasses to the table and sat down at the right distance. Barnabas popped into the back of my mind asking questions, and almost as though he could hear them, Davey reached across and put his hand over mine. I heard myself say, 'How's Ilona?' A really adult reaction – well done, Dido.

He took it at face value. 'Fine. Flourishing.'

'I was surprised to see you.' (In the old days too I always used to make the first move. It always was my mistake.)

'I've missed you, pet.'

I got my hand back and used it to pick up my glass. 'What have you been doing? Are you working?' I meant, What do you want?

He laughed. 'I'm painting like crazy. I don't sleep, I do a canvas every night. I have an exhibition in Hampstead next month. And I'm doing this and that – hustling. You know.'

I made my voice sound amused. 'Nothing's changed, then.'

'Not much. What about you? How's Barnabas? I heard he was ill.'

It was still too close to think about. 'He died,' I said carefully. 'His heart actually stopped beating. He's all right now, but it's made him cautious. It frightened him. It scared me stiff.'

He said something that I missed, because for a second I was back in the darkness of that winter evening when Barnabas had slipped out of his chair at my table and huddled on the carpet, changed incredibly into a grey-faced stranger whimpering with pain.

'Sorry?'

'How's the shop doing? How are you managing?' There was a quality in his voice that I didn't quite understand. His face was attentive, concerned.

'Oh, I do the book fairs by myself, of course, but Barnabas comes and goes in the shop. I had a catalogue out a couple of weeks ago, and he wrote most of it.'

'Somebody showed it to me. But you have to do all the fetching and carrying? I've been past once or twice, and I saw that you seemed to be on your own.'

18

'You should have come in,' I commented with what sounded even to me like meaningless cordiality.

'I thought you'd throw a wobbly. Didn't want to risk my neck.'

It was just idle conversation, like tossing a bubble back and forth. 'Very sensible,' I said. 'I suppose that I might have broken your knee-caps if you'd caught me at an awkward moment.'

He left it then, but there still seemed something evasive in his look. I stared back. I'd forgotten how light his eyes were: the kind of luminous blue that you see in a midwinter sky.

'You always were tough, for somebody so small and pretty. Anyway . . . today I risked it.'

I smiled sweetly. 'Us lady booksellers have to know how to take care of ourselves.'

'What do you mean by that? Trouble?'

I couldn't stop smiling. 'Not particularly, but you know what booksellers are like: gropings behind the cases at book fairs, drunken knee-bangings under the tables, invitations to hotel rooms in Bristol. Some of them seem to think I'm a pushover.'

'Really?'

'It's my size and my feminine nature.' I breathed down into my diaphragm. 'And being divorced. Jimmy Fox . . .'

'Oh, that little shit. You don't want to worry about our Jim. Do you want me to have a word with him?'

I said coldly, 'I'd do it myself if I thought he meant it . . . which I find improbable.'

Davey seemed to consider Fox. 'Yes, it is unlikely. But I think you need a minder. And handyman and runner. Are you hiring?'

'Not you!' I felt something like panic. 'I'm my own minder now. And it's your round.'

'Lend us a fiver?'

'Bugger off,' I said, and handed over the money.

I watched him walk across and lean over the bar to talk to the pale girl, who turned pink and smiled into his blue, cajoling eyes. I could feel a laugh rising. Or hysteria. You bastard. It's so automatic. Davey Winner: the man who gives promiscuity a bad name . . .

But there was always a purpose behind Davey's moves. *Minder?* Even if Barnabas was right, it was hard to believe that Davey would have undertaken last night's elaborate and dangerous ploy just in the hope of convincing me that I needed him back. Or was it hard? Wasn't there something of Davey's incurable optimism and, yes, naïvety in the idea? The only question was whether he would tell me what was going on, or whether I'd have to find out. That much hadn't changed.

In the end he told me. It came after he'd spent an hour at gossip and anecdote and charm – *Do you remember? Do you remember?* – and after the lunchtime crowd had faded back to their antique shops and offices, leaving us nearly alone in the mid-afternoon gloom. 'Dido, I meant what I said.'

'What about?'

'Don't be smart. About the shop.'

I said slowly, 'The shop's fine.'

'It was fine when we ran it together. It was a good shop. It might even have been a good shop still after Barnabas rode up on his white horse and saved you from me. At least he could help you then – God, he knows books all right! I have an eye for a deal and what looks pretty, but Barnabas knows.'

'Exactly.' My tone sounded dry enough to mop up a swimming pool. 'And he comes in still, when I'm going to a sale or something like that.'

'So he's well enough to babysit the shop.'

I felt myself scowl at him. 'It's all that's necessary.'

'It isn't all you need, pet.' His voice dropped confidentially. 'Look at it when you go back. One person can't run a shop and do catalogues and the fairs. Your stock is tired, those silly little prints are gone, you . . .'

'Not you,' I said. I meant it. 'No way.'

'I won't even take a salary. Commission, half of the increase in your profits, that's all! Say, ten per cent of anything I run for you. I still know all the book people.'

It felt like being hypnotized. The panic in the pit of my stomach pushed me to my feet, and I banged my thigh hard against the edge of the table. Davey's glass was empty. He picked up his black leather jacket and walked ahead through the heavy doors. Over his shoulder he was saying, 'Don't worry, I just need the money.'

'Not from me you don't!'

'Why not? I know the business. I did it for three years – remember? – and full time after Barnabas set you up in that place. It's something I can *do*.'

In the street he turned, waiting.

'You can do lots of things. You can do that for somebody else. As you say, you still know all the dealers.'

He looked curiously at me and shrugged. 'They aren't as much fun as you. But if you can't handle it . . .'

But I could handle it, and I knew just the right way. 'Let's say I can't handle it,' I said. I made my fingers straighten out; the nails had been digging into the palms of my hands.

He was watching me. Wanting something. He always had been unreadable. 'You're right,' he said, sounding agreeable. 'Well – perhaps after all I just wanted to see you again.'

'Don't – just don't!' I remembered suddenly how he enjoyed making scenes. 'What do you really want?'

He said, queerly, 'What do I ever want? Listen, let me just prove to you that I mean it. I don't even want a cut. Well, anyway, not from you. I've told you I still know people, and I can get you buyers for at least three things in your catalogue. No, don't interrupt! There's the Wordsworth: you've under-priced that, and Jimmy Fox has been advertising for one. And the *Tom Jones*? – I'll lay you ten to one I can run that to Griffiths. I'll ask him sixteen hundred and take fourteen. I didn't realize you still had the Ireland stuff, but I happen to know that Heritage has a pet Jap customer who pays over the odds for anything English with a provenance. You just have to sell him a romantic story. I'll handle the whole thing. I bet Heritage can get twice your catalogue price for that. I'll get you twelve thousand, and take anything over that as my cut. What do you say?'

The vision of these flying thousands made me hesitate. Luckily or unluckily, however, they were out of reach.

I said patiently, 'The Fielding has gone, as a matter of fact, and when I offered the *Poems* to Jimmy he said he didn't like the condition. And the Ireland is on order too – at last. Do you remember that nice American librarian who used to come over every summer from Massachusetts? He'll be here next week on a buying trip, and I'm keeping it for him. You see? I'm managing!'

Davey mimed anguish. 'Did you get the full price for everything?'

I almost lied. 'The usual discount,' I said firmly. 'They're both good customers.'

'Tell your American not to come,' Davey urged. 'Tell him that the cat pissed on the manuscripts.'

'Mr Spock never pisses on manuscripts. He has manners. And I can't do it. Anyway, Barnabas wouldn't stand for it. He and Job Warren are friends.'

Davey said slowly, 'Professor Warren – that's it, I remember. Come on, Dido, you can't just throw away three thousand pounds.' His voice was hoarse. But money had always been Davey's true love.

I said, 'Go away. Thanks for the drink.' But when he bent down and looked at me carefully, as though my face were a half-finished crossword puzzle, and kissed me on the mouth, I felt as tired as though we'd been fighting.

'See you later, pet.'

I watched the back of his black jacket vanish around the corner of the street. I'd forgotten his habit of carrying his left shoulder a little higher than the right. Today it suddenly made him look as though he were on the point of twisting on his heel and running for his life.

At the shop, I flipped the sign which still shamefully said CLOSED and phoned Barnabas. I felt as though I needed his kind of reality for the moment. Through his greetings I told him, 'You may be right. Davey's back. I don't mean "back", I mean he turned up. We've been to lunch.'

Barnabas's voice came thinly down the wire: 'What did he want?' I felt a flash of annoyance. If only Barnabas had left things alone . . .

'I don't know,' I said lightly. 'Money, I expect. He seemed bright. Not exactly happy – bright. The way he used to be when he had a scam on. He was full of ideas.'

'Dido, I wish you weren't so bored.'

'I'm not bored! What's that supposed to mean?'

'Good.'

Silence. Then I was angry. 'I'm fed up with men! You all patronize me.'

Barnabas said, 'I'm your father, you foolish child!'

I hung up. That conversation was going nowhere. Besides, I was considering whether or not I wanted to cry.

4

Turn-up

I lay on my bed watching the lights of passing cars whiten and fade on the bedroom ceiling. Davey's breathing was deep and regular. He was probably asleep, but I couldn't be sure: typically, he was giving nothing away. But his body felt solid and warm against mine. I lay still against his back.

When I woke, my body remembered his so vividly that I wasn't sure I'd been dreaming until I rolled over and looked at the empty and unwrinkled space beside me. Funny: I still always slept in my own half. Relief that it hadn't happened fought with . . . panic because it had seemed so normal? Shame? Disappointment? Anger? Stupid cow. I got up slowly, feeling like an invalid, and wrapped myself in the green terry bathrobe because I felt cold.

In the kitchen I could grind coffee beans, watch Spock eat, wait for the kettle to boil. With the water dripping through the grounds, I switched myself on to automatic, splashed cleaner over the worktops and wiped at the week's accumulation of crumbs and grease. Then I remembered to check my answering machine, discovered I'd forgotten to set it, and gave myself the whole morning to drink coffee and read the Sunday papers.

By eleven o'clock, when the telephone rang, I'd climbed far enough out of the cloud of uneasiness to be able to go and answer with only the smallest flutter in the pit of my stomach. But of course it was Barnabas's voice on the line. 'Dido? Are you all right?'

I focused on the dust motes which hung in the sunlight – it wouldn't hurt to mop over the sitting room as well as the kitchen – and took a deep breath. 'Why shouldn't I be? What about you – has something happened?'

Barnabas's voice said, 'Oh – no, I'm gorging aspirin, nothing to report. But I was worried. I tried to phone you last night.'

'I was out.'

'Good . . . Good?'

'I got back late.'

His voice hesitated. 'You wouldn't like to fill me in?'

I wanted to laugh. 'Davey took me out for a meal last night. As a matter of fact, he took me to an unusually flash restaurant in the West End – and even paid the bill himself.'

Barnabas said, 'What does he want?' in a tone so anxious that I nearly forgave him for asking.

'He says he misses me. Ilona is visiting her parents, and I suppose he's lonely.'

'You wouldn't!'

I said, 'Of course not. Oh, Barnabas, do you really think I'm such a fool?'

'It just seemed,' he said slowly, 'rather a waste of a good divorce. When I bought it for you, little did I think . . .'

I took a grip on my temper and said relatively mildly, 'Shut up, Barnabas! Or talk about something else.'

'If I'm competing with Davey again, I'd better take you out to lunch. Rocca's?'

'Provided you'll stop acting pitiful,' I agreed, 'I'll pick you up at one o'clock.'

'You ought to be having your meals with *somebody sensible*.'

I hung up. It was a kind of joke between us, that type of conversation, but suddenly this morning it felt as though our relationship was out of hand.

When I left university, I'd wanted to try something or somewhere entirely new. An American girl at my college had suggested we should go to New York together, and we'd both wound up working for a publishing firm and sharing an apartment near Columbia. That was where I was when my mother died. I moved back to London after the funeral without even consulting Barnabas, because it felt like the only thing to do.

I knew he'd expect me to move in with him. Pat, my older sister, had remarked with tearful sentimentality how convenient it would be for both of us. I hadn't been so daft, but a kind of jokey pretence grew up between us then – especially in him – that we were looking after one another. Of course for nearly two years there had been Davey, and then things were different. But I was determined not to let either Barnabas's heart or my divorce become the excuse for something false. I have always loved my father, but I value my independence, and so does he. Realistically, I reckoned that we would have been at one another's throats.

Rocca's Restaurant, down by High Holborn, was Barnabas's favourite – partly because the food is pretty good, and partly because he liked the Italian family who run it and keep it unswervingly postwar with its brown walls, plastic grape vines, and real table cloths. They didn't mind us sitting there all afternoon, even on a busy Sunday. Barnabas maintained that Armagnac is better than coffee for a man with a heart condition. If only they'd stocked Irish whiskey, he would have gone there every day.

I'd refused to discuss Davey, so Barnabas talked about his work. Then, over his brandy and my espresso, he got on to the sub-topic of Tullett's edition of love sonnets, but even in my slightly distracted state I knew that his mind wasn't on it. I could feel a wall of unsaid things beginning to rise up.

'All right, spit it out.'

'I've been mulling things over for the past couple of days while we were waiting. I presume that the pranksters in the white car have been totally silent? And yet if they are trying to put pressure on one or both of us, they ought to have let us know by now what it is they want. It's not very effective to let up.'

I was surprised for a moment to find that I'd stopped worrying about the episode. 'Are you really looking forward to being blackmailed, then?'

My father assured me that his desire for excitement was limited.

'Well, then, just be grateful. Maybe it was a joke. Someone who knows me was passing and just happened to recognize the car. There are people with a warped sense of humour who might consider it funny to give me a scare. I'm waiting for one of the lads to snigger at me in a pub so I can chop him down.'

'A joke?' Barnabas mocked. 'It might have been someone's idea of a joke, I suppose – although I hope you aren't too familiar with such humorous individuals – but what about the note? Having taken advantage of a wild and wonderful coincidence, your joking friend extends the joke next morning to give us all an even bigger laugh?'

Well, I'd tried. I sighed at him. 'All right, I'm listening.'

'Either someone will contact you or me any hour now – can't think why it's taken them so long – or something else frightening will happen.'

'Oh.' I tried to focus on that. It wasn't a reassuring thought. 'Barnabas, you wouldn't go and stay with Pat for a while, would you?'

He shuddered visibly, but otherwise ignored my suggestion. 'I'm afraid we should talk to the police. Also I think that you'd better move in with me for a few days. I don't want you alone at night.'

'Oh, but . . .' I meant, Oh no. But that was in normal circumstances. So far as his suggestion was concerned, I wasn't too happy about him being alone if there was really to be a 'something else frightening'. 'You're as vulnerable as I am, Barnabas. I just can't think why anybody would seriously want to . . . to scare *me*. I know you thought it might be Davey, and for a while I thought you must be right. But why? That's all finished. I'm not doing him any harm, I don't have any money . . . it really doesn't make any sense. Perhaps somebody's after you, not me?'

'There have been . . .' Barnabas gazed elaborately at the ceiling. '. . . several students and at least half the English staff who might have wanted to harass me at one time. But not now. Nowadays, I am only a poor old bore. Half of the rest of them have left the university too and are also poor old bores. Unless we're postulating a mad research student who believes that I blighted his career and has been plotting fiendish revenge in an attic in Whitechapel? I don't *remember* actually blighting any careers, though I often wanted to, as a kind of public service to future student generations. I still think . . .'

He hesitated, but I knew perfectly well what he meant, because when Barnabas held a grudge he never made any secret of the fact. Whatever bee he had in his bonnet, I could only hope that he would avoid turning it into a campaign.

'I suppose that you're going to give me the usual speech on the usual topic? I suppose you're convinced that Davey has kept some terrible rage because of the divorce? For God's sake, Barnabas, why should he?' I heard my voice rising and took a deep breath. 'He got what he wanted – don't interrupt, I've always known that you paid him off – he went off to Ilona which is where he decided he wanted to be, and as far as I can see he's perfectly happy there. I'm not bothering him! What would be the point of his messing with us now?'

To do him justice, Barnabas blushed and covered his uneasiness by taking a long, considering sip from his brandy glass. 'Well then. I suppose that fathers never know about their children, although the police are bound to ask: do you have any murderous ex-lovers? No doubt you were mixed up with the Mafia in New York?'

I breathed in a mouthful of coffee and spluttered, 'What an incurable romantic you are! I'm actually as hard-working and harmless as I appear.'

He fixed me with a sharp stare. 'Perhaps you are. I'm not sure that, at your age, it's entirely healthy.'

'Oh, Barnabas, stop playing.'

He said softly, 'I'm afraid that I am genuinely anxious about this. You see, I hate not understanding things.'

I said, 'I can't believe all this . . . fairy tale.' At that moment, I meant what I said. 'There's a shamefully silly explanation for the whole business.'

'Beware,' said Barnabas, 'or reality will tap you on the shoulder . . .'

'The waiter will tap you on the shoulder if we sit here any longer,' I pointed out. 'He might like to have a little time off. Anyway, it's time for your nap.'

But after I'd delivered him to Crouch End and pretended to supervise his settling down to rest, I drove home and left the car around the corner from George Street, away from the shop. That gave me the chance to walk back. I shook myself mentally. I asked myself what I thought I was doing. Because even then I couldn't believe my father's theories. And yet I found myself watchful. The sky had clouded over while we were eating, and a gust of wind brought a promise, almost the touch, of raindrops; but that was the only visible threat. Stop it! You'll be seeing things in doorways next.

And then when I got there, the doorway was wrong. It took me a moment to understand the reason: the CLOSED sign that had been there had vanished, so that the glass in the door appeared darker and plainer than when I had left. Wrong. Beyond it, something else had changed.

I fumbled at the door (later, I could remember unlocking it) and pushed it back with a thud against the case of prints.

The mounted engravings slid along the floor under my feet. Beyond them, books had been ripped from their shelves and flung in heaps, the pages fluttering sadly in the breeze from the open door. I fought my way inside, trying to avoid doing any more damage as I moved. Someone had pulled down one of the free-standing bookcases in the middle of the room. I edged past the Literature section, where not a book was left shelved, towards the door of the office. I always leave it closed; now it was slightly ajar. Moving lightly on the balls of my feet, I reached out and touched it, listened . . . pushed. Something soft first gave way and then resisted. I shoved.

It looked as though a pack of monkeys had been imprisoned inside. I'd been pushing the door against the mounds of my Banbury purchase, which had been thrown across the floor like the books in the front room. The chair lay on its side, and the drawers of the old desk had been pulled out and emptied on to the floor. The computer monitor lay on its face. Anxiously I fought my way over, set it up and switched on, to find with relief that the menu came up normally. But the parcels I'd spent hours preparing for the post had been ripped apart, their brown paper wrappings shredded. Why? I picked my first edition of *Tom Jones* out of the mess and stacked its six volumes gently on the table. One of the spines was cracked, but it could probably be fixed. The telephone lay on the floor, wires dangling, and my little cash box sat upside down beside it, empty. The thought slid stupidly into my head that at least I'd gone to the bank on Saturday, so I couldn't have lost more than eighty pounds in cash and a sheet of second-class postage stamps.

And how many valuable books?

I reached out to pick up the cash box and stopped myself: anybody so mindless might well have left his fingerprints. Instead, I pushed the empty drawers off the chair and sat on its legs.

No, no use clearing up yet. No use crying. No use being angry. I locked up without looking back.

I turned without thinking to the door at the side, the door up to my flat. I'd even put my key into the mortise lock before I realized that whoever had broken into the shop might just have gone upstairs afterwards, might just be there still . . . My first reaction was anger: I wanted to roar up the stairs, only I could hear Barnabas saying, the way he used to when I was little: 'Temper, Dido! Count to twenty-nine . . .'

And then I remembered Barnabas saying that something else frightening would happen.

I made sure that the mortise was still locked. No easy escapes . . . if you are up there. Then I eased the key out of the lock again and walked to the phone box in the main road to dial 999.

5

Nothing

It took some time for the long, strangled clamour of the doorbell to penetrate my sleep. I focused blearily on the clock. For a moment the fact that it was past nine meant nothing. Then a wisp of memory returned. I said '*Damn!*' to the clock and screamed 'WAIT!' to the bell. Then I wobbled out of bed and struggled into the grey tracksuit extracted from the mound of laundry I'd dumped on a chair after my last visit to the launderette. I stuffed my feet into a pair of clogs and ran a hand uselessly over my hair, which needed a lot more than smoothing. It could wait.

When I opened the door, I found myself staring from my five-foot-three height at the diaphragm area of a white shirt. Stepping back mentally, I moved my gaze up over the ranges of a weight-trainer's body in what looked like a rather expensive grey suit jacket – I'm rarely too sleepy to appreciate good things – and located my caller's face nearly a foot above mine: big brown eyes, wedge-shaped face, and a tan that at that time of year had to be from a lamp. Only the shortness of the dark hair and the fact of the grey suit betrayed that this was either a stockbroker or a policeman, and circumstances favoured the latter. I could feel myself blinking at him. As I blinked, a warrant card was flourished in front of my nose. The photograph did not do him justice.

'DI Grant. Sorry I'm late.'

Suspecting sarcasm, I made sure that his expression was professionally blank. 'No problem,' I drawled, emphasizing gracious coolth and wishing

29

I was more awake and less unwashed. 'You'd better come up. I was just going to make coffee.'

'I'll need to see the shop. Afterwards, coffee would be fine.'

'I'll get the keys,' I said.

By the time I'd climbed the stairs again, the one thing I knew quite clearly was that my cotton-wool brain required first aid. If he couldn't take a hint, he'd have to wait. I set the electric kettle to boil and found the instant coffee. The milk in the fridge was sour. I extracted a sticky jar from the jumble in a cupboard, dumped a spoonful of liquid honey into the black brew, and descended carrying both keys and mug.

The uniformed policeman who'd arrived the previous day in response to my emergency call had told me to leave everything untouched until the CID could examine it. In the light of Monday morning, the mess was unspeakable. It was hard to imagine I'd ever owned a functioning bookshop, and even harder to believe I ever would again. I sipped my coffee gingerly, trying not to burn my tongue, and watched Whatsisname – the thought drifted past me that if I'd forgotten the name of such a dishy bloke, I was clearly past the prime of life – prowl along the edge of the chaos. He couldn't have a clue. Nothing useful was going to come out of this; his visit was a gesture the police had to make before they allowed me to get on with my life. I relaxed grumpily, drank sweet coffee, dozed on my feet, and waited for something to happen. It would be nice, I told myself, *if somebody actually did something.*

The detective produced a small black notebook and a large green pen from an inside pocket and threw me a quick look. 'I'll take some notes, and then I'll have to ask a few questions.'

'The uniformed policeman filled in a report yesterday afternoon.'

'Just preliminary,' he said. 'I like to do my own looking.'

I watched him idly as he wandered through the mess, looking at something or other from time to time and scribbling without pause.

'Miss Hoare, can you tell me what's missing?'

I looked at the mess. 'Not yet. Your man told me not to touch . . .'

'Of course.'

'He told me not to clear up until you'd been here to have a look at it. I've plugged the phone back in and picked up the computer, that's all. He said it would be all right.'

'Well, there's no reason why you shouldn't go ahead and clear up. Apart from the phone and the cash box, there's no point taking fingerprints – it's a shop, after all, so there's not much chance of finding anything meaningful. We'll send the phone and the box to the forensic people, just in case one of the local villains got careless.'

'Money,' I said. 'They took the money from the cash box – it wasn't locked – and the stamps. I can't see what else is missing. I mean, I can see some quite valuable things that are still here. I told the constable . . .'

'I know.' He was gingerly retrieving the cash box and sliding it into a plastic bag while at the same time watching me through narrowed eyes, and I noticed irrelevantly that his nose was crooked. Presumably somebody had broken it for him. It made him look more human. My telephone was unplugged again and went the way of the box.

I said, 'I won't know for sure until I've got everything back on the shelves, but . . .'

'What?'

'Look,' I said, suddenly realizing what I had been thinking since the moment I'd walked in on the mess, 'whoever did this didn't know anything about antiquarian books.' Saying it aloud made me more sure about it. 'For example, see that *Tom Jones* in six volumes? That's a first edition. I've just sold it for twelve hundred pounds – it was wrapped up, waiting to be posted, with the invoice in it. It's the kind of good, collectable eighteenth-century work that's – well, almost like money. Whoever broke in found it and just tossed it on to the floor. Do you understand? Everybody knows that an old six-volume novel is worth something, and pretty easy to sell. Or . . .' I thought. 'Did you notice the low case under the front window? I keep some nice illustrated books there – two signed limited editions of Rackham fairy tales, an Ackermann's *Oxford* . . .' His feet shifted, and I realized that he had no idea what I was talking about. Booksellers lead introverted lives, I guess. 'Well, those three volumes together could sell for two and a half thousand – three, with any luck. They're fairly common – anybody who knows anything at all about old books knows what those are, and they wouldn't be terribly easy to trace. And yet they didn't touch them.'

'You think that's strange.'

I corrected him: 'It's unbelievable.'

'Can you think of a reason for it?'

I looked at him hard. 'Well . . . of course, they took the money – eighty or ninety pounds. And a sheet of second-class stamps. But why break into a bookshop if that's all you're looking for?'

31

He flipped his notes shut and said slowly, 'An off-licence or an electrical goods place would be a more likely target, yes. You don't think of a second-hand bookshop having a lot of cash. Of course, you're on a side street. They might have picked an easy target.'

'It's not *that* easy. People live around here. *I* live here! I might have been at home.'

'They probably saw you go out.' He shrugged. 'It may be that some kids took the chance, walked in, had fun making a pig's breakfast, and took the money because it was the only thing they could see of any value.'

'But they didn't walk in,' I said slowly. 'I told your man yesterday – I know the door was locked when I got back.'

The notebook was back.

I repeated for its benefit, 'I know that the door was locked when I arrived. I remember unlocking it to get in. It's a mortise lock – a high-security lock. You can't even copy the keys. You have to order new ones from the manufacturers.'

DI Grant looked amused. 'There aren't any keys that you can't get copied somewhere. It's obviously what happened here – if you're right about unlocking when you got back. There are no signs of forced entry.'

I shook my head.

'And everything is shut up tight back here. The bars on the window haven't been removed, and the rear entrance is bolted on the inside with lockable bolts . . . unless you . . . ?'

I was beginning to feel impatient. 'No! They were still locked, of course.'

'What about your alarm system?'

'I don't have one. I'm not a jewellers – or an off-licence.' They'd asked me the same things yesterday, and heard the same answer with the same air of disbelief. Apparently you don't run a shop in London these days without having all the security arrangements of the Bank of England.

'You realize that whoever did this seems to have had a key?' His face was totally blank.

Yes, I did realize it. I'd spent a lot of the night realizing just that, which was why I hadn't fallen asleep until dawn and was having to cope now with a head like a sieve.

'Who has keys?'

'No one. I do. My father does.'

'Cleaner?'

I looked at him ironically. He must have seen that the present mess couldn't quite hide the shop's normal dustiness.

'Who owns the building? Is there a management agency?'

'My father and I have a long lease on the whole thing.'

'When did . . .'

'We've been here for four years. We changed the locks when we took it – the insurance people insisted.'

'Have you ever lost your keys? What about your father, might he have . . . ?'

I said impatiently, 'Of course not.'

'At least you're insured. You'd better let them know what's happened.'

'Yes, of course. I'll phone as soon as we've finished.'

He looked at me and closed the book once more. 'You know, that's the only thing that seems important, and we're going to have to go on asking the same question: where did the key come from – the one they used? Frankly, this looks more like a grudge than a robbery. You haven't fired an assistant lately?'

I sighed. 'Not unless you want to count trying to discourage my father from coming and moving books around the place.'

'I'll need to speak to him.'

'Why?' He looked at me. He put his book down on the table beside his plastic bags. I said slowly, 'My father and I have the only keys, so you think that he or I or both of us together did it.' I understood. 'Oh . . . an insurance claim.' I looked at him with distaste. 'Look . . . sorry, I've forgotten your name.'

'Grant. Detective Inspector.' He grimaced. 'I'm sorry, but it's going to have to be cleared up. You realize that your insurance people will be on to me first thing. They'll look at it in exactly the same way.'

I decided that the two of us were unlikely to get on very well. 'Mr Grant, *if* I were trying to defraud my insurance company, I wouldn't have to be very clever to think of leaving the back door open into the alley. Also, I'd be weeping buckets of tears and telling you about the incredibly valuable books that are missing.'

He looked at me closely and had the grace to grin. 'I take your point. So far, you've only told me about the incredibly valuable books that are still here.'

'They aren't even incredibly valuable,' I observed sourly. 'Unfortunately, I don't have any incredibly valuable books.'

'Even so, I need to check with your father about his keys. I do need to make sure that he still has them.'

I hesitated. Confession time. 'I haven't told him about this. He had a heart attack a couple of months ago; I keep trying not to upset him. I suppose he has to know?'

Grant grimaced. 'My father's had a couple of heart attacks, as a matter of fact. You can't help worrying, but it isn't the end of the world. Dad is living a pretty normal life.'

'I just try to make things smooth for him.'

He said abruptly, 'I take it your father doesn't live with you? We can go together and talk to him, if that'd make you happier.'

There was no help for it. I shrugged.

'Apart from that, you'd better clear up as quickly as possible and find out what is missing – apart from the petty cash. While you're doing that, keep your eyes open for anything they might have dropped.'

I sighed. 'You mean, a clue? Like a box of matches from a little café down at the docks where we go to find a menacing gang of oriental book thieves?'

Grant looked at me with obvious distaste, and I decided I didn't like tall, handsome men who couldn't laugh at themselves. He said, 'Exactly. I see that you read old books as well as selling them.'

'When I was a little girl,' I observed coldly, 'I used to read Edgar Wallace. You're saying that there's nothing you can do about this.'

'We'll do what we can, obviously, but unless we find out something about your father's keys, we probably have to wait for your stuff to turn up somewhere. As soon as you get things cleared up, give me a list of every item that's missing. I'll consult one of our people who's an expert in stolen antiques – she might have some ideas. We'll circulate the second-hand bookshops. If we're dealing with your usual opportunist, he'll probably try to sell your stuff somewhere in the area.'

'I can do that myself,' I said coldly, 'through the booksellers' association. And that's it?'

'That's it. Let's just go and call on your father, and then I can write this up and get the wheels turning. No – wait. I'm supposed to be somewhere else in ten minutes. What if I call for you at about four o'clock? Give you a chance to make a start here, too.' He was looking with distaste at the rubble. 'Do you have somebody who can lend a hand? There's a lot to shift.'

'These days,' I remarked as much to myself as to him, 'my whole life consists of moving books by the ton. I'm strong. I take it that you aren't offering?'

'I'd love to, but I have to go and solve crimes.'

'Like this one,' I muttered, and locked him out of the shop.

I stuck the CLOSED sign on the door, and turned and looked and sighed and levered the display case back on to its legs so that I could begin to stack the prints in their compartments. Never before had they looked so shabby, so . . . remaindered. I said, 'Bugger it,' and went back upstairs to make a pot of real coffee.

For the next hour, I pushed books back into roughly the appropriate places, picking out the ones that had been damaged and putting them to one side so that I could look at them later and decide what was worth mending and what I should toss out. A few spines had been torn by someone pulling them roughly from tightly packed shelves. Half a dozen volumes had suffered more serious damage, and an ornate nineteenth-century *Burke's Peerage* had lost its red gilt covers. The Ackermann and the Rackhams were safe, and the other few dozen books which any respectable thief would recognize as worth a hundred pounds or so.

After a while I stopped expecting to miss anything and began worrying about Barnabas. I'd brought down my upstairs phone and plugged it in, but put off phoning him yet again. I wanted to tell him about the burglary before DI Grant did, and yet the more I sorted, the more uneasy I felt. I took the time to phone the insurance company for a claims form and then went back to it. By the time I'd finished with one long wall, I was almost certain that nothing was missing.

I should have been relieved, but discovering that somebody had apparently materialized inside the shop by magic and amused himself by spilling books on to the floor had started to frighten me. A good honest thief I could understand, but this was invasive and senseless.

Or rather, it was a kind of terrifying madness.

The reason I didn't want to tell Barnabas was that I already knew what he would say. And I knew, surely, who had broken in, if not how they'd done it: the men in the white GTi. This was their 'next time', and I had to tell the police about the winking car, only how could I? The whole thing was absolutely insane, and who would possibly believe it? Inspector Grant would jump to some logical conclusion. He would be quite sure now that I had planned an insurance fraud and concocted this fairy tale to divert his suspicion. Anyone, including me, could have written that phoney-looking threatening letter. Suddenly I found myself shaking so hard that I had to go into the back room to sit down.

I was there when the telephone rang. My wristwatch said that it was Barnabas's usual time to call me, and I still hadn't worked out what I was going to say to him, so I answered reluctantly.

It was a stranger's voice. 'Dido Hoare?'

Out of a sudden irrational fear of what I was going to hear, I croaked, 'Yes?'

'Halloo, Michael Allyn from Quaritch here. From your last catalogue, do you still have item thirty-eight? We have a customer who may be interested.'

I'd almost forgotten that I was supposed to sell books. The master catalogue was still lost somewhere in the mess. 'Sorry,' I said, 'which . . . ?'

'Item thirty-eight,' the voice repeated, tinged with reproach. I could imagine the voice's owner thinking that you can't get the staff nowadays. ' "Ireland, W . . ." '

'Sorry,' I interrupted him. 'Yes . . . I mean, no, it's gone. Sorry.' I hung up, reflecting that it was par for the course that the only buyer in sight today wanted something I'd already sold. Or maybe it was luck, because it was hard to imagine actually being able to find any particular book in this tip. My temper lurched from bad to atrocious, and didn't improve with two more phone calls from people who wondered whether I could sell them some Enid Blyton first editions or buy some paperbacks from them. There are some days when you just aren't going to win.

By this time I couldn't touch the mess any more. The books had been handled by the men from the white car, and a kind of sliminess seemed to stick to their covers. Only what choice was there?

I was still hesitating when the door rattled. I expected to see Whatsisname – Grant – or the beat constable checking up on me, but it was Davey who stood silhouetted against the pale sunlight of the street.

'Have you buried a customer under that lot?' he demanded, edging his way inside. 'What happened? This is spring-cleaning gone mad!'

'Burglars,' I croaked.

He strode through the chaos and gripped my upper arms. 'God! Are you all right, pet? Have you got the police? Are you okay?' The tenderness in his voice nearly finished me off.

'It happened yesterday,' I explained, my voice cracking. 'It's all right, there's not much harm done. I'm all right. The police have been here. But I have to . . .' The description of what I had to do failed me. I could only gesture at it.

Davey strode through the chaos, looked into the office, whistled. 'How much did they take?'

'I don't know yet. A bit of money from the cash box, anyhow. I'm making a list for the police.'

'Want some help?'

I slumped against a wobbling book case. 'Yes. Aren't you busy?'

'I'm busy helping you. I *was* going to take you for a drink . . .'

'I'll take you for a drink afterwards,' I said weakly.

'Then I'll take you for a meal.'

I asked, 'Have you inherited a fortune?' The Davey that I knew had always been free with money, but especially when he knew there was something to gain. Did he think there was something to gain?

'I had a horse,' he said shortly. 'I'll do this side, you do that. You haven't changed anything since I was here, have you, pet? Never mind, I'll look at the labels if I get lost.'

We worked into a rhythm of bending and picking up, moving in tandem up one side of the shop and down the middle, close but not touching. Dust hung in the air, and the shelves filled more quickly than I could have believed possible.

'Filthy as ever,' Davey said. 'The Environmental Health ought to close you down. I'd forgotten what it was like.'

'I'll need a bath.'

'We could have one together,' Davey suggested. 'There's nothing like a good bath to start an evening. What next?'

I was drifting back along the rows of books. The shelves looked both familiar and strange – things near their usual places but not quite in order. No good trying to judge from the general look of the shelves: better think of valuable items.

I had known from the first that the rows of illustrated books were untouched. Now I wandered up and down the side aisles, looking for my best volumes. Davey stood, watching me prowl. The good Bewick was in its place. And the Grandville. For a moment I hoped that some of the four-decker Victorian novels were missing, but then I found where he'd shelved them at knee height.

'Well?'

'I can't see that anything's missing.'

Davey hesitated. 'In my day we used to keep the good stuff in that little locked cupboard with the glass door. Where is it?'

'Someone leaned on the glass a couple of weeks ago. It's away being reglazed with something shatterproof.'

'Where's the stuff?'

'I had it on two shelves over the desk. Not even touched. I made sure yesterday when the police came.'

'Manuscripts? Signatures?'

'No. Only a couple of sheets, all rubbish. Don't go on about it, it doesn't make sense.' It did make sense in a mad way, but Barnabas believed it was Davey's mad sense, and I couldn't be sure Barnabas was wrong, and I couldn't say that, because it had to seem like an accusation. I shivered. 'Let's just finish, and maybe I'll see some hole in the stock.'

But I gave up eventually. Davey had vanished into the office, and I could hear the rustle of papers being piled together. I followed him, walked round the edge of the door, and found myself held and kissed slowly in a way that – like my reshelved books – seemed both familiar and unfamiliar. He raised his head and I felt his breath in my hair. He said, 'It's time to leave the rest of this. I'm going to buy you a drink. Then I have some business to do, but after that, I'll come back. I don't want to leave you alone.'

I buried my face in his black jacket and closed my eyes, and for a moment was able to stop thinking. If I spoke, I'd find myself saying something stupid, like *If you don't want to leave me alone, why did you, and what the hell are you doing here now?* Confused, perhaps, but appropriate. Then he would say that I had thrown him out, and we'd quarrel – or maybe not this time, maybe we'd both grown up a bit? But I remembered him as being absent for months before I'd stopped pretending.

I moved away. 'It's nearly finished. Then I'm supposed to tell the CID what's gone. They won't do anything until they have a list.'

'What *has* gone?' he asked.

I turned helplessly from desk to table. 'I don't know. Nothing. I mean, nothing except the cash. No books.'

'You're lucky.'

'I know. It must have been someone who doesn't understand about books.'

Davey said softly, 'Or someone who knows enough to reckon he couldn't easily shift them? London antiquarian books are a small world.'

The suggestion stopped me. Yes, but if you were going to worry about that, why do it at all? The key . . . I hadn't explained yet about the key. 'Davey, why would they make such a mess on the way to the cash drawer?'

He was watching me, eyes narrowed, oddly serious. 'Perhaps somebody wanted to make trouble for you.'

'The inspector said it looks like a grudge,' I admitted, thinking, *Who could hate me so much? I haven't hurt anybody. Is it you? I haven't hurt you – you hurt me.* Again I felt a frisson of panic.

Davey held me again. 'Don't. I'm here for as long as you need me.'

It was restful. Which was strange in itself, because whatever our relationship had been, restful was now how I'd describe it. I buried my face in him again and said, 'I'm tired.'

He laughed and ran a finger down my cheek. 'Amazing. Then it's time to lie down.'

I didn't have a chance.

6

You Always Call It an Accident

I stopped in the doorway to make sure that my shop looked like a business again, rather than a rubbish tip, and flipped the sign to OPEN. Then I turned round and watched Davey's back retreating towards Upper Street and whatever it was that he had to do that afternoon. He rounded the corner without looking back, and I stood for a moment breathing the fresh air. I felt drunk. The pub had been postponed, but we'd shared a bottle of Muscatel that I'd been keeping, sitting together on the bed wrapped in the duvet, laughing.

The memory warmed me until I'd closed the door. Then I was frozen by the thought that I'd never again step into this place without wondering whether somebody had been there, or was waiting there still.

Little fingers of panic squeezed the air from my ribs. I pushed them down. I could see perfectly well that the place was empty and untouched. Only the memory of another presence remained; because even the process of clearing up hadn't erased the uneasy feeling that everything was changed, and all bets were off. And I recognized the feeling. It must be like being raped: you would ask, Why me? What's lurking around the corner? When will it happen again? Who can hate me so much?

What I wanted to do was run away. But you can't, so instead I let the impulse push me into being busy. Why on earth hadn't I already arranged for the lock to be changed – was I waiting for somebody to tell me what to do? And I was supposed to contact Inspector Grant. And I still hadn't

41

phoned Barnabas, who'd be full of instructions, but I had to put up with that.

I found a local locksmith in the telephone directory and persuaded him that he could be with me in two hours, As I was hanging up, the bell on the door tinkled and Mrs Acker crept in apologetically. Mrs Acker is one of my locals – a browser. She never says anything, and almost never buys a book unless I'm having a clear-out and have set up the one-pound bin, but I was glad to have somebody else in the place. I left her to it and phoned the number that Inspector Grant had given me. After twenty or thirty rings, a woman's voice said he was out and took my message.

Which just left Barnabas. I didn't want even Mrs Acker overhearing what I anticipated would be a difficult conversation, so I left it again and began sorting the Banbury books once more, with the office door wide open so I could keep an eye on the shelves. After twenty minutes, my customer smiled her apologetic smile at me and left.

I took a deep breath and dialled.

He said without preamble, 'What's wrong?'

'How can you be psychic on a Monday afternoon?'

'I've been phoning,' he said. His voice was plummy with indignation. 'Upstairs. Downstairs. Even your machine wasn't on!'

With a little start of guilt I remembered that my flat was now indeed without a phone. Just as well, that afternoon, but I must start to carry it up and down with me until the police returned the other one. 'I've been in and out,' I said. 'I've been busy. Now look, Barnabas, there's no harm done – in fact, it seems nothing was taken – but somebody broke into the shop yesterday while we were having lunch. And the reason I haven't phoned you is that they pulled every book off the shelves and chucked them all over the floor. I've been dealing with the police and clearing up.'

I was ready for a torrent of questions or exclamations, but he said simply, 'I'm coming,' and hung up before I could argue.

He was stepping out of a taxi just as Inspector Grant's car inserted itself into the row of illegally parked vehicles on the yellow line across the road. They jostled one another in the doorway, both requiring an immediate report. I introduced them. My father gave Grant that little calculating stare with which he always favours any appropriate-looking man he finds in my company. Look out, Grant.

'Nothing,' I told them both. 'There is absolutely nothing missing except for the money in the cash box. I'm not sure how much, but certainly less than a hundred. And about fifty second-class stamps – and some of those were probably useless because I spilled a bottle of buckram cleaner into the drawer last week, and believe me, you wouldn't want to lick something with that on it.'

'I meant to mention the smell,' Grant said.

Barnabas said, 'Impossible. If they were after money, they wouldn't stop to pull the books off the shelves. Why, anybody could have looked in and seen them at it.'

It wasn't a new thought, and I was feeling a little tired of arguing about what had happened. 'Well, they did,' I said flatly.

Barnabas shrugged it aside. 'If somebody just wanted to destroy the business, why not throw petrol about and set fire to the place? Much quicker and safer, I should have thought. You agree, Inspector?'

Grant threw him a curt nod which implied that he did agree, but would prefer not to have to discuss it with the customer.

'There was damage,' I retorted, 'but . . . I don't know how to explain this: accidental damage. It seemed as though they were just in a hurry: pages crumpled, hinges split . . .'

Inspector Grant looked as though somebody had handed him a mysterious parcel containing something as yet unidentifiable, but obviously noxious. He said to Barnabas, 'You're saying that the whole thing was some kind of practical joke?'

My father considered that. 'Or casual vandalism?'

'Not so damn casual,' I said sourly. 'It must have been hard work pulling everything off the shelves, almost as hard as picking it all up again. It's as though somebody was mad with anger or fear or . . . Why would a burglar make such a mess . . . ?'

Asking the right question can lead to the right answer. Something made me remember my sister, Pat, and her burglary a year or two earlier. She and her husband, John, live in a detached house full of possessions in the sort of road where people keep themselves to themselves. They'd come back from France one day to find their patio door forced, their smaller electrical goods removed, and assorted gold charm bracelets and wristwatches missing from the bedroom. The intruders had searched for valuables by the simple expedient of emptying every drawer, shelf and cupboard on to the floor. Insured to the hilt, Pat had complained more about the mess than the actual loss. John said they were lucky: he had heard of burglaries where blood and worse had been smeared on walls and furniture for the luckless victim to find, whereas in this case the mess was merely the simple, unperverted product of a vigorous and hasty search.

' . . . unless he was looking for something?'

Inspector Grant fixed me with a kind of schoolmaster's stare. 'Are you sure there's nothing gone?' He looked around eloquently. Eight or nine thousand volumes now filled the shelves around the shop.

'You do get to know your stock,' I told him coldly.

'If you say so. Look, I don't disagree with your suggestion – it could make sense. But if we're going to get anywhere with this, you'd better tell me what they were looking for and why they thought it was here if it wasn't.' He was staring from me to Barnabas with an unfriendly expression. He'd stopped talking about how the intruders had managed to get in, but I realized that he still thought we were hiding something.

In his shoes, I might have been equally suspicious.

He produced his notebook and scribbled briefly. I could see Barnabas's ironic expression and said quickly, 'What next?'

He turned to Barnabas. 'I understand that you have the second set of keys to this place?'

Barnabas nodded.

'I suppose they aren't missing?'

Barnabas raised an eyebrow, removed his key-ring from a pocket, and held it up. 'No, all correct.'

Grant shrugged and turned to me again. 'Can you come down to the station later? We'll go through the whole story again, I'll get it typed up, and you can sign a complaint.'

'And?' Barnabas enquired.

'I'll ask around. Somebody in the street might have seen something.' His tone of voice said that he doubted it. 'I'll talk to your neighbours while I'm here.'

I pointed out to him that there aren't many people loitering outside my door on a Sunday afternoon.

'All the more likely that somebody would remember seeing them. On a Saturday afternoon around here, they could have carried your whole stock out through the front window without anybody stopping to ask. Shall I expect you at about four thirty, say?' I explained about the locksmith. He smiled sunnily. 'Never mind, come as soon as you're free. I'll still be there.'

When he had departed to do his asking around, Barnabas faced me. 'Why?'

'What?'

'Why didn't you let me know?'

'I was busy.'

'Too busy to pick up the telephone?'

'You couldn't have done anything.'

'I could at least have come round and sat watching you work. Always a pleasure and a surprise to fathers, you know, seeing their children's exertions. I would probably have seen something you missed.'

I felt a spurt of anger. 'There was nothing to see.'

His voice rose, and I realized that he was angry too. 'Will you credit me with still having some mental capacities? Just tell me what all this is about! Even that infant who claims to be a detective inspector, God help us, doesn't believe a word of your story.'

I controlled myself. 'Barnabas, you have no reason to think I'm lying. *I do not know what is going on.* Frankly, I think that somebody simply came in looking for money and found there wasn't much. Saturday was slow. So they messed things up out of spite. Isn't that how burglars are supposed to behave?' I didn't believe what I was saying, but I wished that Barnabas would. 'You hear about people being burgled and finding that the most horrible damage has been done. Remember what the police told John?'

'But the most horrible things *weren't* done here,' Barnabas said coldly. 'Almost *nothing* was "done", was it!'

My souvenir of the reshelving remained in my every aching muscle. 'You should have seen it,' I assured him.

Barnabas glared. 'Be serious. If I were an insurance adjuster, I'd be waiting for you to claim for a dozen books and ten thousand pounds in cash.' He stopped abruptly. 'What was that about keys? How did they get in?'

'I don't know. It was all locked up tight when I got back.'

The news seemed to make my father more angry. 'You'd certainly be advised not to make an insurance claim. Clearly it's a fraud, and we'll both wind up in jail. I speak, of course, on behalf of that imaginary insurance adjuster.'

'If it's any comfort, your "infant detective" and I have already been through all this. He agrees with you. For a moment he almost convinced me I'd left the door unlocked – but I didn't. The back door was bolted inside, so they must have gone in and out through the front. I suppose they had some kind of master key.'

Barnabas hesitated. 'Did you ever send off for an extra one?'

'Of course not. There were never more than two.'

'There *are* three,' he said impatiently. 'Logic, logic!'

I said apologetically, 'Only the registered holder is supposed to be able to order more keys.'

'I'm sure that anything can be copied if you know how,' Barnabas said loftily, once again echoing the official line. 'Don't you make an impression of the original in soft soap, or candle wax, or something else unlikely? I never understood what happens then. Well, that's it, isn't it?'

'That's what?'

'You must know that it was Davey. He's the only person apart from the two of us who ever held a key. Have you told that policeman?'

'Whatever goes wrong, it's always Davey!' I exploded. 'You don't have to go on! Your key, there – that's the one he used to have. He gave it back when he went. How can you say it was Davey?'

I knew he was right, though. It was Davey's way to have copied his key somehow, months ago, when things started going wrong. He wouldn't have had any particular reason in mind; he just liked to feel that he always had a hold on situations.

Barnabas shook his head. 'Obviously it's no coincidence that he's suddenly turned up. What does he want?'

I almost snapped, My body, of course, but I couldn't quite do it to him. I watched my fingers move along the front of a shelf. 'I think he might want to come back.'

There was a silence, then: 'Don't.' Despite it all, Barnabas's voice was gentle. 'Don't please even think that. I'm sorry, I really hoped that you were over it.'

I smiled. 'I am over it. But you never liked him.'

'You know,' he said slowly and still gently, 'you're wrong. In a way, I do like him. He's amusing, attractive . . . What do I mean? A pity that he's about ten years old. I hoped, when he left, that you could get on with your life better without having a ten-year-old child to look after.'

You were wrong, weren't you, Barnabas.

I said, 'I don't seem to have had much to get on with, do I.'

'There's time. When you've really finished with him, things will get better. I think your mourning is nearly over.'

I waited.

'But I still wonder what it is he wants. Hasn't he said anything?'

'Nothing sensible.' I was remembering Davey upstairs in my flat, in what had once been our bed – remembering my discovery that I had been missing him. It was like unwrapping a Christmas present to find that it was already broken. For a moment I almost hated Barnabas. I think he realized.

'What will you say to Mr Grant when you see him?'

'Nothing. Not about Davey. We don't know.'

'What will you do about it?'

I said again, 'Nothing. I don't know. Try to work it out.'

Barnabas sighed. 'I'm very sorry, my dear.'

I said, 'I know. You don't have to be, though. Will you go home now? I have a lot to do. The locksmith is coming. I don't want to talk just now. Shall I phone for a taxi?'

'I'll find one in Upper Street.' But he stood in the doorway, and we stared at one another until the locksmith's van edged up the street and hovered in front of the shop. 'I wish I didn't feel you were in some kind of physical danger here,' he said, and left abruptly.

I spent the next hour following the locksmith around, watching him put a new lock on the shop door and another on the door of the flat. I would have had it done even without Barnabas's parting shot. While the man was there, I got him to install lockable bolts on the upstairs windows. I hated it, but I hated even more the idea of being unprotected. He recommended an ultrasonic security system for the shop and grilles on the kitchen windows overlooking the flat roof, and I let him measure up with Mr Spock making plaintive enquiries.

'You,' I said to my cat, 'will be on velvet, mister. We'll be able to leave the windows open. You can go hunting day and night if you want to.' The locksmith threw me a peculiar look which said, Another mad old woman talking to her cat, and promised to have them ready by Friday. I wrote him a deposit cheque large enough to put my bank account into overdraft and saw him out.

It was time to go down to the police station. Brushing my hair, I looked with distaste at the face in the bathroom mirror. I was just about to let myself out when I remembered that I'd brought the telephone back upstairs and forgotten to plug it in. Do it now, Dido, or you'll forget about it and Barnabas will turn up again – what had Davey said? – on his white horse. And (at the back of my mind) Davey may phone . . .

It rang just as I was plugging the jack into the wall, and when I picked up the receiver it was indeed my father's voice. He said without preamble, 'Is it done? I wanted to make sure.'

'I'm in a bloody fortress,' I assured him.

There was a silence. I waited.

He said, 'I wanted to know . . .'

'Well?'

'Have you told the boy detective about the other night?'

'What other night?'

'Dido!'

'All right, No. Not yet.'

'But you will? And the note – don't forget about that, it's much more important than what did, or didn't, actually happen at the time. I have it here safe. You'd better give it to them.'

I clutched the sideboard. 'All right, I will.'

He hadn't finished. The little voice in the earpiece tickled and nagged. 'There's a pattern. Consider this. First, you're followed, chased, frightened; not robbed, raped, beaten, killed, or any of the things that happen to women alone on empty roads at night. Then I get a note which goes to the trouble of pointing this out, just in case we weren't bright enough to think of it for ourselves. A few days pass. We are burgled, but not robbed, beaten. You do see what I mean?'

Yes, of course I did, because this was only what had been at the back of my mind ever since.

'Now, they must have been in the shop for some time, to judge by your description. They could very well have been seen – there are passers-by even on a Sunday, even shoppers . . .' I listened to an abbreviation of one of Barnabas's diatribes against Sunday opening and the materialism of our culture. He broke off. 'So there is something worth the risk. Listen. I want you to consider that Davey is involved.' I started to speak. 'Just accept that he might be. Otherwise, you won't be thinking clearly about . . . about whatever is going to happen next.'

I took a deep breath. 'Nothing else *is* going to happen.'

'My dear child, don't pretend you are stupid. You must keep your eyes open. You are in danger. You must defend yourself.'

My stomach lurched. There was nothing to say.

'Dido? Listen, you are going to talk to that policeman now. Tell him about the car business. You must. It might make him a little more inclined to take things seriously, which at the moment he is not doing.'

'I wish I knew whether things should be taken seriously,' I said. My voice didn't give anything away about panic. I was quite proud of it.

Our local police station had recently been refurbished. Great wooden hoardings had just come down, revealing a glum-looking yellow brick building indistinguishable, as far as I could see, from its previous incarnation. The enquiries area had seats along the side which seemed to have been newly upholstered, but the walls were the same institutional cream that I'd always seen when I walked past the glass doors.

I gave my name at the desk. Grant appeared, nodded, and led me through the inner doors. We negotiated a little knot of uniformed police in front of the lift and turned right down a corridor lined with closed doors. The place looked like the offices of some unprofitable service company. In the green-painted room that Grant shared with two untenanted, paper-laden desks, uncountable grey metal filing cabinets, a dying pot plant and a computer terminal, I spent half an hour answering questions with a tape machine whirring and a woman police constable sitting silently against the wall. I guess she was supposed to protect me against male brutality. The statement, when I signed, said everything that I had given him. The truth, a bit of the truth, and nothing but the truth so far as it went. I hadn't told him about the white car. I made excuses to myself, but perhaps my only reason was that I knew I needed to talk to Davey first.

I'd walked there to clear my head; going home, I hopped into a taxi in front of the supermarket because it was after six and he was due at seven and I needed time to think of all the things we had to sort out. Or maybe just to get my courage up.

By eight o'clock, he hadn't arrived and hadn't phoned. I sat with my television tuned to a programme I wasn't watching, remembering a thousand other times just like this, rehearsing old speeches. Why didn't you just phone me? No, above all not a wifely whine. Perhaps instead: Davey, what made you turn up just now? Davey, do you know anything about a little white GTi with two men in it? Davey, Barnabas thinks it was you who . . .

When the doorbell rang, I picked up my bag, looked briefly at my white face in the mirror by the door, decided that I had neither the time nor the desire to do anything about it, and went down the stairs.

My first impression was of too many people, but there were only two: DI Grant and the woman PC who had been sitting in his office that afternoon. They were so unexpected that I must have gaped at them. He said, 'We'd better come in.'

'I was going out.'

'We'd better go up,' he persisted, and pushed in. I turned away and led them upstairs before I faced him and said fatuously, 'Aren't you ever off duty?'

'As a matter of fact, I was going, but I was still in the station when something came up on the computer, and since I knew you, and everybody else is flat out at the moment, I said I'd drop off on my way home.'

The dread welled up. I thought I'd drown in it. '*Barnabas?*'

'No! No, it's about David Winner.'

Barnabas! What have you told him? I said, 'Yes? As a matter of fact, we were going to have dinner tonight, but he's late.'

He gave me a sharp, odd look. 'There's been an accident . . . Funny how you always call it an accident. His car blew up. I'm very sorry. He died on the way to hospital. Your name was in his wallet as next of kin, and . . . Are you all right?'

7

Tell Dido

The sunlight slanting through the windows bathed a bank of filing cabinets, and the wilting ficus on top of it, in a brightness that did them no favours. Someone had brought me a plastic cup filled with cardboard coffee, and I sat wondering how to get rid of it, looking at the dying plant and trying to work out what I was going to say to the man behind the desk.

Grant cleared his throat. 'I'm sorry to bring you in again. Are you all right?'

I said, 'Yes, of course I'm all right. I want to thank you for coming and telling me yourself last night. After you left, Barnabas made me take two of his sleeping pills. I'm fine now.'

I lied. How to say that I sat in his chair talking, holding a cup of something distantly related to coffee, with the memory of Davey Winner's eyes, voice, hands enveloping me so strongly that it was somehow physical.

Inspector Grant seemed to find it necessary to make a study of the wall behind my head. 'I'm sorry. If I'd known . . . you had different surnames, you see. I didn't realize what the relationship was.'

I said, 'You were fine. Anyway, I hadn't seen him for nearly two years, not until the last few days. I don't know why he was still carrying my name around in his wallet.'

Grant hesitated. 'Do you mind if I turn the tape recorder on? It might save time later.'

I shrugged and shifted in the slippery chair. I didn't want to be in a paper-cluttered office in a police station, talking about Davey. I didn't even want this man mumbling apologies in a sympathetic, embarrassed voice. I sat breathing through my mouth. I've found that it makes control easier.

Grant finished his own coffee, hesitated fractionally, and tossed the cup at his wastepaper basket. When it missed, he frowned at it, then at me. 'It wasn't entirely because he was carrying your name around that I came to tell you. He didn't die in the blast. One of our people went in the ambulance with him. They were keeping him sedated, of course, and I gather he wasn't making much sense when he tried to talk to them.' He paused. 'They knew he wasn't likely to survive.'

Another nightmare is made up of images of blood from the movies. I took a breath right down into my diaphragm and let it out and was able to ask steadily, 'I don't understand. What did he say? What happened?'

'I have a photocopy of our man's notes.' Grant pulled a sheet of paper closer without looking at it. 'There were a few confused words. Your name – that was the thing. When I saw . . . I've never known anyone else called "Dido".'

My parents named me after a heroine in an obscure Elizabethan play. Dido was a queen of Carthage. Also unlucky in love. 'You mean he was talking about *me*?'

'About you, maybe *to* you. Nothing very clear. He said, "Tell Dido it's really." '

It seemed somehow characteristic of Davey to appeal to reality and then evade it. '*Really*' what? 'Is that all?'

'Nothing else makes sense. A certain amount of, well, cursing – he was in some pain at first, despite the morphine he was getting.'

I stared into my coffee, facing what was literally unthinkable. If I allowed it, I'd only find myself drowning in what had happened and how I'd felt about Davey, whether he really . . . although in cold moments of course I knew that, really, Davey wasn't the man to leave deathbed confessions of eternal love. Not really. Now if ever was the point when pretending ought to stop.

I said flatly, 'It's not much of a message, is it.'

'No. I wish we knew what he started to say. We need anything that might throw a bit of light on this business. What was he up to?'

There was something here that made no sense to me. I abandoned my cold coffee on the corner of his desk. '*Up to?*'

Grant leaned back abruptly in his swivel chair, looking as though he would like to dissect me – I felt a preliminary twinge in the belly.

'When a car blows up, it has to do with something nasty. Terrorism or serious . . .' Then he must have seen my face. 'It was a device. A bomb. Didn't you understand that?' I got my jaw under enough control to let out some kind of squeak. He looked genuinely astonished. 'Then we've been at cross-purposes. It *was* a bomb – the kind you see in films, under the engine, set off either by the ignition or by a remote control of some kind – we'll know by this afternoon what sort of device it was and – maybe – where it came from.'

The phone on his desk rang. He snapped, 'DI' and began a monosyllabic conversation which lasted long enough for me to get ready to speak intelligibly. When he hung up I said – unnecessarily – that I'd assumed it was an accident. 'That old van he drives . . . I thought it had finally . . . He never had it serviced properly, you know, he always asked some mate of his to . . . I assumed it caught fire.' I heard myself babbling and stopped.

Grant was silent for so long that I had time to think of a dozen questions. I held back only because some woman poked her head around the door, took a look at Inspector Grant's face, and retreated.

'First,' Grant said, 'it wasn't a van. I guess you are out of date, at that. It was a car, a new car.'

New? I was indeed out of date. Where did Davey Winner get the money for a new car?

'Point two: of course it wasn't any accident. That kind of thing means either protection, drugs or terrorism. The liaison officer from the anti-terrorist squad doesn't know anything about a connection.' He cleared his throat again. I was learning that this meant he was coming to the point. 'It had to be drugs, given Winner's track record. The Hornsey police thought he'd started dealing the past couple of months – cannabis, Ecstasy, speed – not just little deals for his mates, but something bigger. They were waiting to identify his sources, but they weren't getting very far. I guess they missed something. As a matter of fact, they were thinking of pulling him in and applying pressure. As for a terrorist connection . . .'

I said, 'No. He talked politics sometimes, but he didn't even bother to vote.'

'He's not on the central computer, so I'm sure you're right. So . . .'

I started to say, As for drugs, he never had that kind of money. And remembered.

Grant noticed. 'Yes?'

I said slowly, 'He had money. I don't understand about the car. Usually Davey was skint. He even asked me for a job the other day. But you say it was a new car? And then he took me out to dinner on Saturday at The Restaurant. That's . . .'

'I've heard of it.'

I thought, So much for neighbourhood cops. 'I mean that he actually paid the bill. Cash.'

'So?'

'Look, he never bought a new car in his life. I'm surprised that his credit rating would stand it. You should find out whether he was keeping up the payments.'

'There's no charge recorded against the car.'

I didn't understand the term.

'It wasn't financed. He owned it outright.'

No. Not my Davey.

He was watching my face. He said, 'Good! We're getting somewhere.'

'Maybe he'd sold a painting.' Davey did sell paintings sometimes.

Grant scribbled a note. 'We'll ask.'

'Or he might have . . .'

'What?'

It suddenly seemed important to explain. 'Davey was . . . I don't know how to say it. He was only dishonest in certain ways. He felt that he had the right. He didn't like work – except painting. He wasn't very good at that, but he was very serious. He thought other things were a waste of time. He could always borrow money from people, and he always paid you back if he could, if it wasn't too much, if he counted you as a friend and not just a mark.'

Of course that was it: Davey was a man you could safely trust to certain clear boundaries; but it was never a good idea to place too much confidence in him, because it was easy for him to get in too far and too deep, and then, as they say, he would make an excuse and leave the room. I suddenly saw an image of Davey twisting and turning in a maze, getting more and more lost. He'd been that kind of man.

And I'd finally spoken his epitaph.

I looked up to find Grant watching me. I took another breath. 'I could certainly see him dealing in soft drugs, or in things . . . trading. Stolen goods, if you want to know. He didn't have much belief in ordinary honesty. But . . .'

'But?'

I tried. 'But his being murdered doesn't make any sense. I mean deliberately murdered, not killed in . . . in a fight or something. An accident. I could easily see him being killed in some kind of accident. He was careless, you see.'

He nodded slowly. 'Out of his league. Yes – we thought that too.'

Well, if you want to put it that way.

'Unless he was moving into something. There's a lot of crack on the streets these days. Half our work here ties in with drugs one way or the other. If somebody saw him as a threat . . . But street dealers don't use bombs – yet.'

'You can't ask me,' I said. 'In the old days I would have known, or at least guessed. But we haven't kept in touch. He only turned up again last Friday.'

'So it was a friendly divorce. But why did he just "turn up"? How often have you seen him since you split up?'

No, not friendly; but that wasn't police business. And just why had Davey turned up? 'Never, and I haven't a clue what made him turn up now,' I said honestly. 'Anyway, for up-to-date information, you'll have to talk to Ilona Mitchell. He was living with her. He said she's visiting her parents, but I imagine you can find out where that is.'

I thought he looked at me speculatively. 'We've talked to her. You're mistaken. She was at home. Hysterical, and not making a lot of sense. She said they'd been going out somewhere, and then he cried off at the last minute – said he had to do something. So they'd had a row. She's still sedated to the eyeballs. One moment she's in tears because she could have been in the car with him, and the next she's crying because he's dead and she isn't. Constable Franks – one of our WPCs who's been with her – doesn't think she had the foggiest idea that anything unusual was going on.'

I almost laughed: he'd been going out with Ilona, and then changed his mind and decided to spend the evening with me. I was familiar with that pattern, though mostly from the other side of the fence.

At last I said, 'By the way, it doesn't make any difference any more, but while we were married, he had the second key to the shop. Barnabas got it from him when he left.' I was on my feet before I knew that I was going, but I'd had enough. I said, 'I need to go away and think. If I remember anything relevant, I'll get in touch.'

He was on his feet too, switching off the recorder. 'Would you like a lift home?'

I shook my head. 'I have the car. I put it into your car park – I didn't fancy risking a ticket.'

I thought his face changed. He said, 'I'll come down with you.'

He led me back to the entrance and out of the main door. In the street, he took my elbow and steered me along the front of the building and round the corner to the big gate I'd driven through. As we stepped on to the asphalt of the car park, he was almost pushing me to the left, towards the Volvo in the far corner. I stopped. I don't like being pushed. 'It would have been easier to come out the back entrance,' I said, and saw it.

Near the door at the rear of the station, a green tarpaulin covered something more or less car-shaped. I'd seen it on the way in, but it hadn't registered.

He said, 'Damn! Sorry. That's supposed to have gone off to the lab in Lambeth, but the transporter hasn't turned up from Traffic. They'll find anything that can possibly help.'

I must have gone white, because his hand was holding my arm hard enough to hurt. I said, 'What colour is it?'

'What?'

'Davey's car. What . . .'

'White.'

'A little white hatchback.' It wasn't even a question. Oh, Barnabas, you were right all the time. I said, 'I need to look at it. I'm not being morbid. I just need to see the rear window. Please.'

At least he had the sense not to ask questions yet. We crossed to the distorted shape, and I stopped ten feet away because I couldn't go any closer. The car had been dumped with its rear end outward. Inspector Grant hauled at the straps and edged the tarpaulin up to the roof. The glass of the rear window faced me. It had shattered and sagged out of its frame, but I found what I had expected. You could still read the pathetic, silly joke on the fire-blackened sticker. CAUTION: MOTHER-IN-LAW IN BOOT.

I heard my voice say from a distance, 'There's something else I need to talk to you about, but I have to go home just now. Barnabas was right, after all. I have to go home.'

He was staring at me, eyes narrowed. I could see him decide to go with the flow. That, I thought vaguely, was nice of him, probably.

'I'll take you back,' he said. 'You'd better not drive. You're as white as a sheet.'

So there was no way I was going to get out of telling the whole story, not any more.

8

Personal Storm

The coffee was too strong, but at least it would obliterate the memory of the powdered-milk stuff at the police station. We sat at my kitchen table, as though we were friends, until I was ready to tell everything.

Almost everything.

The white car with its unamusing winking headlight which had been Davey's car; the note delivered to Barnabas; Davey's reappearance; the wrecking of the shop. Laid out in chronological order, their meaning still escaped me. And yet Barnabas was right: these things were somehow connected. Anything else was impossible.

Grant asked questions – dozens of unanswerable questions which all boiled down to the one unanswerable question: why? In the end, he left. He promised to speak to me soon. I believed him.

It had been days since I'd had the time to do any shopping. Perhaps I should take the car and stock up with enough to keep me alive until I'd managed to get my life into some kind of order? Or perhaps I didn't care to. I dug the dry heel of a loaf out of the bread bin and carved two hard slices off it to shove into the toaster. Half a jar of marmalade lurked at the back of one of the cupboards. I scraped off a thin layer of mould, and the rest was fine. I ate standing at the window, watching Mr Spock prowl restlessly along the edge of the flat roof.

When I went to check my answering machine, the light was flashing, and Barnabas's voice was on the tape saying, 'Oh Lord, Dido, why are you

57

never in?' After a second or two of silence there was a sound remarkably like a giggle. 'Well, at any rate, be warned: there's a thunderstorm heading your way. Call me if you need an umbrella!' Beep.

I really wasn't in the mood, and why couldn't Barnabas ever learn to give the time of his phone calls? I should phone him back. No, I should go downstairs to phone, There was, I reminded myself bitterly, a kind of fairy tale about how I was running a business. My trade customers were used to irregular hours, most of them being guilty of their own irregularities, but there was always the outside chance that a millionaire might wander in off the street and give me thousands of pounds for some obscure book he'd always longed for.

What I really wanted to do was go to bed with a gin and the television set, but my conscience was at work. I bought it off by pouring half an inch of Gordon's into a clean mug, finding my keys, tucking my telephone under my arm (why couldn't the police have returned my other phone by now?) and heading downstairs.

I was unlocking the shop door when a shadow at my back brought my heart into my throat. I whirled . . . and saw that the thunderstorm had arrived.

'Pat!' I said faintly. 'How nice to see you.'

Barnabas's description of my elder sister as a storm referred to her manner only. Pat is older (by four years), bigger, fairer, more straightforward, and probably altogether tougher than I am. She stood, wrapped in a mac and head scarf against the wind-driven drizzle that had begun during my elaborate lunch, looking determined.

'It *says* that you open at eleven. I've been back twice. Where on earth have you been?'

'Lunch, cup of tea,' I said indistinctly, hastily swallowing the evidence to the contrary in my mug.

'All morning?'

Pat is a well-organized lady; her lunch-hour is 12.30 to 1.15 on weekdays, and she doesn't even go out to work.

I said, 'Police station. I couldn't help it.'

Pat's handsome pink face stiffened. 'I know. Dad told me. Dido, why in heavens didn't you let me know what was going on? I would have come in to look after him. I knew there was something wrong the minute I phoned this morning, but I had to drag the whole story out of him. Why didn't you let me know about the robbery? And Davey being killed? Oh,

Dido, what is going on here? Are you all right?'

I finished unlocking the door and got us in off the street, because when Pat decides to take me in hand, the consequences can be lengthy and abrasive.

'I've been so busy with the police – really, Pat, I haven't had a minute to think. Anyway, I wasn't seriously burgled; they broke in, but they only took a bit of cash.'

I turned my back on her plaintive, 'And what about Barnabas? He must have been worried sick. It's not good for him, you know. And what's this about Davey?'

I said, 'Thank you for your condolences,' and swept ahead of her into the office, looking furtively around: it looked all right now.

Pat was exploding again. 'Condolences? Well, of course it was a shocking accident, but I can't say that I ever cared for him much one way or the other, and you know you hated him!'

'Of course.' I took a deep breath, wondering what made Pat my keeper, but knowing the answer all the same. Our mother's death had pushed her into feeling ultimately responsible for her old father and her flighty younger sister, and she couldn't get herself out of the role. She plonked herself down on the second chair, radiating dissatisfaction. I caught myself casting another furtive look around the office, as though I expected critical comments about my housekeeping. I placed the empty mug with its tell-tale smell of gin on a high shelf. Damn it, why did I always react this way to Pat's presence? I'd think it was just her being my elder sister, except that I knew she affected Barnabas the same way.

'Tell me,' she demanded, 'all about it.'

I temporized. 'What did Barnabas say?'

'Nothing at all. Just about the shop being wrecked – it looks all right now – and then Davey. His car caught fire?' I felt myself relaxing a little: apparently Barnabas had confined his account to the basics. In the background, I heard her voice going on. 'Well, it's terrible and I'm sorry – of course I am, really. You have been having a time of it! But Dido, why on *earth* didn't you phone me? I'd have come down right away! I'm your sister, you know. You should let me take care of you a bit more. And Daddy – somebody ought to have been keeping an eye on him. In the circumstances.'

I sighed. 'Barnabas has been wonderful. I think he's enjoying the excitement, really.' I described the great bookshop burglary mystery, and gave her a selective account of Davey's death. I didn't have to say much about that: it was understood that I found the subject unexpectedly painful.

'Heavens!' She thought. 'I'll take Dad back with me for a week, just for a rest.'

I was tempted to agree, only I could imagine Barnabas's face. 'He'd worry about me,' I said. Worrying Barnabas was the one thing that Pat would not allow even herself to do.

'You come too.'

I shook my head firmly. 'I have a business to run, and it's been disrupted enough as it is. I really think that Barnabas is . . .' I groped for the right words. ' . . . better off staying quietly at home. It's always so exciting for him having the boys around. At his age . . .' The feeling of hypocrisy stopped me in mid-sentence.

Pat was always inclined to want to put Barnabas safely to bed for nursing. But I went on emphasizing the value of normality and the dedication with which I kept in contact with our father by telephone almost continuously; so that by the time Barnabas opened the shop door, she was weakening.

'In here,' I called. He poked his head around the end of the book cases. I said meanly, 'I thought you'd turn up. We were wondering about taking you to St Albans for a rest . . .'

When Pat left, Barnabas lingered. Remarkably, two customers arrived and it took me a while to deal with them. Even more remarkably, they gave me several hundred pounds between them, and one of them expressed a credible interest in the Ackermann. He might come back. Barnabas hovered in the background, waiting for a report of the morning's visit to the police. When the shop was empty again, I told him.

'So now we know,' Barnabas said. 'Not that any other explanation was possible.'

'But it doesn't answer any of the real questions, does it.'

'No. Still, it's good.'

I said, 'Just what does that mean?'

'It means . . . well, it means it's finished. He's dead. You're – safe.'

His choice of words made me stop short. 'No more burglaries? No more funny notes through your door?' I hoped that I'd spoken quickly enough to stop him thinking about it, because there were two things I might have said. One: there had been a second man in Davey's car that night. Two: until I found out who could possibly have any interest in murdering Davey

Winner, I couldn't be sure whether he might also have an interest in me. I'd happily leave Inspector Grant to sort out mad bombers, but that second man worried me.

Barnabas said abruptly, 'Dido – leave it!'

'Are you reading minds today?' I asked him sourly.

'Your face,' he said sternly, 'is a picture. Oh Lord, Dido, I hoped that you didn't care about him so much.'

So much? I'd been surprised when Davey had turned up, surprised I could want to see him again. I'd assumed for over two sore years that I hated him because he had somehow shamed me, and then he'd turned up as though nothing had happened between us.

'I'd forgotten how nice he could be . . . I don't really mean "nice".'

'I trust not!' Barnabas switched to donnish indignation. 'Davey wasn't at all nice. Dido, wake up! Your mother and I did not want our daughters to be victims. I thought we'd raised you not to be sentimental!'

I said bitterly, 'You did. Just give me time. I'm trying to cope!'

Suddenly he said, 'I wish that you'd had a child.'

I felt myself glaring. 'Ouch! So I just felt motherly towards Davey, did I? That makes me a real fool!'

Barnabas glared back. 'You're allowed to have loved him.'

I said, 'I need to know what's going on. I have to understand what this is all about. The police – do you think that boy detective is good enough to find out?'

Barnabas looked sour. 'He seems to be young for his rank, so I suppose he's passed his exams or whatever it depends on nowadays.'

'He thinks that Davey was mixed up in drugs. He thinks it's something to do with that.'

'Then he's probably right.'

'But what does that have to do with me?'

Barnabas hesitated. 'He couldn't have . . . I don't know . . . hidden something here in the shop?'

I considered that. If Davey had suddenly needed a place that his new contacts didn't know about to hide his stash, that could perhaps explain his sudden reappearance. It might even explain the break-in, if he'd been trying to retrieve something. I shook my head. 'If he'd done that, I would have seen it. He was with me all the time on the Friday. Unless of course one of his mates brought it in. I suppose he might have come looking for a . . . delivery. But it all seems pretty casual.'

Barnabas considered. 'Since the entire place was upside down, he, or they, presumably didn't find what they were looking for.'

I gave up. 'I've looked at everything in the place – moved everything – in the past couple of days.'

I was lying. What about the flat? I'd have noticed if something had gone missing, but what about something extra that didn't belong there? A full search seemed to be the next step. And I needed to do it myself, right away. I'd get in touch with Inspector Grant when and if I found anything.

For a moment I could hear Davey's voice saying, *Tell Dido it's really* . . . Perhaps, after all, he'd had a message for me.

If he did, there was one other person who just might know. I locked up twenty minutes before closing time and was in the street before I remembered that the Volvo was still down at the police station. Pure frustration made me kick the kerb, and I received a very odd look from a passing woman with a pushchair who quickened her steps, obviously thinking that London was full of madwomen and nobody was quite safe. I relieved her anxiety by hailing a passing taxi and removing my bad-tempered self from her presence.

I didn't look forward to calling on Ilona Mitchell, but if anybody knew about the second man in the car, she did. She might even know what I had at the shop which was so important.

I'd be damned if I didn't at least try to find out.

9

Misery

I knew Ilona Mitchell's address because I'd been politely forwarding Davey's junk mail ever since he'd walked out on me. Wilding Road is one of the late-Victorian terraces that fill the southern edges of Wood Green. The house was divided into flats and, like the rest of the terrace, had a neglected, flaking look. I managed to wedge my recovered Volvo into a space just opposite, turned off the engine, and examined the building's lifeless face. I'd expected a police guard, yellow tape, or at least some horrifying marks on the road to show where the car had exploded and burned, but there was nothing. Davey's death had not left so much as a mark on his world.

A painted sign said that the entrance to 12A was down the flight of narrow, litter-strewn cement steps. I followed the arrow down and rang the bell above the WINNER-MITCHELL name card: Davey's work – I recognized the elegant India ink lettering. A bell rang inside but nothing happened. On the fourth ring a noise, or a stirring, made me put my eye to the letter-flap and peer into the darkness. Perhaps there was a movement, I wasn't sure, but it occurred to me suddenly that Ilona might be too frightened to come to the door, so I called into the shadowy hallway.

'Ilona? Please, let me in. It's Dido Hoare. I need to talk to you about Davey.'

This time I was sure that something moved just out of my line of vision. I waited. 'I'm by myself and I have to see you. Let me in – please!'

For a moment I thought she would ignore me, but then I saw something red. I let the flap close. The door opened a crack, on the chain, and I could just make out two expressionless eyes. I'd seen her a few times, but I don't know that I would have recognized that frozen face. I said again, 'Let me in, please. We have to talk.'

The voice was as frozen as the face. 'I'm not seeing anybody.'

I said, 'I understand, but I really have to talk to you about Davey.' I thought that the door started to close. I said quickly, 'I'm not going away.'

The crack narrowed, but the chain clattered down. 'All right,' she said. 'It doesn't matter.'

I took it as an invitation and stepped in, slamming the door behind me. 'Are you on your own? You should have somebody with you.'

She shrugged and walked away, and I followed her into the sitting room of the basement flat.

Davey's big canvases were stacked around three walls. Painted faces, distorted and black-lined, stared out at the unmatched furniture in the middle of the room. I slid round the corner of a coffee table whose surface was filled with dirty mugs and two big overflowing ashtrays, and sat myself down on a sagging sofa. Ilona drifted into the chair opposite, not looking at me. She was wearing an old red wrap, too big for her. There was a stain on the chest. She fumbled at a cigarette packet on the table.

I said again, 'You should have somebody here to keep you company.'

From behind a cloud of smoke she said tonelessly, 'I'm going home in the morning. They've been in and out all the time, asking questions, but I'm going, I don't give a fuck what they say. I don't know anything. I don't even know why you're here. If they want to talk to me any more, they can come to Stafford.'

I said carefully, 'Is that where your family is?'

She shrugged again, and I took it as assent. Her silence made light-hearted conversation difficult. I said, 'They can't stop you going home.'

'What do you want?'

All right, then. 'I want to find out what's going on. You know that Davey got in touch with me a few days ago?' There was no response, but something in her expression changed: she'd known, all right. 'He was in trouble of some kind. I saw that.' Anyway, I should have seen it. 'He said that he wanted to start working at the shop again, but he didn't really, did he? He wasn't short of money.' She shifted in the chair and stubbed out the half-smoked cigarette, and I knew that was it. 'There was some trouble about the money, wasn't there!'

'I don't know sod all about the money.' Her voice was tight.

I let my tone grow sarcastic. 'I'm not the police, you know.'

She looked at me directly for the first time. Her eyes were red and haunted. She'd been crying for Davey or for herself. Her hands twisted in her lap, and I saw the bitten fingernails.

'Do you have any cigs? I'm out.'

'I don't smoke.'

'What do you want?' she asked again.

'I want you to tell me why Davey was killed.'

She let out a little bark of hoarse laughter. 'If I knew.'

'Maybe you don't know, but we can work it out, if you'll just talk to me.' The hands went on twisting, but she showed no sign of wanting to respond. The silence dragged until I began to think we would sit there together for ever. Not a happy future, 'For example – last Thursday. Do you know where Davey went last Thursday evening? Who he was with?'

She said, 'Don't be stupid.'

The answer threw me. I shifted to a straight attack. 'I want to know who was with Davey last Thursday night up in Buckinghamshire.'

Again the explosive, hoarse laugh. 'Come off it!' She threw me a quick little look, furtive and yet somehow triumphant, and it occurred to me for the first time that Ilona had always hated me. I tried to digest the insight. Half by instinct I said, 'All right, but I just want to hear you say it.'

She stared at me bleakly with her pink-rimmed eyes and made a dismissive gesture with one hand. 'Okay, you know it was me. So what? It was just a silly joke. No harm done.'

I breathed very softly. 'I was pretty pissed off at the time, but you're right – no harm done. Only what were the two of you doing there in the first place?'

She said, I thought a little more readily, 'We went for a drive. Country pub, or something. Davey saw your car heading into Banbury, and he said it was you, let's tag along and see what you were up to.'

'Funny thing to do,' I said mildly.

She laughed hoarsely again. 'Well, it wasn't my idea of a good time, but what the hell, he made it seem like it might be fun. You know?'

I knew. Davey had always been full of surprises. 'You didn't wait all the time I was buying those books and loading them, did you?'

This time it was the shrug. ''Course not. We peeled off and spent the evening in a pub. You were still there at closing time when we went past, so we stopped, and then you moved off, and Davey said we might as well go home. Then you took the wrong turning, and Davey said we'd go along in case you got lost.'

'Very kind of him,' I drawled. 'It's a shame you didn't wave me down and say hello. Anyway, why did he start playing silly games?'

'I don't know.' Tears began to slide hopelessly down her cheeks. 'It was just a joke. He was always a silly bugger, wasn't he – but funny.'

'Yes,' I said, 'pretty funny. Weren't you scared at all?'

'I was scared when you pulled that stopping trick,' she said, sounding indignant. 'I wasn't scared with Davey, he's . . . he was a wonderful driver.'

'So it was just accident that you happened to see me?'

Ilona appeared to be intensely interested in the hands she was holding in her lap. After a moment, she peered at me from under her eyebrows. 'Sure.'

I shook my head, and she flushed a little but remained silent.

'It's a shame about Davey's car. Or was it yours? It was a new car, wasn't it.'

Nod.

'Where did Davey get the money to buy a new car?' I asked mildly.

'How should I know?'

'Did he borrow it?'

There was something in her face that suggested I'd probably found the right answer, but she shrugged again and said she had no idea.

'He never used to have any money. The police told me he'd got mixed up in drugs.'

She shrugged again. 'Yeah? Well, so what? They can't prove it.'

I pushed down against rising impatience. 'They don't *have* to prove it! He's dead. It can't do him any harm now.'

She said distinctly, 'Let sleeping dogs lie, then.'

'Why do you think I'm here?'

'I don't know,' she mumbled. 'I keep asking you.'

'And I'm going to tell you. I'm here because somebody burgled my shop, and I know for sure that it was something to do with Davey.' No need to accuse him outright, not in her present mood. 'I want to know what they wanted. Listen, Davey must have told you something about what he was doing, and now I just want you to tell *me* what was going on. Why shouldn't you? It can't hurt either of you.' I thought she was going to laugh. 'Somebody murdered him. Don't you want them to be caught?'

'What would that help?' she asked.

I groped for the right answer. 'I think it would help me.'

Her hands twisted restlessly in the thin cloth of her wrap. She reached for an empty cigarette packet, then threw it down and stirred in the overflowing ashtray for the longest stub. 'I have to go out and get some fags. Trust you not to have any.'

'In a minute,' I said.

She almost interrupted me. 'Look, I don't know, Davey never told me, just said mind my own business, so I did! Yes, he was getting money somewhere just lately. I don't know what it was for. Yes, it had something to do with you. He didn't say so, but he went all shifty a couple of weeks ago. He said . . . about your shop, that's all.'

I didn't understand. 'What about my shop?'

'He said . . . I thought he was going to get a share of the shop. He said something a little while ago about his share from the business, getting his share . . . something like that.'

I digested this. I knew – Barnabas had never talked about it, but I knew – that at the time of the divorce Davey's solicitors had asked for a division of assets. My solicitor had put an end to that somehow. At the time I had the feeling Barnabas had bought Davey off – Davey was always impatient, always wanted everything right away without waiting. I never brought myself to ask because it had felt too shameful, but the business had remained mine – mine and Barnabas's.

I shook my head. 'That couldn't have happened, you know. It was all settled at the time of the divorce.'

'Well, if you say so, but that's what I thought.'

'It was settled in court,' I assured her. 'Signed, sealed, finished. So what could he have meant?'

She gave one of her dismissive shrugs.

A share in the business? I struggled. 'Do you know whether he'd been talking about it to anybody? I mean, anybody else besides you?'

'Maybe. Davey was always hanging around with people.'

It made no sense, and I suddenly felt that Ilona had been trying to divert me from the real story. If so, she'd nearly succeeded. 'What are you afraid of?' Hang on to that – because I knew from her reaction that I was putting a finger on a sore spot.

She looked up at me from under a tangle of unbrushed blonde hair. 'I don't know what you're driving at.'

'You're frightened of something.' I made it straight and confident. 'Anybody can see that. I think that's why you're going away – to get away from trouble. I can't blame you. You aren't responsible for Davey's messes.'

When she spoke, it seemed she had changed the subject. 'I need to go out and buy some cigarettes. You wouldn't walk down to the corner with me, would you? And back? I don't like to be alone. I'll just go and put some clothes on. I won't be a minute.'

I wasn't sure what to expect – to hear the back door slam, perhaps, or to catch a glimpse of the old red robe fleeing up the steps, but she went into the bedroom and I could hear her rattling hangers. It seemed like a chance to look for . . . what?

I heaved myself noiselessly out of the low sofa and stood inspecting the room. It was a mess of paints, old newspapers, books, dirty dishes . . . a perfect hiding place for anything smaller than a set of the *Encyclopaedia Britannica*. Perhaps if Ilona was really going to leave, I should come back and do a little breaking and entering of my own?

There was an old oak sideboard against the wall, the kind of piece that can be found in any junk shop in the country. It looked especially promising. I walked over silently and slipped a finger under one handle. The drawer was difficult to pull out and, as I'd expected, was stuffed to the top with old papers, bills printed in red, and broken pens. It would take a while to go through it, but if Davey had any secrets to be revealed, they were probably under my hand, Something thudded in the bedroom. I pushed the drawer in quickly and found myself looking at the top of the sideboard. Tucked almost out of sight under a week-old Sunday newspaper was the corner of a sheet of second-class stamps. I lifted up the newspaper. It was half a sheet of stamps, with one end stained and discoloured. Even without leaning closer I could smell the pungency of my buckram cleaner.

She said, behind me, 'I'm ready.'

For a moment I wondered whether I was going to be sick. No. I put the newspaper down so that it hid the stamps entirely. I said, 'Let's go.'

We walked silently to an off-licence where she bought five packs of cigarettes and a bottle of vodka. Supplies for the night, I supposed. And silently back. Sitting again in her cloud of smoke, she talked a little about Davey. There was nothing else, or nothing she would agree to remember or to guess at. Outside the windows, dusk was falling, and the cigarette smoke was beginning to get to me. So in another way was my consciousness of the stolen stamps sitting a few feet away.

In the end I gave up. I wrote my phone number on a slip of paper from my notebook and tucked it into the bag she had taken to the shop.

'Phone me,' I said, 'if there's anything that you think might help.'

She shrugged for the last time and said, 'Sure,' and I left her in her tobacco haze. I thought she was probably full of guilty secrets, but I wasn't going to get at them tonight.

I sat in the Volvo for a long time, trying to think with a brain fogged up by cigarette fumes and Ilona's helpless misery. I had found out more than I'd expected, and been left with more questions. I knew that Davey was not only the joker in the car, but the intruder in the shop. But I'd known that already – hadn't I? And with the second person I'd seen in the hatchback turning out to be Ilona herself, even that avenue had been blocked. I'd got the confirmation, not an explanation. What I needed was explanations; let the police bother about proof.

There was a telephone box beside the road halfway up Crouch Hill, and I pulled the car over and dialled the number in my notebook before I knew what I was doing. I was tired. I couldn't keep hold of all this any more, not without help. When I asked for Inspector Grant, I scarcely expected him to be at work, but they paged him and put me through. Did the man live on the job?

'I need to talk to you.'

'I was just going off . . .'

'I've been to see Ilona Mitchell. It was Davey who trashed my shop, and it was Davey and Ilona in the car last week. I think it must have something to do with what's happened.'

I thought there was a rather long pause. Then his voice said, 'Right. Can you meet me at the bistro on the corner of Almeida and Upper Streets? I'll buy you a meal.'

The day was proving to be full of surprises. This one threw me off balance for a moment. But why not? Two unbroken hours of Ilona Mitchell had left me needing food and a drink. Probably a couple of drinks. Still wondering, I said, 'I'll be there in half an hour.'

10

Hard Times

Somewhere, a bell was probably ringing – unless it was just a part of the throbbing in my head. I opened one eye cautiously. From his seat on top of the wardrobe, Mr Spock enquired after my state of health. I said, 'Don't ask,' and set about discovering whether I could get myself upright. I could, but a strange thudding, like mercury reluctantly adjusting its level in my head, brought back the memory of the evening. Something about one bottle of Côte du Rhone following another and being followed by a brandy or two. There had been duck. And a tiramisu. Oh.

The bell stopped for a moment or two, and I contemplated collapsing; but when it started again I padded slowly out to the sitting room to answer the phone.

'Ummm . . . Dido? How are you?'

I examined my face in the gilt-framed mirror above the fireplace. I thought it looked smug, but there was a certain darkness around the eyes. 'I'm alive. Just.' I closed my eyes to rest them and tried to think about the evening. It had gone on for hours, and there were quite a few blanks in my memory. I said, 'I think I overdid it. How are you . . . Paul?' Yes, I definitely remembered us reaching first-name terms quite early on.

His voice came drily. 'I'll live.' Well, good. I glanced painfully at my wristwatch, Nine thirty. By now, he'd presumably set up a rota of constables to ferry canteen coffee to him at ten-minute intervals.

'Thanks,' I told him. 'I needed to unwind. From the way I feel at the moment, I must have done a lot of unwinding.'

'We both did.' I tried to read the expression in his voice, but gave up. 'Do you remember about getting home?' Slightly alarmed, I wondered whether I did. There was an impression of the back seat of a car, a certain warmth, a rather lengthy kiss at the downstairs door. I was pretty sure it was the downstairs door. 'The minicab,' he said. 'Neither of us was in a state to drive. Your car's still on a meter near the bistro. I've asked somebody to go down there and put some money in for you – can you pick it up before eleven?'

I almost made a joke about the convenience of police corruption, but I wasn't sure whether we were on those terms yet so I cut it to, 'Yes, of course. And thanks again.'

'I'd like to do it again.'

A policeman? My generation is cynical about policemen. 'I'd like that,' I said.

I went carefully into the kitchen to find the Alka-Seltzer and heat up yesterday's coffee. Mr Spock's tin was opened and emptied – I realized with a guilty pang that he hadn't been fed last night – and then I set about the business of turning myself into a human being again, which involved a large mug of coffee and a hot bath. Lying submerged, with my eyes closed and the coffee mug balanced on my breastbone so that it wouldn't be too difficult to lift as far as my mouth, I contemplated the situation. The memory of the doorstep kiss was positive, if vague. Well – why not? I finished the coffee, closed my eyes, pinched my nose, and sank under the surface, then rose in a fountain of warm water that drove Spock from his companionable perch at the foot of the tub, and groped for the shampoo. Clean, moist, and in my right mind, I left to rescue the Volvo with half an hour to spare. I was actually feeling cheerful.

The positive mood barely faltered in response to the bank statement lying in ambush on the floor of the shop when I got back. If I were properly interested in money I'd be running a bank, not a bookshop. I checked the account charges, decided that they were correct though excessive, and set about digesting the fact that Dido Hoare Books was deeply in the red and that Dido Hoare Proprietor had to do something about it.

The rest of the mail consisted mostly of catalogues, junk mail, and small bills. There was one order for a twenty-pound book from the last catalogue, which I virtuously invoiced and started to wrap while waiting for better things and keeping an eye on a remarkably tall, bespectacled young man who had wandered in and was drifting through the philosophy section. He looked to me like a reader, not a buyer, and confirmed it by departing (after much internal debate) with the slightly damp-stained three-volume edition of Russell's *Autobiography*. I'd let him have it for eight pounds – my bank manager wouldn't cheer, but at least Mr Spock would eat for a fortnight.

And then the phone rang.

'Ms Hare?'

I blinked. 'Dido Hoare Books. Can I help you?'

'My name is Cynthia Coxall? On the local paper?' I opened and closed my mouth. 'I am so sorry to bother you at such a tragic time, but I wondered whether you'd have a moment to speak to me about the tragic death . . . ?'

I switched off. When the voice stopped on yet another question mark, I said, 'I'm afraid I'm too busy. Anyway, I've had very little contact with my ex-husband for several years. Of course it's *such* a tragedy, but I'm afraid I can't help you?' The question marks were catching. I pinched myself sharply and concentrated on ending the conversation.

The next caller was my friend Susie Bates. I've known her since we were up at Oxford together. Our paths have diverged – she went into teaching, and was lecturing in sociology at a run-down technical college in Kilburn. 'Dido! I just saw the newspaper – I wanted to say how awful. It must have been a shock, even if . . . you know. Are you all right?'

I wrenched my mind to the deduction that the news about Davey had spread. What was for me a kind of miasma of gloom was fresh news for everybody else, and I realized that I hadn't even thought about this situation. I said, 'I'm fine.'

'What happened? Why on *earth*?'

I demanded to know what the newspapers were saying. It wasn't much: car bomb, police investigations continuing . . . I suddenly thought that I needed to talk to someone I could trust, but not over the phone. I blessed Susie for the thought, and we arranged to meet in the evening at her flat, which solved her babysitter problem.

After Susie, there was a series of calls, mostly from people in the trade agog for information but hesitant about what to say on the subject of a spectacularly slaughtered former husband. I formed the paranoid impression that two or three of them were wondering whether I'd put out a contract on Davey. After half an hour I went upstairs and brought down the answering machine. That freed me to deal with the old customers who drifted in hesitantly, remembering Davey, and enough sightseers to make me feel like a tourist site. I was tempted to behave like a grieving widow and shut up shop; instead, I set myself the goal of selling at least one book to each of the tourists. It seemed only fair to make them pay their way.

I had just decided that I would in fact close for the afternoon on the grounds that I didn't need all this, when Barnabas phoned. He was abrupt: 'Dido, my dear, I've called a minicab, and I thought I'd let you know I'll be there in fifteen minutes.'

'*Barnabas . . .!*' But he hung up before I had the chance to say that I was going to a movie, which meant that I had to wait for him. I used the time and my charm to shame a man who'd been goggling at me with more than usual persistence into paying thirty pounds for a minor Doré, and I was just reflecting ruefully on the value of publicity when the doorbell jangled once more. Not a customer. Paul Grant.

He surveyed the scene of battle and threw me a sharp glance. 'I should have warned you that you'd get curiosity-seekers.'

I shrugged. 'I'm going to get out of here. I might throw a book quite soon. Or a wobbly.' As Davey would have said.

'Good. Then you won't mind coming with me. Professor Hoare will take over.'

I mouthed, *What?*

'I phoned him. I hope you don't mind. I told him that I needed some help from you this afternoon and as it's a business day I thought you might want somebody to mind the shop. He seemed quite keen.'

It wasn't a bad idea giving Barnabas something useful to do; but I don't like being organized. 'I can make my own arrangements,' I pointed out. 'What help?'

'I'll tell you in private. There he is.'

I noticed that he exchanged a look of complicity with Barnabas, who was just sweeping through the door, and realized that I was the victim of a conspiracy. My father arrived with a more sprightly step than I remembered seeing for some months. He aroused customer speculation by planting a kiss on my forehead. 'Off you go. Good luck.' He grinned at Grant. 'Make sure she gets lunch.' And he turned his attention to a hovering woman to whom he set about selling a book on gardening.

'Lunch?' Grant repeated as though the word was foreign to him. 'Maybe later. They're waiting for us. Come on and I'll explain as we go.'

I said, 'I think I need a drink and a sandwich now. Who's waiting? You'd better phone them and tell them that you'll be late.'

'It's my superintendent; you don't do that to superintendents. He's in charge of the case.'

I said I'd thought that *he* was in charge of the case.

He said that it didn't quite work like that and embarked on an explanation about superintendents and Area Main and incident rooms.

'Oh well,' I said in tones of the deepest humility.

I thought that I caught the ghost of a grin, but it was overlaid with something else – a kind of abstracted worry which might not have been entirely friendly. He said, 'As it happens, there's a really good fish and chip shop on our way.'

11

Realism

Paul Grant double-parked his old Ford outside the house in Wilding Road – another of the policeman's privileges? – and I tried to wipe the grease off my fingers with the paper that had held my cod and chips. There is something comforting about fish and chips, especially with enough vinegar, but it always leaves me needing a bath.

'What about explaining?' I suggested.

He switched off the engine. 'Look, it'll be better if I don't tell you until we're inside. You were here last night. You left at about – what, eight o'clock?'

'Just before I phoned you. Has something happened to Ilona?'

'No – she's arrived at her mother's.' He was watching me, but I couldn't read his expression. Was I supposed to have done something? 'Don't ask anything else for a moment. Just come inside with me and look around, all right?'

All right, Detective.

I followed him down the uneven steps to the front door. It swung open before we got there, and a uniformed policeman recognized my companion, stood straighter, and stepped aside. In the sitting room were two men. The older one, bald, besuited and rumpled, stood in the middle of the floor flicking cigarette ash in showers around himself – Superintendent Colley, The younger one, introduced as DS Baden, pasted himself to the wall by the door as though he'd been ordered to make himself flat.

Colley flung his expiring cigarette into an already overflowing ashtray, where it smouldered unpleasantly. 'Miss Hoare. Good. Thanks for coming. Has Inspector Grant explained?'

I said that he hadn't.

'I thought,' Paul put in, 'it might be better if she looked at it first.'

Colley grunted. I raised an eyebrow at Paul.

'Right! Can you please look around and tell us whether you can see anything different about the place today?'

I looked obediently and grimaced. 'Not particularly.'

'Are you sure?'

So it had been a serious question. I let my eyes stray over the room. There was an unfamiliar blue scarf lying over the back of the chair in which Ilona had sat – presumably she'd left it behind at the last moment. Dirty coffee mugs still sat among overflowing ashtrays and old copies of the *Mirror* – she'd made no effort to clear up. In the cold light of today, the place looked abandoned.

'Yes, I think it's more or less like last night. I didn't take an inventory. Perhaps it's a bit messier, but I don't think she'd started packing when I left.' I went over to the sideboard. The Sunday paper lay where I'd left it.

'Don't touch anything,' Paul warned softly.

I drew my hand back. 'That's where I found my stamps. Under there. Are they . . . ?'

Colley came across and lifted the edge of the newspaper with his forefinger. I caught a glimpse of the sheet before he replaced it.

'You can definitely identify them?'

I assured him that there was no doubt and explained why. Oh no, Davey Winner was my burglar.

There was one other thing worth looking at. I pulled out the drawer I'd opened yesterday. This time it slid open easily because it was half empty. Would Ilona have packed that jumble of old bills? Then I saw the slew of papers on the carpet under the coffee table. They looked like what I'd seen in the drawer, and they certainly hadn't been down there yesterday. It looked as though she'd been sorting them and given up halfway through.

I said, 'What's the joke?'

'I can assure you it isn't funny,' Colley said loudly. 'Were you in any of the other rooms?' Obviously the kind of tough cop who prefers asking the questions to answering any.

I got the impression that he found me disappointing.

Impressions . . .

I had another impression: that Davey's canvases had been disturbed. They still leaned against the walls, but they were no longer stacked by size so that they would not damage one another with the rub of a stretcher or a sharp corner against paint. They staggered carelessly, as though somebody had been flipping through them.

'You've searched the place.'

'Not yet,' Colley said. He was lighting another cigarette. I wondered if his intention was to smoke me into co-operation.

Grant said slowly, 'A woman who lives upstairs saw two men coming out of here at about ten thirty this morning. She didn't recognize them, but she'd seen Mrs Mitchell leave in a taxi with her cases, so she had a look and found the front door open and dialled 999.'

'Thieves?'

'Maybe.' Paul hesitated. 'But it would be quite a coincidence, and the video recorder hasn't been touched – that's usually the first thing that goes in a break-in.'

I said, 'I'm sorry, I can't be sure. She could have left things lying around when she packed.'

Colley growled, 'If my wife kept a place like this . . .' and apparently thought better of it.

'Is it all right if I look in the bedroom?'

The men exchanged a glance which I decided to assume meant agreement, and I slid past the sergeant. Every drawer in the bedroom had been emptied on to the floor. I didn't go inside. No one in her right mind would leave her clothes in that state, no matter how upset she was, and Ilona had always been in her right mind. Unless you counted her taking up with Davey, but then she wasn't the only person mad enough to do that, was she?

Suddenly the realization that Davey was gone for ever hit me with a sense of desolation so strong and unexpected that I staggered and had to clutch at the door frame. I issued instructions to myself to stand up straight and went back to the others.

In the doorway I stopped for the overall view. 'The paintings have been shifted, that's what it is: they were stacked with the largest ones at the back, and now they're all mixed up. Why would anybody do that?'

'Looking for something,' Colley said. 'Miss Hoare, thank you for coming down. I appreciate that. I'll get somebody to drive you home. We'll be in touch.'

'I'd better drop her off,' Paul said. I thought that Colley gave him a warning look before we retreated.

'What were they looking for?' I asked when we were alone in the car. 'Money? Drugs?'

He hesitated. 'There's a little screw-topped jar on the kitchen table. Empty, but it smells of marijuana.'

'Oh.' I stopped myself saying anything else. Often in the days of my marriage I'd found similar little jars in the flat, sometimes empty, sometimes not. I said cautiously, 'There wouldn't have been a great deal in a little screw-topped jar, surely?' I knew where the missing stash was: Ilona wouldn't have abandoned Davey's personal stock.

'Perhaps there was more,' Paul said softly, 'but if there was, it's gone. They ransacked everything.'

'It doesn't fit,' I said before I could stop myself. Talking out loud was getting to be an awful habit.

'What do you mean?'

'Are you seriously saying that somebody killed Davey to get an ounce of cannabis?'

'Colley thinks that your ex had got mixed up with one of the south London gangs. Either Mrs Mitchell will tell us about it, or somebody on the street will pass the word along, or we'll find fingerprints we can recognize in that mess back there. He might have owed somebody money – the new car suggests bigger money somewhere, and the contents of that flat suggest it arrived recently. Incidentally, the car was a demonstrator from one of the local car firms; he bought it a fortnight ago. So the best guess is that something didn't work out, or some outsiders moved in on him.'

But Davey had not been the kind of man to be killed in some gang war. He had been too . . . I sank back in the seat. Not clever. Too shifty? That was better. Too cowardly? If a man had come to him and said something like, 'Winner, hand over that pound of heroin or I'm going to blow you to smithereens,' Davey would have caved in. He had too much imagination to do anything else. He would have given the man the package, grinned cheerfully and ruefully, and vanished. He'd been the very model of the man who lives to fight another day. And yet he was dead – he'd run out of elbow room at last.

Grant's car stopped outside the shop, and when I looked up, he was watching me again. 'The only thing is,' he said when he saw me looking, 'that it doesn't explain how you're involved.'

'Ilona said . . .' I stopped.

'What?'

'Is she in danger?'

Grant looked at me with narrowed eyes. 'You think that she might have been the target, not Winner? Is it likely?'

'I know, but when I talked to her yesterday she was so frightened she'd hardly trust herself to speak to me. She was sitting there with the chain on the door. She made me walk to the corner shop with her – as though she was afraid of being attacked in the street.'

'You think the bomb was meant for her, not him? But whoever broke in was looking for something, and she has no form, so we assume it was something Winner had stashed. They searched the whole place – you didn't look into the kitchen, did you? – so we suspect they couldn't find what they were looking for. The obvious thing would be to lean on Mrs Mitchell now. From what you've said, I'd guess that's what she was afraid of. Anyway, we're happy to have her out of the way.'

A car drifted along the road, looking for a parking place. The driver hesitated hopefully behind us, and then accelerated off when she saw that we showed no signs of moving.

I said, 'Davey told her that he was going to get some money. I'm sure I told you this last night. She thought he had a plan to get a share of the business.'

'Yes, you said something about that. You also said that it wasn't on.'

'It wasn't, and he knew that.' Didn't he?

'But we know now that he was responsible for trashing your shop.'

'None of this explains why Ilona is expecting somebody to come after her. You haven't found my key in the flat? You don't think they were looking for that, do you?'

'We haven't seen it yet. But if Winner had any sense, he'd have dropped it into the nearest storm drain last Sunday. He'd have known you'd change the lock anyway.'

'It makes sense,' I admitted, 'except that I don't understand his motive. Unless . . .'

'What?'

'He asked me for work. Perhaps he just intended to demonstrate that I needed him.'

81

Grant shrugged. 'It's a pretty elaborate way to go job-hunting, but it would be nice to think that's all, because that would mean you're out of trouble.'

'Why shouldn't I be?'

Grant twisted in his seat and stared at me. 'I don't know. Just like I don't know whether Mrs Mitchell is safe. But everything in your shop was turned over, just like the flat, and to me that means somebody was looking for something in *both* places, and probably didn't find it in either.'

I said, 'We know that the shop was Davey's doing.'

'We don't know that he was on his own. It bothers me that something's loose and we still don't have any idea what it is.'

I couldn't find an answer to that. I'd been feeling that I'd come out of the woods; and now he'd pointed out that the trees were still everywhere around me. I put my hand on the door handle.

'What about this evening? I should be clear by seven or eight o'clock.'

I told him I couldn't.

'Tomorrow, then? I have a couple of days off. Would you like to drive to the sea for the day? There's a place I go to on the Suffolk coast when I want to breathe air and look at waves for a while.'

The sea. I said, 'There's the shop . . .' and he responded with a kiss. It was a nice kiss. I decided that Barnabas wouldn't mind standing in for me just one more time.

12

Walk in the Wind

Paul Grant's seaside turned out to be a sweep of shingle in Essex with the Sizewell nuclear plant squatting on the northern point. We left the car at the end of a deserted car park and walked south under a flat grey sky. The wind blowing from the east had an icy centre, like a memory of the snow still lying on the Urals. I raised my collar to shield my left cheek from the bite and thrust my hands deep into my pockets. The dry shingle underfoot shifted and rustled.

When we got cold, we drove inland to a pub with a fire in the bar and thick toasted ham and cheese sandwiches. By silent agreement, Davey's name was still unspoken.

Back in George Street, he stopped the car in front of the shop and we sat for a moment.

'I'm going to visit family this weekend, but I'll be back on duty on Monday morning,' he said abruptly. 'I'll ring you then and let you know what's turned up in the meantime – if anything.'

I could see him wondering whether to say something more and deciding not to, and stood in the street watching his car pull out into the thick Friday traffic. It was as if he'd suddenly decided to back off, and I couldn't guess why. Davey?

Through the window of the shop I could see my father on patrol between the rows of books. We were busy, even for a Friday afternoon, and I guessed that we were still profiting from our notoriety. Barnabas looked cheerful, so instead of rescuing him I went upstairs.

The locksmith had come and gone, and my vulnerable kitchen and bedroom windows now wore white-painted metal grilles. The keys sat on the kitchen table, and I wasted five minutes worrying what to do with them. In the end I hooked the ring over the handle of one of the wall cupboards, where I was unlikely to forget them, and tried to resign myself to living in a cage. It didn't even seem necessary now, and the locksmith's bill propped against the teapot was for a frightening sum. I ought to go and inspect the arrangements in the shop. Instead I made tea.

Just after six o'clock, Barnabas arrived with the cash box and an air of open curiosity.

'Good day?' he enquired significantly.

I yawned; the hours in the sea air were beginning to affect me. 'You?'

He shook the cash box, which rustled. 'I've taken nearly eight hundred pounds, and there is a magnificent burglar alarm which makes a truly unspeakable noise. I'd better show you, or you'll be arrested when you open the door tomorrow morning.'

'Eight *hundred*?' I repeated stupidly.

'I turn out to be a salesman!' He sounded smug. 'Furthermore, Job Warren phoned. He arrived at Heathrow this morning, and I invited him to eat with us tomorrow evening.'

Tomorrow was Saturday, the busiest day in the week, and I said, 'Oh, but . . .'

'Leave it to me,' Barnabas said expansively. 'I'll buy American-sized steaks, and ice cream, and a bottle or two of the kind of claret that I can never afford to drink in a restaurant. You won't have to do a thing.'

I laughed. The day at work *had* put my father into a sprightly mood, and the holiday had relaxed me. 'I suppose that you've also arranged to show him the stock?'

'Sunday,' Barnabas said. 'He'd prefer not to have to compete with all your Saturday market customers.'

'Busybody,' I said contentedly.

Professor Warren was head librarian of the Constance Hance Research Library at a small New England university – a large building in the colonial style (we had seen photos), extraordinarily well endowed in memory of a formidable American matron forty years deceased (we had also seen the reproduction of her portrait, in mink). He seemed to have a free hand when it came to acquisitions, and turned up in London every spring with a chequebook and a thick computer print-out of his library's catalogue. Thus armed, he toured the antiquarian bookshops. He usually spent one or two days with me, moving methodically along the shelves, spreading his selections over my packing table, recollating, and checking his catalogue, until he had chosen a few thousand pounds' worth of books. He paid on the spot. For the past four years, Constance Hance had been my best single customer, bless her.

Not only that, but Barnabas and Professor Warren got on together like old mates, which explains the special treatment: my father did not provide old wine and well-hung Scottish rump steaks – he regards rump as the only cut suitable for a serious steak man – for just any big spender.

'You look much less tired than you did this morning. The boy detective must have taken care of you all right?'

I said quickly, 'Not *really* eight hundred pounds? You're a marvel. You don't want a job, do you? What with this and Professor Warren, I'm going to get some new stock. It's time I did something about the prints. Right?'

'Excellent,' Barnabas purred. 'I shall come into the shop more often, now that I'm well. It's too much for one girl . . . person. If I were to do a couple of days a week . . . ?'

Well, perhaps it was time for that.

I woke late on Saturday morning, feeling like a human being: an invalid, perhaps, but mending. I even found the energy to throw on my clothes and go down the road to shop for croissants, fresh orange juice and cat food. Mr Spock and I breakfasted together before going our separate ways.

My good mood wasn't even punctured when I listened to the tape on the answering machine and found another sequence of messages from people I barely knew, or didn't. They included somebody from a radio station asking whether there was any news about the investigation, and the woman from the local paper who was apparently trying to prove that female reporters can be just as intrusive as their male colleagues. Pat had phoned, having got no answer from the flat, and there were a few calls from book dealers who had actually known Davey, asking about the funeral. I made a note of the names of those who needed a reply and promised myself I'd deal with them on Monday. Then the first of the browsers arrived.

Saturdays in Islington are usually busy. Today the mixture of sightseers and genuine shoppers at times jammed the aisles. I took a chance at about

1.30 and closed the shop for a twenty-minute break. I closed again at five when the crowds had started to thin, gingerly setting the combination of key and switches that was designed to defend the shop from all evil-doers, and fled upstairs. I was feeling happier than I'd done for a week as I put on my most respectable skirt and silk shirt in accordance with Barnabas's instructions, brushed my hair until it shone, put on some lipstick, and set off for the party.

Barnabas met me at the door. I saw him do a quick check. 'Good! You're wearing a skirt, and you look very nice.'

I cast a deliberate look over his sitting room. He had cleared the papers from his dining table, and three places were set. 'Good!' I said. 'You've made enough space for normal human beings to eat dinner, and it looks very nice. When is he due?'

My father had the grace to look momentarily embarrassed, but it passed. 'A quarter past six.'

'And what about the dinner?'

Barnabas sniffed. 'Perfectly under control. Even I can manage smoked salmon plates and a couple of steaks with mushrooms. All we need to do is have a glass of wine while we wait. How was it at the shop today?'

I told him that it was fine, although I hadn't equalled his incredible takings of yesterday, and we went through into the kitchen.

The evening was planned as a repeat of the ritual that had developed over the past couple of years: a leisurely dinner that would go on for hours as the two men kept breaking off to flit from one volume of Barnabas's library to the next, commenting, arguing and reminiscing about the Tudor poets. I always brought over a few choice volumes from the shop as a foretaste of what (I hoped) Professor Warren would think of as the delights awaiting him. Most of the time I was simply expected to play dutiful daughter and domestic stooge. I was usually the one who prepared the unhealthy meal full of red meat and puddings – Job Warren was an American of the old breed who considered cholesterol and jogging to be inventions of a degenerate age.

Barnabas lit the grill, left the red wine near it to breathe, poured two glasses of a cold and spicy Gewurtztraminer, and led the way back to his sitting room where we sat for a while, Barnabas talking about his book and me only half listening to him, sipping the golden wine, yawning, thinking of nothing.

A smell of hot fat roused us.

'What time is it?'

I looked at my wristwatch: it was well past 7.30, and our guest was an hour late. 'Do you think he's been looking at books somewhere and forgotten the time?'

Barnabas dismissed my suggestion with scorn. 'The man is a titan of punctuality, as you know very well. I hope nothing has happened. It's astonishing that he hasn't phoned.' He went to the telephone and lifted the receiver to check the dialling tone.

Not being a titan of punctuality myself, I felt disinclined to worry. 'He's probably in a taxi in some traffic snarl. It *is* Saturday evening, remember.' The streets of central London would be full of people driving around like lemmings. I braved the heat in the kitchen long enough to turn off Barnabas's smoking grill and open a window.

'I'll try the hotel and see whether they can tell us anything.' Barnabas strode to his desk, paused to peer out into the street, and then shuffled things until he had found the necessary telephone number scribbled on one of a thousand scraps of paper. He dialled; I eavesdropped on an unilluminating conversation with a desk clerk.

'He's not there, his key is in the rack, and they can't remember when he went out,' Barnabas reported. 'You heard: I've left a message for him to phone, and the number in case he's lost it; but I presume he'll arrive at any moment.'

At 8.30, we finished two plates of the smoked salmon and put the third one back in the fridge. Then we watched the news on the little television set that Barnabas affects never to turn on. A Cabinet minister was reported to have sold something, probably himself, to an arms dealer; Kurds were being bombed somewhere in the Middle East; a child was missing in Hull; Kenneth Branagh and Emma Thompson had gone to the preview of a friend's new film.

Barnabas telephoned the hotel again at 10.15 to no purpose.

'Not there?'

'No. I shall phone the police.'

I hesitated. 'What for? There's probably a very simple explanation. Barnabas, are you dead certain you arranged it for tonight?'

Barnabas said with dignity, 'There is nothing wrong with my mind, or even my memory.'

I'd have to agree with that. 'Obviously something has gone wrong.

He'll phone you in the morning, and we'll take him out to Rocca's tomorrow evening, instead.'

Barnabas hesitated. 'I don't know why, but I don't like it.'

I said gently, 'If the hotel hasn't heard anything, then he can't have had an accident, or anything like that.'

Barnabas shrugged slowly. 'Of course not.'

'Have you taken your aspirin?'

'Not yet.'

I said, 'Then I'll heat some milk and you can have it now.'

'He may still phone.'

'Well,' I said, 'he probably will, especially when he hears that you've been on to Reception all evening. Unless he thinks it's too late.'

The phone, however, remained stubbornly silent. At midnight Barnabas went to bed and I went home. My chief feeling was of annoyance about my father's disappointment. But after all, plans do go wrong.

13

Coincidence

When the telephone woke me, I looked at the clock in disbelief and pulled the covers over my face. After a while the ringing stopped and began again, and pretending I was in Timbuctoo wasn't working. Wrapped in the duvet, I navigated uncertainly into the sitting room: five and a half hours' sleep does not fit me for either a new day or rational communication.

Because I was still only half conscious, I recognized Barnabas's voice without really hearing what he said. Panic. 'What's happened? Are you all right?'

He was not all right. I'd gathered that much.

'Dido, will you just come quickly? The police are on the way. I don't know that I can face this on my own.'

My mind sped in the only direction it could imagine. 'Is it Pat?'

There was a little silence, and then my father's voice came more strongly. 'No, no – Job Warren is dead.'

I started a 'How . . .' but stopped myself. 'Don't worry, I'm coming,' I yelled at the phone. I dropped the duvet where I stood, and ran to pull on some clothes and get my keys.

I couldn't even think where I'd left the car, but instinct kicked in and hurried me round the corner. During the night, some idiot had pulled up within six inches of my rear bumper, boxing me into my space. I dealt with the matter a little more fiercely than I normally would. As I get older, my behaviour is certainly becoming less ladylike. I gunned the car across Upper Street – this early on a Sunday there was no traffic to speak of – and headed north.

I'd expected police cars with flashing lights, but Crouch Hill was quiet except for a curtain twitching on one of the upstairs windows, which confirmed that Mr Stanley, on the first floor, had noticed something – as he always did, whatever the hour of the day or night. As I rang the bell, I could just hear the rumble of voices from inside, and the door was opened by a thick-set, red-haired man in a tired blue suit whom I'd certainly never seen before.

'Barnabas?' I pushed in and was relieved to find my father sitting at the dining table in his dressing gown, looking subdued, being served tea by a blonde girl in uniform who was beaming at him respectfully and probably reminding him of one of his students of old.

'Dido! Good.' Barnabas flourished his cup in greeting. 'You've been quick. The tea is fresh.'

Simultaneously, the redhead was saying, 'DI Gillespie and DC Wilcox, Holborn CID, Miss Hoare,' and Constable Wilcox was asking whether she could get me a cup and did I take sugar.

I replied, How do you do, Yes, No, and What happened? in a single breath and went to hold Barnabas's hand.

'What did happen?' Barnabas echoed, which told me that I hadn't missed much. 'Yes, yes, do sit down, both of you.'

Inspector Gillespie took the third dining chair and edged his clipboard cautiously down on the table among the teacups; Constable Wilcox cast a wary eye around the room, realized that she could not compete with the books, and wisely gave up the quest for a chair and positioned herself by the kitchen door.

Gillespie struggled visibly to decide where to begin. 'A few hours ago, we found the body of a man identified by staff at the Hotel York as a Professor Warren, an American who registered on Friday. He hadn't returned to the hotel last night, and Reception told us that there'd been a couple of messages from Professor Hoare. Lucky that you left your phone number, sir. We'd like to confirm the gentleman's identity, and we'd be glad of any other information. I don't suppose that the American Embassy know anything about him, and it might save time if you can help us to contact his family.'

'Professor Warren is in his late fifties,' Barnabas said almost inaudibly.

'Tall – about my height. Considerably heavier than I. Blue eyes, greying hair . . . I haven't seen him for a year, you understand. I don't know his home address, but he is the senior librarian at a university in Massachusetts – I'll write down the details.'

I said, 'What do you mean, you found him? He didn't die at the hotel? He was supposed to come here for dinner last night, but he never arrived, and it wasn't like him not to let us know.'

I thought that Constable Wilcox threw a quick glance at the inspector. A chilly finger played down my spine.

'One of our men found the body in Bloomsbury Square just before daybreak. It was under some bushes and may have been there for a few hours. His pockets had been emptied except for his room registration card – that's how we got on to the hotel.'

'Mugged?' Barnabas asked tonelessly. He was struggling. I squeezed his hand.

'We assume so.'

Barnabas was quiet for a while. He shook his head. 'He was supposed to come here to eat at six fifteen yesterday evening. I suppose he went out to get a taxi . . .'

I was watching the inspector's face. I said, 'What?'

'Well, the square was full of people at six o'clock, and it was light until nearly eight. Nobody reported a disturbance, much less an attack. Of course we'll have a better idea of the time after they've examined him.'

Barnabas was wearing his stubborn face. 'He was always very punctual. We've known him for several years, and I don't think that he has ever been more than five minutes late for an appointment.'

'You're saying that at six o'clock he must have been on his way to you?' Gillespie's eyes narrowed. 'That's odd.' He scribbled a note.

'Possibly so,' Barnabas was saying in his most measured tones, 'but Job Warren would certainly not have been wandering around Bloomsbury Square after dark instead of coming for dinner as arranged.'

I said, 'We see him every year when he comes over to London; I think my father is right.'

Gillespie's face expressed the sour realization that his life was not going to be as simple as he had hoped. The rest of us waited for him to come to terms with this. After a long minute he said, 'It might have been an accident. There is a head injury . . . we can't rule out an accident.'

Barnabas emitted a sarcastic snort.

I said, 'What kind of accident?'

'If he fell, perhaps nobody would have been alarmed. The square is full of street people these days – kids, old drunks. Nobody pays much attention. It wouldn't be surprising if one of them found him dead and cleaned out his pockets. It might be that.'

'Perhaps,' Barnabas said in a tone of voice that became more acid with every word, 'he was hit by a car, staggered into the square, and dropped under a bush to die without the crowds noticing?'

The inspector stiffened visibly. 'You'd be surprised, sir, how many people don't like to interfere. They want to avoid trouble.' He looked accusingly from me to Barnabas: apparently we private citizens made life difficult for the police, one way or another. 'We'll look into it. If you could kindly give us the address of Professor Warren's university, we'll get on.'

Barnabas went to his work table to look for his notebook. In the momentary silence, I said, 'Have you told DI Grant about this?'

I was half expecting to get a blank look, but DC Wilcox threw the inspector a glance that made me wonder.

Gillespie hesitated and nodded. 'We picked up the reference to the murder up here, of course, when we ran Professor Hoare's name in the computer. I've been on to the superintendent in charge of the Winner case. I gather they haven't contacted Grant yet. He's off duty. Do you have any reason to think that the two might be connected? Did the deceased know each other?'

I said that they had met a couple of years ago; Gillespie seemed inclined to dismiss the link, and for once Barnabas held his tongue. He handed Gillespie a note of the library's address.

'One thing,' Gillespie said after he had been politely grateful. 'The people at the hotel didn't actually know Professor Warren personally. If his passport isn't in the hotel, I wonder whether one of you would be willing to make a formal identification?'

'Me,' I said quickly. 'No, Barnabas, of course I'll do it.' It wasn't a happy prospect, but my father couldn't go through that. I gave the officers my own telephone number, saw them off the premises, and then returned to where Barnabas was sitting staring into his cooling tea.

I heard my voice whisper, 'Barnabas! Oh, no!' We looked at each other.

My father got up slowly and came close enough to pat my shoulder. The touch was meant to be comforting, but somehow it had the opposite effect, like a switch opening floodgates of anxiety.

He said, 'Dido, don't.'

'Barnabas, *what is happening*? That poor old man . . .'

'Yes – I know. I have an awful feeling that he was killed because of us.'

I tried to pretend I hadn't been going to say the same thing, tried to shape the word 'nonsense', to say that it was just bad luck and a terrible coincidence, nothing to do with anything; but suddenly I felt too wretched to speak. Of course it was no coincidence. The idea was laughable. I could feel myself start to shake, and Barnabas was pouring something into a glass.

'Drink it.'

I lifted it and smelled whiskey. My stomach heaved.

'It's not even breakfast time!' I protested when I could speak.

'Who cares?' he asked stiffly. 'It's my thirty-seven-year-old Jameson, and it will do you good. Sip it slowly. Go on!' His eyes were fixed on me and his face was grey. Things seemed to be out of control, and I had to do something.

'I'm going to phone Paul Grant.'

'It's Sunday.'

'He gave me the number of his mobile phone. He said he'd be away, but it's worth trying.'

Barnabas hesitated. 'Yes – I take it back. You're right.'

In my wallet I located the scrap of paper on which I'd written the number of Grant's mobile. It was a while before the phone was picked up: when I looked at my watch I saw that it was still not quite nine o'clock. His voice was thick with sleep.

The silence after my story stretched so long that I had to say, 'I hope you don't mind my phoning,' although I didn't care whether or not he did.

'Don't be silly.' His voice was abstracted. 'Look, I'll ring in and try to find out what's going on. I'll get on to the Super. They'll probably want him to oversee this case, since there's a possible connection. He probably won't get much for a few hours, but I'll let you know when I hear anything. In fact, I'll come round.'

I said, 'I'll be at Barnabas's. Do you have the address? I want to keep an eye on him.'

In the background my father was mumbling about not letting me out of his sight, and Paul's voice in my other ear said, 'Right, stay there until you hear from me. Take care. And don't worry, there isn't necessarily any connection.'

'What?'

I thought he laughed a little. 'Try not to worry. Coincidences do happen. You were right to phone me.'

I heard my voice rising. 'It's not a coincidence.'

'Probably not. Look, I'll take care of it.'

'Will you?' I asked. It sounded as though I doubted him, so I said, 'Thanks' to make it better before I hung up.

I wished I could believe him. I certainly needed somebody to take care of it; but I had a nasty feeling that it just wasn't going to turn out like that.

14

Dead Man' s Bluff

In the dream, I wandered through a grassy park enclosed by iron railings. The ground was frozen; it splintered where I stepped. Leafless bushes grew around the perimeter of the place. Without looking up I knew that it was not sky, but something that resembled a low grey ceiling over my head.

Somewhere among the straggling bushes there lay a terrible thing. As soon as I remembered it, I saw – or half saw – out of the corner of my eye a grey, featureless horizontal form at the far side of the rectangle where I walked. It kept shifting and fading, and I turned away because if I got too close I knew that it would stand up. I was afraid to turn my back, and walked diagonally away, crossing two stone paths as I went.

Ahead were the pillars of a gate; but something blurred, and the grey shape lay between me and the way out. I turned right, making another long diagonal. There was another shifting change. Ahead of me stood a man covered in blood. He had no face, but I knew it was Davey, so I said, 'This is just a dream.'

In the confusion between sleeping and waking, the faceless man turned into Barnabas, leaning over the couch with a cup of tea. I sat up quickly.

'What time is it?'

'Nine o'clock. We have a visitor.'

'Visitor?' I yawned blankly and tried the tea which, as usual when my father made it, was mysteriously cool and weak.

95

'In the kitchen. Your policeman.'

I swallowed another yawn, put the cup and saucer down on the floor, and struggled out from under the tangle of blankets. I had gone to sleep wearing yesterday's tracksuit, which meant that I felt disgusting. I pulled on my socks, wished that my mouth tasted less like the inside of a shoe, and ran my fingers through my stubborn hair.

'It's all right,' Barnabas assured me with more than a touch of irony, 'he says he's been "running around" half the night – I expect he'll enjoy sitting there quietly for two minutes.'

Thus admonished, I crept into the bathroom and applied soap, warm water and a towel to appropriate places and ate a mouthful of toothpaste while I plied Barnabas's hairbrush.

In the kitchen, I saw that Barnabas's judgment had been well founded. Paul Grant had propped his elbows on the table; his eyes had the strained look of somebody trying not to yawn.

'What's happened?'

'Not a lot. I've been down in Bloomsbury Square, and I've talked to the people in the district. One thing: they know now that he wasn't attacked in the square, although he might still have been alive when he was dumped.'

'How can they tell?'

'Not enough blood.'

'Oh.' The remembered image of the bloody figure in my dream swam towards me for a moment. I pushed it away.

'What happened to him?' Barnabas was asking.

'He was knocked on the head with the traditional blunt instrument and then, presumably while he was unconscious, he was . . .' To do him justice, Grant hesitated. 'His throat was cut. Very neat, very quiet. Very deliberate. Then his body was taken to the square and dumped.'

'Very odd?' Barnabas asked.

Grant looked at him quickly. 'Yes. Yes, it is.'

I felt as though I were in the nightmare again. 'What do you mean, odd?'

Grant turned to me. 'Suppose that somebody wants to rob him. They hit him over the head, he passes out. They take his wallet and run for it. That makes sense. Or they hit him, he's still conscious, they panic and batter him badly and he dies and they run for it. I'll wear that. Or they threaten him, he yells or tries to fight them off, they panic and pull a knife and stab him in the chest and stomach, and cut his hands and arms, maybe, when he tries to push them off, and then they grab his stuff and run . . .'

'But he was robbed?' Barnabas said.

'Oh, yes – pockets cleared out. They were too busy to notice his watch, though. Nothing fancy – just an ordinary eighteen-carat gold Rolex worth a thousand or three. Holborn is very, very unhappy about that part of it.'

'Not a real robbery?' Barnabas asked.

I thought I ought to get into the conversation. 'Are you saying that he was murdered for some other reason and they stole his money to make it look like a mugging?'

Grant hesitated, and alarm bells rang. Finally he asked, 'What kind of a man was he?'

'Be specific,' Barnabas urged drily.

'All right. Holborn thinks . . .' Grant hesitated, looked at me, looked away quickly to Barnabas. 'Holborn wonders whether there is some kind of sexual element. Could he have come on to one of the kids – one of the rent boys – in the square?'

Barnabas looked blank.

I found myself glaring. 'Professor Warren's wife died two years ago. He has two daughters and three grandchildren. He's an eminent head librarian of a New England university.'

Grant grimaced. 'None of that makes him exempt.'

'What is a rent boy?' Barnabas asked.

Grant looked at him in utter disbelief, saw that he meant it, and hesitated. 'It's an American term,' he said, and stopped.

'Professor Warren,' I said loudly, 'was a quiet, friendly, but quite experienced man. He travelled a lot, all over the world, and he lives near Boston, which is a big city with a lot of violent crime. I don't believe that he would come to London and do something naïve or dangerous. All right?'

Grant looked depressed. 'Well, there is always the possibility that he met a nutter, or . . . Might he have been carrying a lot of cash?'

I tried to remember from other years. 'No – traveller's cheques or credit cards for his personal expenses. He paid for purchases with ordinary sterling cheques on a London bank. Was the chequebook still in his briefcase?'

Grant became alert. 'Briefcase?'

'He always carried it when he was over here.'

'Even if he was going out for the evening to visit friends?'

I thought about it. 'Probably. We weren't just friends – it was business too. We always talked books, and he carried a copy of the library's short catalogue and his wants list. I've never seen him without the briefcase.'

Grant pulled out a sheet of paper and consulted it. 'No briefcase. Not in his room, either. His passport was at the hotel. No traveller's cheques. No wallet, so you wouldn't expect to find any cards. You can't describe this briefcase, can you?'

'It might not be the same one as other years,' I pointed out.

Barnabas disagreed. 'It was always the same case.'

'It was about a hundred years old . . .'

'There was nothing wrong with it!'

Paul Grant cleared his throat.

'It was a leather satchel,' Barnabas said loudly, 'very like mine, in fact. Dark brown calf. Rubbed at the edges. Brass fittings and . . . initials, I think. It would have been very heavy, because he carried a thick computer print-out of the library catalogue around with him, also a loose-leaf notebook in case he wanted to jot down details of books he saw that he needed to look up in the British Library, or appointments to view stock – anything to do with his schedule.'

'There's certainly no case and none of those things on the list of his belongings.'

'Then it was stolen.'

'Seems so. Maybe they thought the case was so heavy it must hold something valuable. Anyway, it will have been dumped by now. Unless . . . unless it was left at the place where he was attacked. Can I use your phone? I'd better let Holborn know: they'll need to put the word out about it.'

'It was quite a polished leather,' Barnabas was saying with interest. 'Fingerprints – I'm sure it would show fingerprints very well. The phone is on the desk, but mind my papers.'

He led the way into the sitting room and located the telephone by his usual means of following the cord through the labyrinth of documents. I sat down among the mess of blankets on the couch where I'd passed my restless night. Barnabas sat beside me, listening to the detective's side of the phone conversation with undisguised interest.

Hanging up, Grant let his eyes survey the room. He took in the temporary bed. 'Are you moving in here, Dido? Good.'

I shrugged. 'I'll probably sleep here for the time being. Just until . . .' Until what? Once I'd started to say it, I wasn't sure. I decided: 'Until things are a bit clearer. I don't open the shop on Mondays anyway. There are things I ought to do there, but I'll leave them for the moment.'

Grant hesitated. I noticed what dark, deep brown eyes the man had. Nice.

He said, 'Look, I'm going to make sure that somebody is keeping at least a passing eye on both this place and the shop. All this business with the professor might not have anything to do with the other, but it's hard to believe. Take care, eh?'

'I will,' I said.

Barnabas sniffed but held his tongue until Grant had gone.

'Pigs might fly.'

I scowled at him; I hadn't slept well. 'What?'

'If anyone thinks that Warren's death and Davey's aren't connected . . .'

'How can they be?' I growled. 'They barely even knew each other.'

'They both knew you,' Barnabas growled back.

'*And* you.'

'Fiddlesticks. At any rate, until the police know why at least one of them was killed, I want you to be extremely careful.'

'You mean . . . *I'm next*!' It came out in a hard-boiled Humphrey Bogart voice. 'That's silly . . . just because Davey broke into the shop and stole eighty pounds and half a sheet of postage stamps?'

Barnabas glared. 'Don't pretend to be addle-brained. Until we know the reason for all this, you can't be sure. Better safe than sorry.'

'A stitch in time saves nine,' I mocked him. 'There's no use crying over spilt milk. Many a mickle makes a muckle.' The thing is, I agreed with him. 'Barnabas, perhaps you really should go and stay with Pat for a little while after all.'

'If you'll come too.'

'How can I?' I'd rather spend a holiday in a kindergarten. 'With Pat's au pair, you know that they only have one spare bedroom. Anyway, I'll be perfectly safe at the shop now that I'm all barricaded in and burglar-alarmed.'

'But you can't stay locked up all the time,' Barnabas objected. He stopped abruptly and looked as though an idea had come to him.

'What?' I demanded.

'Idea,' he said unnecessarily. 'We'll have another pot of tea and something to eat, and then we'll creep out together and go shopping, I think.'

When I suggested that a shopping trip was inappropriate to our present worries, he threatened to go alone. I gave in to blackmail, of course.

Two hours later we were illegally parked in the Tottenham Court Road gingerly examining my new mobile telephone, juggling instruction booklet and connection agreement. I felt as though I had finally joined the late twentieth century. Barnabas had provided an impeccable credit rating and a masterful insistence on immediate connection, and it really hadn't cost him very much.

'Now . . .' Barnabas was giving instructions and looking like a child with a new but terrifying Christmas present. 'If you will programme my number into your phone, and also 999 and the boy detective's numbers, I shall feel almost certain that you are going to be safe. We can call each other every half-hour if we want to, and you get help anywhere, any time.'

Being phoned up every half-hour wherever I happened to be was the terrifying prospect that had always before prevented me from taking this particular technological leap forward. There had also been another reason.

'Barnabas, do you know how much one of these costs every time you use it?' This point had escaped his attention. I told him. He looked a little subdued. I said, 'Never mind, you're right: it's wonderful being able to get help in an emergency. Let's just not go overboard.'

'Business expense?' he suggested tentatively.

'With luck,' I agreed, reminding myself to put the receipt into my accountant's file.

'Well . . . it's worth every penny. In the circumstances. You'd better read the leaflet and find out how to work it.'

I said, 'I'll take you home first. This should keep us both amused for hours. I hope you have some food in the fridge.'

'There's some smoked salmon left over from Saturday,' he said slowly.

Which killed that conversation absolutely dead.

15

A Patron of the Arts

After I'd bullied Barnabas for a while, he agreed to keep his door on the chain so that I could go home. I wanted to check the shop to see if anything had turned up; and more than anything else, I *needed* to change and collect some things, because if I was about to spend another night on my father's sofa, then I wanted to be prepared.

The Volvo was just south of Highbury Corner when the mobile shrilled unexpectedly from inside my bag. I recklessly pulled the car up on a double yellow line and dug for the thing.

'Barnabas?'

'Good! It's working!'

Charity won out when I reminded myself that Barnabas was anxious about me. 'Of course it works.'

'Excellent! Well, now that we're sure, I can relax. I wanted to ask you . . .'

There was a gap in the line of traffic, and I drove on slowly, one-handed. 'What?'

'I'm almost out of milk.'

'Message understood,' I intoned. I switched off. Then I conscientiously switched back to stand-by and drove on. Perhaps the real answer was to teleport myself to some other planet?

The door of the shop swung inwards against the slew of mail on the floor: catalogues and bills, orders and bills . . . I was bending over in an

101

undignified way to gather them up when a demonic voice began to scream at me. My first impulse was to run. On second thoughts, I hurtled the length of the shop, fitted the correct key into my new and unfamiliar alarm system, and silenced it. Then I leaned against the office door jamb until my heart sank back into place.

The post looked wholly uninteresting. But there might be cheques – probably were some cheques – and if I couldn't even bring myself to open a few envelopes for the sake of money, where had I got to? I snarled, tossed the stuff on to the desk and relocked the door without bothering to set the alarm – one shock a day was quite enough – and let myself into the flat. I was dirty. I had a rising suspicion that I actually smelled. I needed a bath, clean clothes, coffee . . .

Mr Spock ambushed me at the head of the stairs with one of his dirtiest looks. Then as always he offered his saintly forgiveness in return for immediate food. I opened a tin, refilled his water dish, dumped and replaced the cat litter.

'And that's you,' I said. 'You'll be all right until tomorrow. I'll make it up to you. We'll spend some quality time together.' If I ever got myself out of this incredible nightmare.

While the bath was running I wandered into the bedroom. The naked bed reminded me that I'd dropped the duvet on the sitting-room floor the previous morning, and I went to find it. The light on the telephone answering machine was blinking: one message. It could wait until I'd got myself organized.

I'd got as far as the bedroom doorway when I allowed myself to remember that Davey and I had been there together in that bed – how long ago? Last Monday. Seven days. As suddenly as a heartbeat his death was there in my bedroom.

I'd tried to avoid thinking of that afternoon, but now the memory had invaded my head. I wondered whether I'd ever be able to get rid of that ghost. He had been there alive, and now he was dead. He had sat on that bed, and now . . . Suddenly it became absolutely essential to erase the nearness of his presence there, of his touch. I wanted to set fire to the place. As though that would change anything. As though I could burn it away. As though death were contagious.

I was shivering.

I'd actually pulled out one corner of the sheet when a kind of retrospective uneasiness stopped me. Because something was wrong. The

102

wrongness was connected with the bed – or rather the sheet, smooth and unwrinkled except for the corner that I'd just pulled out. It had been *tucked* wrong.

I wanted to laugh wildly. I also wanted to run out of the flat and never come back. Instead, I made myself look. *Wait: think . . . What is it?* The sheet had been folded at each mattress corner in two sharp creases. Not my doing: I'm an impatient buncher, not a folder. Not me. Somebody else.

That was ridiculous, of course.

Also, I'm what you might call a busy sleeper. When I get up in the morning, the bed is always a mess: bottom sheet rucked up, duvet rolled around me. Yesterday, when Barnabas's phone call had woken me, I'd left everything and rushed out. Today, the bottom sheet of my bed was as smooth and comfortable and absolutely wrong as it could be, and I knew as clearly as though I had witnessed it that a stranger had walked into my bedroom, breathed my air, searched my things . . .

I gritted my teeth to stop a scream – or a sob. Wardrobe door open – messy, normal. Chest of drawers – underwear scattered over the top, hairbrush and make-up tangled in it: normal. I looked into the drawers: the antique gold watch chain with turquoise bead insets, my mother's crescent-moon diamond pin, the baroque pearl and silver engagement ring . . . nothing had gone. Bathroom? Kitchen? Living room?

I stood in the doorway. The sun had come out; dust motes danced in the air. *I must somehow find the time to clean the place up. Don't be stupid, what does it matter now?* The television, the video player, the music centre were there, my camera still in the drawer of the sideboard. I kept thinking that this thing or that was out of place, but I couldn't be sure, *I couldn't be sure . . .*

The flashing light on the answering machine began to annoy me. I pressed a button and listened to the tape rewind. It was a woman's voice, familiar yet momentarily unrecognizable. '*Dido? This is Sally. Will you phone us, pet? In case you don't have the number, it's still 766590. You will phone, won't you?*'

By the time she'd finished, I'd identified the speaker: my one-time mother-in-law, Sally Winner. I started to reset the machine, but stopped because there was a second message, although the machine seemed not to have noticed the fact: Pat's voice starting in mid-sentence. '*. . . and so Father should come to us for a couple of days, Dido, so will you please*

persuade him? And phone me the MINUTE you get back there, yes?'
Click.

I stood listening to the machine reset itself. Not an important message. What was important was that although I hadn't heard it before, Sally's phone call had recorded over it.

My answering machine works very simply. When you reset it, the message cassette rewinds. There is no way that you can prevent subsequent messages from recording over older ones. Somebody had recently listened to the tape and then reset the machine, not realizing how this make works. This 'somebody' was the intruder who had replaced my bottom sheet. *Why? Davey? Why?*

I switched the machine off altogether, because it was my evidence. It felt important not to lose it; or I'd have to phone Paul Grant and say, 'Come quickly, somebody has broken into the flat to make my bed for me': not really a credible complaint.

I reached for the telephone, but at the last moment found myself dialling Pat's number. She answered sharply and I could hear sounds of warfare in the background by which I knew that my nephews were home from school.

'I can't talk now!' she informed me unnecessarily. 'I'll ring you this evening. I want to discuss what we're going to do about Barnabas and all this business . . .'

'I'm going back to his flat quite soon,' I said wickedly, 'so I'll phone you from there and we can all discuss him.'

The pause confirmed my suspicion that Pat wanted another conference about Whether I Was Taking Proper Care of Father, and preferred to keep it confidential.

'He's fine,' I assured her sweetly; 'in fact, the whole business seems to have given him a new interest.' I'd meant to tell her about Job Warren, but my annoyance stopped me: why did she have to assume that Barnabas was no longer capable of knowing what was good for him? 'By the way . . .' This was why I'd phoned, of course; I made my voice casual. 'By the way, when exactly did you leave that message? I may just have missed you.'

'Oh, it doesn't matter. Just after I got the boys to bed yesterday, I suppose. You've taken long enough to ring back.'

I told her truthfully that I'd been spending the time with Barnabas, and hung up. My intruder might have had all the hours of darkness, if he'd needed them. It didn't help.

Next in the order of business was to locate Paul Grant. I tried his personal number without success. At the station, a voice told me that he was out and promised to get him to phone me when he came back. I left the number of the mobile in case it took him a while to get the message, and gave up, cursing.

Finally I pulled myself together to ring Sally.

Sally Winner was a retired blonde bombshell, pushing sixty when I'd known her but still wowing 'em behind the bar of a pub in Leicester. I hadn't spoken to her for three years, and I wondered whether she had changed. I'd always liked her.

'Dido? Dido, dear, it's good to hear your voice. How are you?'

I could hear Davey's tones in her voice, and it took me a moment to reply. 'I'm well, Sally. How are you? I'm so sorry about Davey. I should have phoned you.'

'Thanks, pet. It's a funny business, losing a child. It just doesn't seem right, even with somebody like Davey who was always pushing his luck, eh?'

I told her I knew what she meant.

'I wanted to tell you about the funeral,' she went on. 'They say we can bury him now. We thought Wednesday, up here. Will you come? You and your dad too, if he can? Davey told us he'd been ill, so if he can't make it, we'd understand, but we'd be glad to see you here.'

I said that I wasn't sure about Barnabas, but yes, I would be there.

'The thing is . . .' Her voice trailed off briefly. 'The thing is, I thought I'd better tell you Ilona will be here. I hope you're okay about that.'

I told her that I was certainly okay about it. I was more than okay about having another chance to corner Ilona. I got the details, and we protested our mutual regard. I still liked Sally.

With nothing else crying out to be done, I took my delayed and tepid bath, washed my hair, put on clean clothes, and took both phones downstairs to the shop to sort out the neglected mail while I was waiting for my detective to surface. The catalogues went to one side; by the time I could read them, any bargains would be long gone. There were three orders from my own last catalogue, all for books that had been sold, and bills for telephone and electricity which would have to wait. With only the barest of hesitations I threw everything into the bin, which gave me a feeling of achievement.

In the midst of my self-congratulation, the shop bell pinged. I'd forgotten to lock the door, and somebody had decided to ignore the closed sign. I bounced into the shop.

'Sorry, I'm not open on Mondays. Could you come back tomorrow, perhaps?'

'Dido Hoare?' The voice was soft, with a tinge of East End about it, and monotonous; it turned the question into a statement. 'My name is Campbell, Marty Campbell. I was a friend of Davey's.'

The intruder stood silhouetted against the brightness from the street. I took a step forward, trying to see his face. He was a solid man of medium height, dressed in a grey suit and what looked like a regimental tie. I could see grey hair, but his face seemed too young to fit it. There was an impression of physical hardness, like somebody who spent time in an expensive gym. I decided that he was lying. Davey's friends looked different. Poorer, for one thing.

'Davey's dead,' I said.

'That's why I came. I didn't want to bother Ilona, but I wondered whether you could tell me what happened?'

It made me uneasy to see him standing so still by the door. I couldn't focus. 'I'm sorry, I don't know . . . He was killed. Murdered.'

'We'll all miss him. Do they know who did it?'

'No.' I shook myself mentally. 'How did you know him?'

The answer came without hesitation. 'I met him a year or two ago when he was exhibiting in a little gallery in Camden Town. I bought one of his pictures. I commissioned something else about three months ago: I don't suppose he finished it.'

I tried to adjust my view of this man, to see him as a patron of the arts. 'He owed you money,' I guessed aloud.

'Well, it doesn't matter now.'

I said casually, 'I remember that exhibition. Which painting did you buy?'

There was no hint of the evasion I half expected. 'An acrylic, medium-sized – an interior scene with a lot of red and orange in it. It was called "Senses in Sunlight 4". Do you remember it?'

So the man was legitimate. I duly adjusted my idea of art patrons. 'No, not really. You liked his work?'

'He was lazy, of course,' Campbell said flatly. 'I know he painted a lot, but it often came too easy. But there was power in the best stuff. I liked that. Too bad.'

There didn't seem to be much more to say, though the silence seemed to ask me to speak. But the shop door opened. For some reason, I was overcome with relief when Paul Grant stepped inside. Campbell half turned as Paul hesitated momentarily and then walked past him. I opened my mouth.

'Good afternoon. I'd like to look at travel books, please.'

I closed my mouth, and opened it again to say, 'To your left.' Damn it: my voice sounded odd, and what was Paul playing at?

'Give Ilona my sympathy if you see her,' the man in the grey suit was saying. 'Will you be seeing her soon?'

In other circumstances I might have told him about the funeral, but I wanted to speak to Paul. 'If I do I'll certainly tell her you sent your sympathy.'

He still hesitated. 'Yes, remember me to her. She'll know my name.' And left at last, turning right towards the main road.

Before the door had shut behind him, I was whirling towards Grant, words tumbling. 'Somebody's been upstairs! That's why I phoned you. Nothing's missing, but I . . .' There was only one possible explanation. 'I know it's been *searched*.'

But Grant was leaning against a book case, ignoring the wobble, plainly only half hearing what I'd said. 'Who was that? I know him, but I couldn't place him. I have alarm bells ringing all over the place. Customer? Friend?'

'I *said*, my flat's been searched!'

He looked at me sharply. 'What's missing?'

'I told you: nothing, as far as I can see. My jewellery is still there. But somebody broke in last night, all the same.' I explained.

He said, 'Let's look.'

We looked; and at the end I said again, 'Nothing's gone, you see. Like downstairs. What are they looking for?'

'You're making a habit of this,' he said. It sounded bad-tempered. 'You mean that you can actually be sure that someone removed the sheet from your bed and then put it back again?'

'Of course!' I could hear my voice rising. 'Don't you make your own bed?'

'Fitted sheets. All right, all right. It looks as though somebody wanted to see if you'd hidden anything in the mattress, and they'd prefer you not to notice. So they're still looking. Whatever it is, at least they know now that you don't have it. Winner didn't have it either. I wonder if they thought Professor Warren had it?'

I said, 'This is crazy! What? How could he?'

He sat down on the edge of the bed. 'I don't want to frighten you, but I think I should. Look – I accept that somebody searched the place. I'm going to send somebody round. Nice grilles, but they obviously got in through the front door. You need a better lock. And a security system – like in the shop.'

I said, not particularly to him, 'I hate this.'

'I know, but people are being killed! Look: what if they thought your American had got what they wanted? Christ knows how they found out about him, but maybe they were doing one of their invisible searches in his hotel room when he came back and surprised them. So – did he have what they wanted?'

'No, how could he?'

'Okay. That left you, so they came looking. Unless you just haven't noticed that something's gone, they're still looking. What will they do next?'

'Come and ask me where it is?'

Paul nodded down at me as though I were a clever student. 'Right. The best idea is for you to get out of London until they give up.'

'How long would I have to stay away? What would I do about Barnabas? And the business?'

He said, 'What happens to them if you wind up dead?'

'And you can't protect me.'

He hesitated. 'I could tell you that I would, but you know it's impossible, don't you?'

Did I?

He shifted from a hug to a little shake. 'Nobody can protect you the way you mean. It might work for as long as you were willing to live in a sort of prison – never be alone, always keep the doors locked, have a guard with you in the shop.'

'That's insane! You'll catch them.' Or, at the worst, they'll have to give up eventually.

His voice rose. 'We haven't got any idea who they are or what they want – except that it's worth murdering for. Don't you understand? No clues! Holborn don't have a hope of finding out anything about your American unless something turns up. We're depending on luck, more or less. We're just waiting for somebody to decide to talk. Or somebody else to be killed. I might as well tell you that Holborn don't even accept that there's any link between the two deaths, and my Super – Gillespie, you saw what he's like – agrees.'

I closed my eyes and fought the temptation to lean against him and howl. 'I don't blame them,' I admitted eventually. 'Barnabas and I keep wondering . . .' There was something I wanted to say, so I tried not to think about Paul, but to concentrate on remembering. The thought struggled to the surface. 'Ilona. She *must* know more than she told me. I'm sure she knew what Davey was doing.'

'Agreed. But she's not telling. I'm going up to Stafford myself to interview her again. I don't hope for much, though – I know the type. She's so scared that she doesn't trust anybody, and unless I can persuade her that she's going to be in more trouble if she doesn't talk to us than if she does . . . I can't think what else to do at the moment.'

I said sourly, 'Good luck.'

He laughed and we looked at each other. 'Look, I want you to do me a favour: go over the place once more. Do it now, while I'm here. I'll be phoning a security firm that we recommend.'

I sat down beside him on the bed. 'Most of the time I can't believe that this is happening. You really do think I'm in danger?'

Grant made a grab at my upper arm and pulled me around. 'If I could arrest you, I'd put you away for your own safety. Go and stay with your old auntie or something, even if it's just for a week.'

I said, 'I'm staying with Barnabas tonight.'

'All right. I'll warn the Hornsey station.'

'And Barnabas has bought me a mobile telephone.'

His expression lightened a shade. 'Good! Just keep the damn thing with you. Even in the bath. Give me the number.'

I did, and promised meekly that I would bathe, sleep and eat in the presence of my new telephone.

'And get off to Professor Hoare as soon as we've had another look around here. You'd better not be alone.'

'I have to take some things.'

'Then look and pack at the same time. I have time to drive you up to Crouch Hill – or follow your car, if you'd rather. You can come back to meet the security people – I'll make sure that they get here before this evening.'

He hesitated, and before I could read his intentions, kissed me hard and briefly and let me go.

I searched the flat, half listening to the murmur of his voice on the telephone. Mr Spock woke up and got in my way. Aside from discovering that the missing eight of diamonds from a pack of cards I'd thrown out months ago had been tucked well under the edge of the bedroom rug, there was nothing unexpected. Nor were there any gaps, I'd swear to it, although I suspected that searching for something not to be there was a bad idea.

In the end I gave up. I stuffed a change of underwear, night things, and my mother's jewellery into a shopping bag, and we descended the stairs to the street with the memory of the kiss still there in the silence between us. At the bottom, I double-locked the flat door, then let myself into the shop long enough to reactivate the alarm.

As we reached the Volvo, Grant said, 'The man who's coming is called Moser, from Double-A Security. He'll be here at three o'clock on the dot, and he'll wait for you in front of the shop. Don't get here before he does, and don't go in until he's identified himself – right?'

I said that it was.

Paul put a hand on the roof of the car, waiting for me to unlock it. 'I guess we're lucky your intruder had a moment's carelessness with the answering machine. I'll tell you one thing: I've only once seen a place turned over as neatly as yours, and we got pulled out of that because we were told from higher up to back off. That was MI5, I think. You've pulled some real professionals this time.'

I started to say something and was stopped by the look that came over his face.

'Oh, hell – professionals. The man in your shop – I've got it!'

I remembered then. 'He said his name was Campbell. Davey sold him a painting last year.'

Grant closed his eyes, He seemed to be inspecting a distasteful mental image. Eventually he said, 'Marty Campbell. He was pointed out to me once. The bastard even gave you his real name. He does drugs, gambling, protection, a spot of murder – though I think he hires rather than does nowadays. There's a story that he's the only Englishman with a real line to the Soho Triads. I don't know about that, but I'm damn sure that he's got Mafia connections. Marty Campbell. Shit!'

I was trying to make this fit. 'He said he'd heard about Davey's murder. He asked about Ilona, too – you heard that, didn't you?'

'You didn't tell him where she is?'

I remembered and breathed a sigh of relief. 'No, I didn't. You'd just come in, and I wanted to get rid of him.'

'All right.' He jerked open the door of the Volvo. 'Go on, get in. I'll follow you to Crouch Hill, and I'll ring you later on – about five. Sit tight. Don't do anything, don't say anything, don't be clever. Campbell is a premier-league player . . . I just wish I knew what the hell his interest is!'

I bit back a comment about how much I enjoyed being ordered around, got into the car and locked all the doors before I started the engine. Also, I kept enough of my attention on my rear-view mirror to be sure not to lose his car as it followed mine north. Nothing happened unless you're counting the rush-hour traffic jam at Highbury Corner, and there's nothing unusual about that.

At Crouch Hill, I remembered that I'd forgotten the milk.

16

Tears

A slow train and a taxi driver with an insecure sense of direction delivered me late to the crematorium. I pushed open the door of a red brick building that was pretending to be a church and slid on to a seat at the back.

Twenty or thirty people were scattered about the pew-like benches. I knew a couple of faces: Sally herself, hunched in the front row beside Ron – to whom she had been not-married all the time I'd known her – and Ilona, sitting with a middle-aged woman I didn't recognize. One or two others seemed vaguely familiar, although I couldn't attach names to them – probably old friends of Davey's who'd turned up to our wedding. Most of the rest looked like Sally's friends and customers, come to give support.

One other caught my eye: a blond young man in the seat just across the aisle from me, wearing an expression of harmless boredom. It was only because I was watching him while I tried to remember where I'd seen him before that I suddenly realized he was examining the faces of the congregation, one after the other, quite methodically. That gave me the name to put to the face: Baden – Sergeant Baden. Were the Metropolitan Police in the habit of sending detective sergeants to out-of-town funerals just as a mark of respect, or was he there on business?

Or – the thought trickled in as I started to listen to the eulogy – to keep an eye on me?

Presumably the minister had never known Davey. He made a resonant job of giving what was obviously his standard funeral speech, with

113

inserted references to the 'tragic and violent end' of a 'loving son and talented artist', and finished with an invitation to us to bow our heads and pray. It always surprises me when a gathering of everyday atheists follows this instruction. I controlled my own impulse to do as I was told and spent the time trying to see any others in the congregation whom I ought to make a point of greeting.

There was one rotund figure near the front who looked fleetingly familiar, but he was half hidden by the people between us, and it wasn't until the recorded music welled up and we stood to let Sally and Ron leave the chapel first that I recognized Dan Colbert, of Heritage Books – the only one of Davey's London friends to have made the effort. Dan was not one of my favourite people, but I was touched that he'd turned up. The finality of funerals suddenly made me tearful.

Ron and Sally were standing just outside the door to greet us. Ron, in his Sunday suit, looked uneasy. Sally seemed tired and washed out. She reached between two friends and grabbed my hand as I came up to her.

'Dido! Bless you, pet. You're coming back to the house with us, aren't you?'

I said that of course I was, and stepped aside to allow other people to kiss her cheek and murmur. There was a movement at my elbow. I turned to Ilona. She was wearing a black coat and hat which made her skin look pasty, and had applied liner and eye shadow to try to camouflage the redness of her eyes, so that she had managed to impersonate a miserable clown. When she nodded at me listlessly, I smelled a blast of alcohol on her breath and wondered whether she was carrying a flask and I could ask for a swig.

'Hi. Are you all right? You aren't here on your own, are you?'

She shrugged. 'No, Mum's with me.' She indicated the middle-aged woman in blue who was standing at the edge of the path, now wearing a self-conscious expression. 'She didn't think we ought to come, but Sally asked us both to stop overnight.'

I said, 'Good,' and tried to think of some neutral topic. Most people keep inexhaustible quantities of small talk for use at funerals and christenings, but mine had left me in the lurch. 'It was a nice service,' I embarrassed myself by murmuring.

'Yes. Your father isn't here?'

'I wouldn't let him come. I was afraid that the return trip might be too much for him in one day.'

'Oh. Yes . . .' Her voice trailed off.

I cleared my throat. 'Not many of us here from London. Do you know any of the locals? I don't seem to.'

'Well . . .' She stopped. 'That man over there by the kerb. Do you know him? He isn't talking to anybody, and I wondered . . .'

I looked. 'That's a detective from London. One of Inspector Grant's men. He hasn't said anything to you?'

Ilona shook her head. I thought she seemed relieved.

'And,' I added, seeing the man himself weaving his way in our direction through the thinning crowd, 'there's Danny Colbert. You know him, don't you?'

She seemed startled, and looked at Colbert from under the brim of her black hat. 'Yes. And I don't want to talk to any of Davey's friends today.' She left me abruptly, and I watched her cross to her mother and grab at the older woman's arm. The two of them climbed into one of the undertaker's limousines.

'Dido, love, sympathy – if that's in order.' Colbert had joined me. He had dressed for the occasion in what Davey once called his 'Oscar Wilde mode' – long black overcoat with astrakhan collar, black wide-brimmed hat, grey silk foulard, and a stick. Outside a suburban crematorium in Leicester, he looked astonishing.

I said, 'Thank you, Dan, sympathy is always in order in this hard world.'

He lowered his voice confidentially. 'I trust that Barnabas is well, though absent. Doesn't Ilona look like the bride of Frankenstein, though.'

'Barnabas is fine,' I said quickly, 'whereas Ilona is not fine.'

He changed tack with characteristic swiftness. 'She is bearing up marvellously, too. I must just say hello to her.'

'I don't think you can. She's not feeling well. Her mother's with her. Why don't you drop her a note?'

'Because I don't have her current address, my love. Can you give it to me?'

I shook my head. 'Actually, Danny, I don't have it either. I'll tell you what. See that man over there in the grey suit? The one on his own? He's a detective sergeant from London. I'm sure that the police have Ilona's address. Why don't you have a word with him?'

Colbert raised a quizzical eyebrow. 'How terribly inappropriate. Still, if that's what it takes . . .' He hesitated. 'I suppose that you came by train?

What time are you going back? Perhaps we could travel together and exchange gossip, to say nothing of a few buffet-car gins? Will you be at the fair this weekend?'

I had entirely forgotten about the monthly book fair in central London, at which we both usually had stands – there had been other things on my mind. 'I imagine so.'

'Taking anything that I might be interested in?'

'I hadn't thought about it . . .'

'Dido!' Sally's voice was pitched to reach me over conversations and the sound of cars starting. 'Are you coming, pet? Bring . . .'

I realized that she was going to suggest that I brought my interesting-looking companion, and moved with speed.

'Just coming!' I trilled, grimacing wildly. Sally is sharp; I caught the ghost of a grin as I turned back to my companion. 'I'll see you on Sunday, I guess. 'Bye!'

Sally crammed me into the leading limo between herself and Ron, and we returned to their flat in the mood of chatty relief that always seems to follow when a funeral service is completed, and there is nothing more daunting to face for the rest of the afternoon than tea and relatives. The other passengers were two middle-aged women to whom Ron introduced me. Family. Their names promptly vanished from my memory.

Teacups and plates of food were laid out on the dining table, but preceded gratefully by unlimited quantities of Scotch. I helped myself to a drink of a size appropriate to a near-widow and went looking for Ilona. At first I thought she had lost herself, but then I found her sitting in a corner of the kitchen, holding a drink considerably larger even than mine. I found a kitchen chair and plonked it and myself down between her and the rest of the world.

'When are you coming back to London?'

'I don't know. Might not be for a while. Mum wants me to stay up there with her.'

'What about the flat? All your things?'

'Well, I'll drop back and pack anything I want. Most of the stuff was Davey's. Ron is going down to get that. If I ever go back to London, I'll rent somewhere else anyway.'

'Yes, of course.'

'I'd always be reminded, there.'

'Of course. Look . . . did you talk to Paul Grant?'

116

Ilona looked puzzled. 'Who?'

'Inspector Grant. I thought he was going to see you at your mother's place?'

I thought she looked evasive. 'Oh – him. They don't know a damn thing, do they.'

'Have they asked you?'

She drained her glass. 'What do you mean?'

'Who *you* think killed Davey?'

She looked at me stolidly. 'How should I know?'

'But you must suspect somebody.'

She held out her glass and half stood up, as though she were going for a refill, but I didn't move and she couldn't get past me without a physical struggle.

'You're dreaming. I don't know anything about it.'

I reached out and removed half a bottle of Scotch from the hand of one of the middle-aged ladies who was passing, and filled both our glasses. I wasn't sure that I could actually drink Ilona Mitchell under the table, but I was counting on her having had enough already to be at a disadvantage.

'Ilona, tell me one thing: where did the money come from?'

'What money?'

'Davey's money. The money he bought the car with, the money he took me out to dinner with a couple of days before they killed him.'

She sat very still. 'He was out with you? He said it was business.'

I took a deep, only slightly wobbly breath. 'It was business, actually. You know perfectly well that it wasn't really an accident when you and he found me that night in Banbury. He knew I was going to be there, and you came looking for me.' I hesitated, because I wasn't sure whether I wanted to frighten her or appeal to her for help. 'You must have known what that was about. Why was Davey trying to scare me? What, exactly, did he want?'

She was silent. I saw her knuckles tighten on the glass.

I sighed. 'The police know it was Davey who broke into my shop. What was he looking for?'

She took a sip of Scotch. 'He didn't say.'

'But he was looking for something.'

She examined her drink. 'Yeah.'

'And he never said what?'

A thread of disbelief must have crept into my voice, because she looked directly at me then. 'No, never. But he didn't mean you any harm, not really. He always liked you, you know. If you hadn't turfed him out, you and your dad, he wouldn't never have left you.'

Well, if that was what Davey had told her . . . I let it pass for the moment and concentrated on the story. 'Tell me what you really think.'

She lowered her voice. 'The one thing I do know, he was in a corner. He was working for somebody, yes – don't ask me who, because he'd never say.' She continued to watch her drink as closely as though she were waiting for it to change colour and play the National Anthem.

After the silence had stretched on too long, I said, 'Don't you even suspect who it might have been?'

I was surprised when she flashed me a brief and, I could have sworn, ugly look. Her voice rose a little. 'I swear he never said. The only thing . . .'

'What?'

'The only thing he ever said about it was that he met the man a couple of years ago, while he was still with you. I thought . . .'

'*What?*' It was like drawing teeth.

'Well, I got the idea that some friend of yours introduced them, somebody he was hanging around with in the old days, when he was doing the hand-coloured prints. You know.'

She stared me in the eye, and her chin jutted out. Was *I* supposed to have introduced Davey to his fatal new employment? I stared back until she returned to her contemplation of her drink. 'But I don't know that, either. Davey didn't believe in telling you his business, did he. There was just a lot of money for a little while, more than he'd ever had before.'

'What was he doing for this man?'

Ilona laughed shortly, 'He said, running errands, minder, that kind of things?'

'Drugs?'

She hesitated. 'Maybe. Must have been. He wouldn't say. He owed somebody, and they were pushing him. Maybe he lost something or had it taken off him. He was scared.'

'So he was killed by the man he owed?'

Ilona shivered silently. I poured her a bit more. I poured myself a lot more.

'There's got to be some way of finding out who it was he was working for.'

She shook her head.

But there did have to be a way, because I couldn't live like this. Out of the whisky mist, a memory swam. I said, 'Oh – before I forget: I have a message for you. Somebody called Marty Campbell sends his condolences.'

Her body jerked as though I'd hit her, and she hesitated for just long enough that I knew she was going to lie, and said, 'Who?' As suddenly as though a tap had been turned, tears were pouring down her face. I kicked my chair aside and reached out a hand to take away her glass. As I pulled her to her feet, I felt myself wobble slightly. How much had I drunk?

Somebody came up behind me as Ilona stood there with her head down, weeping and speechless. I turned and saw Ron. 'She ought to go to bed.'

He looked alarmed. 'I'll get her mother.' People gathered and the weeping Ilona vanished.

Sally was there. 'You'd better have a cup of tea,' she said, 'and a sandwich. You two weren't having a row, were you?'

I shook my head, feeling infinitely tired and depressed. 'Of course not. We were trying to work out who killed Davey, though – or why.'

Sally regarded me grimly for a moment. 'Better not find out, maybe? It's not your business. Leave it alone.'

I whispered, 'Maybe,' because I hadn't the time or energy to explain why now it was my business more than anybody else's. I put a spoonful of sugar into my tea. Hang the pounds, I needed something strengthening, and the sight of the little triangular sandwiches just made me feel sick. I wished that I wasn't a two-hour journey and more from my home, because that was where I wanted to be: safe in my own bed with all the doors locked, contemplating my discovery that Ilona did know Marty Campbell, or at least his name, and that she was scared to death of him. And that if she feared him so much, then there was an equally good reason for me to be terrified too.

17

The Knot

'I am, after all,' Barnabas was saying, 'an experienced detective. In a manner of speaking. Not that I'd lay claim to pursuing criminals in the usual sense – retrieving heirs or inheritances or erring spouses.' He caught himself and blushed.

I said, 'Put your finger on this while I tie the knot.'

It had been a confused kind of morning. I'd been woken early by Barnabas, phoning nervously to ask whether I'd made it safely through the night back to my own flat, and only reassured by the evidence of his own ears that I was alive and the mobile still worked.

It was too early to go downstairs and too late to go back to bed, so I crept out into the corridor and carefully disarmed the winking red lights of the new state-of-the-art security system, by which apparently I was linked to the police, the Army, and possibly NATO. Then I made coffee and had a bath.

At that point I made the mistake of noticing the rising tide of grottiness all around. I cleaned carpets, dusted, and put away the dishes that had accumulated in the drying rack over the past week. Finding two black beetles in the cupboard under the sink, I swept them up and tilted them into my rubbish sack – let them live in luxury at the dump, not with me. I even took the sack out for Friday's pick-up. Then I made more coffee, ate toast and the last of the dry-cured bacon lurking in the bottom of the fridge, and listened to the nine o'clock news.

I was so wired by my own virtuous efforts that I decided at that point to go downstairs and begin packing stock for the book fair on Sunday morning. It's unusual for me to get down to this chore before about Saturday closing time, but I know myself: it isn't wise to ignore a rare access of such energy, because it goes away again as suddenly as it comes.

I'd pulled armloads of books off the shelves and was standing, pencil in hand, looking at the copy of the French yachting quarto by Philippe Daryl with the smashing coloured title page (and wondering whether I had the nerve to price it at £350) when Barnabas's second call of the day came through on the office phone: had I remembered that Saturday was Thomas's eighth birthday? No, I hadn't. My younger nephew, a frightening, self-confident child, had barely crossed my mind for weeks. Family is family, though, and a shopping expedition was unavoidable.

Which was why I was now crouching in the emptyish space in the middle of my father's sitting-room carpet, enveloping colourful boxes in a still more colourful spaceship-adorned wrapping paper. If I could get them to the post office on my way home, I'd still be able to open the shop for the afternoon.

'I'm a textual detective. I investigate errant vowels, missing words and unidentified poems. I've never made a bad mistake – at any rate, never published one. That bow looks crooked.'

I said, 'That's the last bit of ribbon, so it will have to do. Anyway, kids tear the paper off birthday presents so quickly that they never notice.'

'And my insight isn't doing a blind bit of good.'

I said, 'This is real life. People getting killed. Sally up there in Leicester thinking that it's indecent for her to be alive when her only child is dead. Ilona scared out of her wits about something she doesn't dare talk about. Job Warren's daughters . . .'

'I know, I know. And if you're running a metaphysical image to its lair, at least you have a text. All you do is gnaw at it until you eliminate the other possibilities and work out what it really is.' Barnabas passed me a sheet of brown wrapping paper and went to sit at his desk under the window. He looked tired.

He'd been brooding, and I knew that Professor Warren's death had touched him in a way that Davey's hadn't. He felt that Davey had gone into things with his eyes more or less open – leaving aside his genius for ignoring life's little realities – and been caught out. His death had been so horrible that I couldn't let myself even think about its sudden violence; but it was the blind unfairness of Job's slaughter that hit Barnabas harder.

Personally, I kept wanting his death to have been an ugly accident of modern life and nothing to do with us. Then Barnabas could stop feeling responsible. Then I could stop feeling pursued . . .

I looked at my wristwatch. 'Nearly one o'clock. I'll drop these off at the post office. They can go first class – it'll cost the earth, but it serves us both right for forgetting. They'll get there by Saturday morning.'

'I'll give you the money for the postage. Do you have to go back? Ever since you told me about your intruder, I've been worried whenever you're out of my sight.'

I gave him a quick peck. 'I know. But I can't stop living. And the way things are there now, I don't think that a cockroach could get into the flat without hordes of policemen turning up. Besides – nobody's actually tried to hurt me. Remember, even the search was done carefully to keep me from noticing.'

Barnabas nodded but still looked doubtful. 'Well, ah, do you want a cup of tea before you go?'

I conceded that I did, and Barnabas put the kettle on, cleared his throat, and said, 'Do you want to tell me about the funeral?'

'Not really. I was glad I went. Sally hasn't taken against me or anything.'

'What about Ilona? I wonder whether the boy detective shouldn't arrest her for questioning and put the fear of God into her?'

'She's too frightened to talk about it.'

'The man from the Mafia?'

I grunted and went to take the milk out of the fridge. He was running out again.

'If . . .' Barnabas began and stopped to pour tea before heaving himself into speech again. 'If Davey was looking for something when he broke into the shop, and somebody else was looking for the same thing when they searched your flat, what, I ask myself, will they do next?'

'Give up,' I said, 'with luck. They must realize, by now, that I don't have whatever it is.'

'Suppose they think that you know where it is? Or that Ilona does, for that matter?'

I drank tea and tried to think. 'We keep going round and round. And anyway, you realize that would let Job Warren out, because he hadn't been near us this visit. You know, Barnabas, maybe he isn't connected after all?'

Barnabas shifted in his chair and raised an index finger. 'I remember what I was going to say before you distracted me: if Davey was looking for something in the shop, it must have been a book. What else would you possibly try to hide in a bookshop? I think we've been postulating something much too complicated all this while. Now: why was poor Warren coming to see us? To buy books! And so they killed him.'

'Books?' I stopped listening, because it felt as though a lot of rusty cogs and levers were stirring and clattering into a new pattern. Something cold grew in the pit of my stomach. I cut the knot.

'Ireland.'

'Dido?'

I whispered, 'The Ireland Collection. Oh God, Barnabas, that's it! I'm such a fool! Davey, I never told you, he said . . . I can't remember . . . He said he had a buyer for the Ireland. Wait. No – he said that . . . that he could run it to somebody who'd give us over the catalogue price. I told you he was full of ideas!'

'What did you say?'

'That it was already on order.'

'And he said . . . ?'

'I don't . . . oh.'

'You told him about Warren?'

'Yes. Yes, we talked about it. Davey wanted me to tell Professor Warren that I'd already sold it. Yes.'

For a long time we stared at each other over the teapot while I tried to dig into my memory.

'He said . . . damn it, I wasn't paying that much attention. You know what he was like. I do remember him saying that we shouldn't throw three thousand pounds away. But *why*? Even for ten thousand pounds, or fifteen – why? Barnabas, it's nothing! He must have been absolutely desperate . . .'

I could hear my voice rising. I stopped myself.

'You're as white as a sheet. Drink your tea. Would you like something stronger? Dido, my dear?'

'Where is it?'

I wasn't talking about his whisky.

'I haven't moved it.'

When Job Warren phoned from Massachusetts to say that he wanted the collection for the Constance Hance, and that he was coming to London, I'd passed on Barnabas's usual invitation. Then I'd packed up the Ireland things in an old cardboard box and dumped it in a corner of Barnabas's sitting room. They were Professor Warren's little treat: this year's conversation piece picked out to show him during the evening, bait for his visit to the shop. Every year there was the little treat.

I slid the box out from under the table and opened the flaps.

The Ireland Collection consisted of thirteen old books and a folder of faded letters and manuscripts smelling of dust. It had turned up a couple of years before on a buying trip Davey and I had made to the West Country just before he had removed himself from my bed, if not my life. I'd found them when I'd opened a box on the floor of a bookshop in Hereford whose proprietor had recently purchased several country house libraries of no very great interest.

The moment I saw it, I knew it was treasure.

Over the next year I'd carted the collection around to book fairs with decreasing enthusiasm. I'd also catalogued the lot, as a collection, twice. At various times people had looked and said how interesting it all was, but nobody had showed the slightest desire to buy it.

When this kind of thing happens – and it happens all the time among antiquarian dealers – at first you think that everybody is blind or mad not to appreciate what a wonderful, exciting, unique find you are offering them. But after a while you decide that you've simply made a mistake and you might as well accept the fact. For my last catalogue I'd decided to make one final attempt before giving in and putting the thing into auction. I'd even raised the price. The collection had been sitting at £6000 ever since we'd bought it. I put it up to £10,000 – five figures is a more eye-catching sum, I thought, and what the hell. I've noticed that raising the price of an unsellable curiosity to ludicrous heights very often succeeds. Magic.

But Davey had said twelve thousand, and probably meant more. That was multiplied craziness. What kind of lies had he told somebody about it?

I pulled everything out, one item at a time, and laid it all on the carpet. The dull pages, rubbed sheepskin and cracked hinges smirked at me. Why on earth had I ever got excited about this mouldering pile? Why had I thought that anybody would pay ten thousand pounds for such rubbish?

A copy of the catalogue entry sat on top of the books, but I scarcely needed to refer to it – I'd used the same paragraph several times, and I almost knew it by heart;

IRELAND, William Henry and Samuel
An interesting collection of books and also autograph mss belonging

to the celebrated Shakespearean forger, W. H. Ireland, whose excuse was, 'I only did it to please the old man' (like Cain and Electra – but I digress) and his father, Samuel, the engraver and *littérateur*. Thirteen books from Samuel's library, all with his elegant signature and date of purchase, three with his bookplate, one (Mrs Elizabeth Montague's *Essay on the Genius of Shakespeare*, 2nd edn., 1770) with extensive annotations, mostly ejaculations of approval. Together with one ms and five als from various correspondents, mostly brief and social, and A LETTER FROM W. H. IRELAND (2pp May 1794) hinting at a forthcoming 'find' ('If it shd be what my hopes predict how it will confound the skeptics'). The books are in rather poor condition, some showing scorch marks, perhaps evidence that they were part of the collection which was in the Birmingham Library fire in 1879. The letters are in excellent order, though that from the son shows traces of a mount.

Full details on request.

As a collection (20 pieces in all) £10,000

This had been written by Barnabas, of course, in his best fusty-academic style. He'd made it sound tempting and romantic – hadn't he? I looked up at the author from my seat on his carpet. 'What am I going to do? I'd better take them away with me.'

'Leave them for the time being. They'll be safe here, and I should like to find out why Davey or anybody else would think that this collection is worth killing for. If he did, of course. He was an obsessive liar. As for you, my dear, you'd better phone the Constance Hance and ask whether they still want this. It's . . . what, about seven a.m. there now? Try in two hours. The sooner this is out of our hands, the happier I shall be.'

I felt too dazed to argue. The box would certainly be safer here for the moment. And – the scheme came in a flash – at the book fair on Sunday, I could buy drinks for everybody to celebrate having got rid of the Ireland Collection at last. Word gets around fast at the fairs: soon forty antiquarian book dealers would know that Dido Hoare had struck it lucky, and that the Ireland Collection had left the country. If that message didn't reach any interested party in about half an hour, I didn't know booksellers.

Clutching my new idea, I felt almost cheerful for the first time since Davey's death. I calculated it: seventy-two hours to go.

18

The Dutiful Son

I turned into George Street and left the car where I could see it from my windows. It wouldn't have surprised me much to come home to a hole in the ground, but both street and shop looked normal, and the security alarm above the window was displaying its diligent little red flash in reassuring silence. I stumbled into the shop, disarmed the alarm system, and burped. Apparently stress affects my digestion. The present situation had to be changed before it changed me into a belching wreck.

On the principle that when you are under attack the best thing to do is call in the guards, I rang the police station and caught Paul Grant at his desk for once. The relief of hearing that odd, barked greeting, 'DI,' left me speechless for a few seconds.

'It's Dido . . .'

He cut through. 'What's wrong?'

'Nothing at the moment.' What, exactly, was I expecting to get from this call? I hesitated. 'I need to talk to you about something that's come up. Could we meet . . . could you come over?'

He echoed my own hesitation. 'Have you eaten?'

'Can you?'

I thought there was another pause before he laughed. 'Even policemen are allowed lunch. Besides, it is business, isn't it?'

We agreed that he would finish what he was doing and pick me up in ten minutes. That gave me just time to phone the Constance Hance, locate a voice that admitted to being Professor Warren's assistant, and find out that they knew nothing about the Ireland Collection, certainly had initiated no purchase order, and had no authority to make any kind of arrangement – and would it be all right if the library got back to me as soon as possible?

'Actually,' I explained grimly, 'somebody else wants it.' Hearing myself use the high-pressure salesman's age-old threat – though more truthfully than usual – I started to babble self-consciously. 'Of course, I consider that you have the first refusal, and I wouldn't dream of giving it to anybody else if you still want it, but I really must know soon. Very soon.'

There was a silence from the other end, and then the politely dubious tone that I would have used myself, finding some complete stranger trying to pressure me into paying fifteen thousand dollars for something I'd never heard of. 'The thing is,' the voice explained doggedly, 'I don't know anything about Job's purchase orders, and nobody knows at this moment in time what the university is going to do about replacing him or extending the acquisitions programme. That kind of thing was always his baby. I guess it could take weeks to sort it out.'

That was more or less what I ought to have anticipated. I promised to fax him a copy of the catalogue entry, and he promised to get a decision from some administrator by Monday; but I suspected that I wasn't going to get rid of my embarrassing possession easily, after all. I had a momentary, shameful impulse to offer him the collection for the price of the postage, but I couldn't quite force myself to take this wise but drastic step. Stubbornness? Or just greed?

I tore the relevant page out of a spare catalogue, stuck it to a sheet of my business stationery, and went around the corner to a print shop with a fax machine. When it had gone off to Massachusetts, I felt as though I'd come to a blank wall. Monday was four whole days away. It felt like much too long to go on living in a war zone.

I stopped to buy some indigestion tablets and was examining my face in the mirror over the hand basin in my office, wondering whether it was middle age or tension that was making my body crumble, when the shop door rattled. I was so worried about wrinkles that I stopped long enough to wipe some face powder over them before I could bear to go and let Paul in.

He was looking depressingly good. He grinned, bent down, and planted a kiss on the end of my nose. I held his hand – a little too tightly, probably – and reciprocated.

'How are things? How's your father?'

'Things could be better, but he's all right.'

'What about you?'

I hesitated. 'Not so good. I'm not used to this drama . . . I keep thinking that somebody's going to jump me.'

He looked quizzical. 'The alarm system should help.'

'It keeps reminding me of things I'd rather not think of.'

'Has something happened?'

'Yes and no. Not exactly happened.' I stopped, because I'd just realized what my problem was: I was wanting somebody like Paul to hold me tight and tell me that everything was going to be all right, that he would see to it and I wasn't to be afraid. It was a rather shameful insight.

As a matter of principle I stepped back and looked up at him with what I hoped was a mature and self-reliant expression. 'I've been talking to Barnabas, and I think we've worked out what this is all about – what they're looking for and how Job Warren got involved.'

He looked at me intently. 'Shall we go and sit down and talk? You look as though you need a drink. Can you close for a while?'

I felt as though I needed not a drink, but about half a bottle of gin, so I explained that I had no problem with that. 'Good. Look, let's get you right away from here. Come back to my place. It's private, there's lots to drink, and we can send out for a pizza. We won't be interrupted there.'

The idea of being both safe and private was so welcome that my indigestion vanished. I could even contemplate the pizza. 'Can you leave work just like that?'

'I can't. I haven't.' He grimaced oddly. 'I'm interviewing you again. You've just told me that you've cracked it – remember?'

'And you've just invited me to your place?'

He jerked his head. 'Don't tell my Super that I'm fraternizing – not until it's all wound up, at least. But I don't believe you've done anything criminal – have you?'

For some reason it hadn't struck me that policemen might be discouraged from personal involvement in their work. Being in a worrying mood, I worried about this complication as I locked up, and went on worrying for the duration of the drive.

It took us twenty minutes to get through back streets to a warehouse conversion overlooking a minor canal just north of the Isle of Dogs. We took the lift to the top floor, standing close, and he unlocked a heavy wood-and-steel door into a bright space with tall, uncurtained windows and bare brick walls dotted with big rock band tour posters. Apart from the tiny bathroom by the front door, the flat was a single big room, maybe fifty feet square and eighteen feet high. I found myself examining the place with curiosity and growing surprise. Books and what looked like Indian objects filled industrial shelving along the far wall, sofa and chairs clustered under a window in one corner, a kitchen with stainless steel cupboard doors fitted into another, and a bed that consisted of a platform on scaffolding above another cluster of chest of drawers, cabinets and a hanging rail sat opposite the windows. Along the wall to our left was a music system with the biggest loudspeakers I'd ever seen outside a rock concert – the neighbours must love this – and a stack of rectangular black cases marked with what I vaguely recognized as trade names of instrument-makers.

'You're a musician?'

Paul grinned. 'No, I'm a policeman. I'm renting this place from a friend who's on tour at the moment. There's a bottle of Chianti I can open, or beer, or Scotch?'

We settled on beer, and he produced bottles of German lager from the fridge. 'And I promised you a pizza. Are you hungry, or should we talk first?'

'Talk,' I said, and told him about the Ireland.

My story left him looking bewildered. 'I'm sorry, but I don't really understand. I've never heard of this Ireland character. Is the stuff valuable just because he owned it?'

'I don't know how to answer that.' I hesitated, wondering how to explain. 'It was a famous scandal at the end of the eighteenth century. Look: Samuel Ireland was the kind of father who assumes that his teenage son is a useless slob, and William needed to impress him. He decided that the way to prove himself was to become a great poet, but he wasn't too bright, and Samuel was not amused. When that didn't work, William decided that he would discover some manuscripts by Shakespeare. Samuel was an antiques dealer by trade, you see, a bit sharp himself – he's supposed to have forged some Hogarth engravings. But the point is, he really was crazy about Shakespeare. William reckoned that as Shakespeare had died only a hundred and seventy-odd years before, it was perfectly possible that somebody might still come up with some unknown manuscripts.'

'Sounds to me like a con.'

'Well, it was just possible. Shakespeare had been almost forgotten until about twenty years before this, you know. The Shakespeare industry was only just starting up, and a lot of people expected that some unpublished work might still turn up.'

'What happened?'

'First, William started to collect antiquarian books – which his father naturally approved of – and then he was tempted by the idea of forging some Elizabethan documents. His father accepted them as genuine right away.'

'Little bugger,' Paul laughed. 'So he forged some plays and presented them to his father with love and kisses?'

'He began with legal papers that he could copy from old documents, because he was working in a solicitor's office where genuine Tudor files were stored. From reproductions I've seen, I'd say that his work was unbelievably crude, but apparently Samuel thought it was genuine. It wouldn't fool anybody today for a second. Then William tried composing letters and poems, and he and a friend concocted a story about getting them from an eccentric old gentleman who insisted on remaining anonymous.'

'And Samuel believed them?'

'Enthusiastically. Not just Samuel, either. In the end William produced a brand-new Shakespearean tragedy which was put on at Drury Lane. It was published – I've read it, and it's dire. A lot of people in the audience realized, and there was very nearly a riot. But a lot of other people still argued it was genuine. There was an awful fuss. Most people finally decided that Samuel was the forger. It all went very public, with everybody taking sides, until Samuel died.'

'So it ended in tears.'

'Well, it didn't lead to a lot of happiness. The saddest thing of all was that when William Henry finally confessed, his father wouldn't believe him. He said that William was too stupid to be capable of writing the stuff. He never accepted the truth.'

'That is a sad story.' Grant finished his lager. 'Would you like another?'

'Not yet. Thanks.'

'All right, I can see somebody who collects old books – eighteenth century, you said? – getting excited about this. But just how excited? How much is it worth?'

'I had it marked at ten thousand pounds.'

'In this last catalogue of yours? And you'd sold it to our American friend?'

'To his library. Well, he said they wanted it. Formally speaking, it wasn't on order, but as good as.'

'And Winner wanted it too. What did he think it was worth?'

'He said he could get a couple of thousand over what I was asking, but he probably thought it was worth more, because he'd have wanted a turn.'

'Was he right?'

That was my problem, the one thing about the situation that bothered me.

Antiquarian books have no 'real' value. They are worth what somebody is willing to pay. Prices are usually negotiable, especially higher prices. So while I could accept that Job Warren had been killed to prevent him taking the Ireland Collection out of England, I still couldn't see how the books were worth two lives. There was still something missing from the equation, something I hadn't worked out.

Paul persisted: 'But it's definitely the only thing that connects him and you and Professor Warren?'

'Yes . . .' That was the only way to read it.

He put his glass down on a battered oak table that stood at his elbow, hauled himself out of the armchair beside mine, and stood looking down at me like a man awaiting my confession. 'Could you be wrong about the value?'

'How wrong?'

'You know . . . very wrong.'

I shook my head. 'No. Possibly. I guess so.'

He gave me an appropriately bewildered look.

'As a matter of fact, I'd priced it up for this catalogue.' I told him how long I'd had the collection, how often I'd tried to sell it, and how many people had looked at it and then regretfully refused the bargain. I wound up, 'So you see, there are all kinds of reasons for saying that the value is up to ten thousand pounds. Except that nobody would do all this for ten thousand pounds, would they?'

'No. Not that there aren't people around who'd kill you for sixty pounds to buy crack. But not in this case. Those two murders must have cost real money to set up. This is ridiculous!'

'That's how I feel. So then I *must* be wrong after all. I don't understand.'

I was circling uselessly around my own confusion, when he interrupted, 'I'd like us to go to bed now. What do you think?'

I considered pretending a maidenly surprise and decided not to be stupid. For one thing, I liked his eyes. Furthermore, it seemed like the best offer I'd had in a long time. Finally, I'd never made love before on a mattress on top of scaffolding. It all made sense.

He turned out to be a good lover – an explorer, gentle. Lying afterwards holding and being held, thinking how long it had been since I'd felt the warmth of a new body, the hardness of bone and muscle against me, it suddenly came to me also that he had been wonderfully tactful. Not only had we somehow got up that ridiculous scaffolding without awkwardness, but a condom had come naturally to hand – careful children of the sad AIDs age that we are now. I'd done a lot worse in the past. So I smiled like a cat and lay in a cloud of contentment, listening to distant sounds in the passageways of the old building and to the pulsing of blood in the veins.

Inevitably, Paul's bleeper ended it. He cursed in a muffled kind of way, stirred, unwrapped us. I closed my eyes against his departure and waited for the murmur of his voice on the phone. His end of the conversation began with an unintelligible exclamation, followed by a series of half-audible questions. I heard the phrase 'half an hour', groaned mentally, and tried to tell myself that there would be other afternoons.

He touched my cheek, and I opened my eyes to find him staring at me over the edge of the platform.

'Emergency?'

'Ilona Mitchell's been attacked. I have to go.'

'What? Is she all right?'

He vanished from sight, and I could hear him gathering our things together from the floor around our elevated nest.

'She was beaten up. She's in the Whittington. They say there's no permanent damage. I have to go and see what she has to say.'

A bundle of clothing appeared over the edge of the bed, and I started to sort things out. 'You mean the hospital in Archway? What's she doing in London?'

'Came back to get things from the flat. Somebody must have been waiting for her and roughed her up.'

'Why?'

'Exactly! Come on. I'll drop you off at your place on the way.'

'Will you let me know how she is?'

He looked up at me and apparently wasn't put off by the sight of my struggles to wriggle into my tights while perched inconveniently at head height, 'Are you going to be at home this evening? I'll drop by as soon as I've finished and we can . . . Oh, damn.'

The thought came to me at the same time. I smiled at him demurely as he lifted me down to ground level and said, 'Maybe there'll be time this evening to phone out for a pizza.'

19

Ilona

When I finally listened to the answering machine, I found that, apart from a call from Pat, the tape was full of Barnabas's plaintive enquiries.

Pat's number rang at length without result, but Barnabas responded on the first ring.

'It took you long enough,' he grumbled.

'I was out. Why? Is something wrong?'

'Of course not. But you didn't answer your mobile when I tried it, and I've been anxious.'

I recalled guiltily that I'd turned the mobile off while I was with Paul and then forgotten it, and wondered not for the first time whether I was up to the high-tech life. 'I'm fine,' I said quickly. 'By the way, Pat phoned me.'

'Me too.' He sounded thoughtful. 'She told me all about the child's birthday party. She had some mad idea that I might take the train out. Sometimes she doesn't realize how tiring – do I mean to say tiresome? – I find ten small boys at once. I told her that there's a . . .' His voice faded for a moment into a line crackle. 'I take it you did post it?'

I reassured him. Then I hesitated, wondering whether I should give him the news about Ilona. On the whole, it seemed better to delay that.

'Look, please don't worry if you can't get me on the phone, it's just that I'm rushing around a lot. I haven't even had time to pack for the book fair yet.' That sounded normal enough. I had no intention of saying anything about Paul at this stage, either.

'What was that? I missed part of what you said. The sound fades.'

'It does seem to be a very bad line. I . . . Hello?'

There was a moment's silence, and then his voice returned. ' . . . the library?'

I said, 'Barnabas, this line is awful. Hang up and I'll ring you back.'

'No, don't bother. I'm looking out of the window, and there are engineers working at the junction box on the corner. I'll ring you later. If you're going out, take the mob—'

His voice sank into what sounded like a background of scratching sounds, and I hung up.

My hand was an inch from the telephone when it rang. I picked up the receiver, expecting to hear Barnabas again, but it was Paul Grant.

'Hi. Are you busy?'

'Not really.' No, no, only a book fair to pack up, but I had no intention of allowing that chore to get in our way. 'How is she?'

'Her face is a mess, and she has a broken arm, but she'll be all right. Look – can you come over here?'

'To the hospital?'

'She says she'd like to see you. It's Queen Elizabeth Ward.'

Nagged by curiosity, I locked up the shop for the final time that day and went upstairs for my things. At the last moment I remembered the mobile, checked that it was on stand-by, and pushed it into my shoulder bag. Mr Spock was out somewhere, so I left his entry window open a few inches beyond the bars, set the alarm, and went out of the door with the inaudible promise that I'd be back to perform tin-opening for him before long.

I drove on past the hospital entrance and was lucky enough to find a parking space a hundred yards up the hill. When I walked back, I found the familiar, tall figure pacing inside the glass entrance. He gave me the kind of quick peck that you could miss if you weren't looking closely.

'Is she all right? Has she said anything about what happened?'

'There were two men. She's given a description: vague, but maybe she'll be able to pick someone out of our photo files tomorrow. They slammed her around for a while, and I gather they've left the flat in a worse mess than before, if you can imagine it. Do you mind if we go straight up?'

He steered me almost silently along a couple of crowded corridors, and up an escalator, to a closed door.

'See whether she has something that she wants to tell you. Take it slowly. She's had a fright.'

136

He knocked on the door and opened it for me, and I slipped inside ahead of him.

We were in a side room, small and dimly lit, but even in the gloom I was shocked into a small exclamation at the sight of the puffy, darkened face against the pillows. Ilona's eyes opened in their setting of bruises and flickered at me.

I heard myself whispering, 'I'm here. How do you feel? Is there anything I can do for you?' I sat down gingerly at the side of the bed. Her left arm was in a splinted bandage. I gently took her right hand. There was a bloody abrasion on the back of it, and bruises darkening over her wrist bone.

'I feel lousy. How do I look?' Her voice grated hoarsely, and the eyes flickered at Paul, standing behind me. 'They've phoned my mum. She'll be here in the morning.'

'Do you have any friends you'd like me to tell in the meantime?'

She shook her head and winced. 'Got to remember not to do that.'

'It must hurt.'

'Unh. Not too bad now. My arm hurts. The rest's just scrapes and bruises. They say I won't be scarred.'

'That's lucky, but who *did* it?'

A grimace passed across the damaged face. 'Never saw them before. My fault. When I got there the front door was on the latch, and would you believe I went in anyway? I saw that the place was a tip, but they were hiding in the bedroom and they grabbed me before I could get out. Christ, I was scared! When I yelled, they bashed me.'

'They didn't . . . ?'

'No, just slapped me around. I could feel the bone go when I fell. After a while they went away. Could hear them in the other room. Kept still. When they left I dialled 999.'

Behind me, Paul cleared his throat. His voice sounded over-loud after our whispers. 'I'm going to get a cup of coffee. Will you sit with her for a while? I'll be in the cafeteria. Just fifteen minutes, all right?'

I guessed that whatever was supposed to happen was going to be between the two of us. We both waited for the door to close. I went on listening to her slightly hoarse breathing. In the end I said, 'Who were they? They weren't just burglars.'

'Don't be stupid, of course not. Somebody's boys. Wanted to hurt me, make sure I didn't talk to anybody. Bloody cops! As if I would . . . only they didn't leave me alone.' The laugh was quiet and bitter. 'Always trouble, talking to bloody cops.'

What about sleeping with one? a small internal voice remarked.

'They'd been looking for something. Didn't find it – I got that much. So they decided to wreck me when I walked in on them. Aren't I a stupid cow?' She stopped.

'You're awfully brave,' I said carefully. 'I'd have been scared rigid.'

'More mad than scared. Anyway, I'm out of it. I'm going home with Mum as soon as I can get myself out of here.'

I breathed in and out slowly, thinking that this was the time. 'Do you remember what you said when I came to see you just after Davey died?'

Her eyes flickered at me again. She was silent.

'These men – they're part of Davey's problem, aren't they?'

There was another silence. I began to wonder whether I'd misjudged. Then a kind of decision seemed to harden in her face.

'And they beat you up because of the same thing.'

She was listening.

'Then shouldn't you tell DI Grant everything you can? At least they wouldn't have anything more to gain from pressuring you.'

I couldn't read her expression until her lips twisted bitterly. 'Don't worry, I'm not going to let them find me again.'

I said slowly, 'Even if you stayed at your mother's, it might not be safe. Stafford isn't so far. If they want to find you again, they'll probably manage it, unless the police can get them first.' I thought about it. 'Somebody searched my flat the other day. If I'd walked in while they were there, I suppose they'd have done the same thing to me that they did to you. My father is an old man with a bad heart, and it wouldn't take much to kill him. I have to end this business!'

'Best keep quiet, then.'

'Don't you understand? They aren't going to let it go. And they killed Davey,' I said.

It was a little while before she said, 'Yes.'

I said, 'I don't even know why. Help me, please. I really need to know what you know.'

A small voice said from the bed, 'I don't know anything. Honest. Davey just said that you had something worth a hell of a lot, and by rights it was half his. I guess he told them about it – that lot.'

'Told *who*?' Her dramatic hints made me want to shake her, except that she looked as though she'd fall to bits if I tried.

'All right, but if you ever tell anybody I told you, I'm dead, because I don't know what, but I might know who. There was this man that Davey met through one of *your* friends – one of the book people. He worked for him sometimes.'

'For the bookseller?'

Her voice grew thinner. 'For the *boss*. I told you that before. Listen, I'm dying for a cig. Can you light me one? They're in the drawer.'

I found the pack, lit a cigarette, and pushed it into her undamaged hand. Ilona dragged and blew out smoke slowly.

'Sometimes Davey'd be out all night, and when he came in he'd have cash. Once or twice, there was quite a bit. I asked once, and he said this man had to be around council estates over Kilburn, surveying or something, and he took Davey along in case he had any trouble from the local lads. Davey could handle himself, you know.'

'Oh, yes,' I agreed. Though never as well as he thought he could. I took the 'surveying' with a whole handful of salt. It was drugs – obviously. 'You say he got this job through a bookseller friend? Who?'

For a moment I thought she had fallen asleep, but then she whispered, 'No, can't remember. Odd name, foreign maybe. I guess maybe sort of French.'

I didn't know of any French booksellers in London. 'Can you describe him?'

'No.' She sounded defensive. 'I met all kinds of booksellers with Davey, when we was . . . were selling the prints – you know.'

'And you really don't know which one it was?'

I caught a trace of disbelief in my voice. So did she, because we were both silent for a while. I thought she'd finished, and I pushed my tired mind into overdrive, but the only name it came up with was Jean-Pierre Tessier's.

Jean-Pierre had a market stall. When he was feeling prosperous, it moved to the fringes of Portobello Market; in bad periods it sometimes turned up in Church Street. Apart from rubbish, he sometimes had nineteenth-century illustrated books on his stall, especially breakers – faulty volumes with the engravings that Davey used to tear out and colour. We'd dealt with Jean-Pierre a bit in the old days.

Another name pushed itself into my head, and the image of that strange, solid, white-haired man who had introduced himself so politely. I knew absolutely certainly that there was no question about this one. I said, 'He was working for Marty Campbell, of course.'

She was silent, but it didn't matter any more. I softened my tone, became ingratiating. 'I still don't understand why all this happened. What were they expecting to find in your flat? They searched it twice, didn't they – once the day you went up north. What had Davey left there?'

'I said, I dunno. Look, I know that Davey owed them money – for the car and things. S'pose to pay them off, like, he'd agreed to handle something for them . . .'

'Hard drugs?'

'Maybe. Anyway, he was out of his league, wasn't he. S'pose he was doing a job for them and it went wrong, and they wanted their investment back. You get deeper in, with them. Or maybe he even sort of stole something from them. Maybe he said he'd lost it, and they thought he'd hidden it. All kinds of things could've happened.'

I waited, seeing that as usual she was circling around the real truth. When it seemed she had stopped, I said gently, 'I guess if you owed somebody like Marty Campbell a lot of money, no matter why, he'd be sure to get it back. Right?'

'If you say so. Just then, at the end, he was worried all the time.'

'And so Davey told them I had something really valuable that he could get his hands on, and when he did he could pay them what he owed.'

You could picture the whole thing: Davey, in over his thick head, getting desperate, squirming . . . All right, pet, don't worry; I'll find a way. Always another scam. Saying, Look, I can get my hands on money. Everything I owe you. My ex has something really great. Must be worth a hundred K at least, and it's half mine. Just give me a couple of days . . .

'He had a key to the shop, didn't he? One that he'd got months ago, without me knowing. And he came looking for this valuable thing. He didn't find it, though. Do you know what it was?'

She stared at me seriously. 'Look, he never wanted to tell me anything about this, you know, 'cause it was dangerous, but I did some guessing, and I asked, and things came out sometimes.'

'He must have convinced them that there really was something good, and then he couldn't produce it. Is that why they killed him? Or . . .' It took me a couple of seconds to work it out. ' . . . they thought that he'd got it and was holding out on them. That's why they killed him. That's why they keep coming back to your flat, looking for it.'

All she would say was, 'Yeah, maybe. I guess so.' I pushed it, but in the end she sighed, 'Look, forget about it, it's all just an idea I had. I don't expect it's right, but if it was you'd want to keep out of it, because it's real trouble. You don't know.'

If only. 'Just forget about it? Forget what they did?'

Her voice became stronger. 'Yes! Davey's dead, but that doesn't have anything to do with you, you're fucking alive, and so am I.' The easy tears were flowing down her bruised and puffy cheeks.

There was a name now. Confirmation. And another name still to find: a French bookseller, somebody Davey had known well enough in the old days, somebody with criminal connections – the missing link. I needed to think. I had to go back over the last couple of years and remember – the necessary link.

There was a tap on the door which opened to let in both Paul and a staff nurse wanting to get rid of us so that Ilona could sleep. I promised I'd come again. Or was it a threat?

Paul bundled me silently away from the door, where a uniformed constable was now sitting motionless and obviously on guard. Down the corridor, he asked, 'What did she want?'

I stopped to consider that. 'I'm not really sure. I think . . .'

'*What?*'

'I think she wanted to warn me to be careful. Not to talk to you. She seems to think that if she keeps quiet it will all go away. She's scared to admit that she knows what's going on.'

I told him the skeleton tale of the French bookseller and Davey's occasional employer, and the hints about their falling out. I gave him Marty Campbell.

Paul stood very still, staring over the top of my head with the kind of absent-minded intensity that leaves you certain that your companion is cursing vigorously inside his own head. It was minutes before he asked, 'What about the other one? We need a tie-in. I'm not saying I don't believe her. In fact I'm sure you're right; why would Campbell have come to see you except to find out where Ilona had gone? But we aren't going to get any co-operation from him! We need the identity of the other man, the bookseller who ties them in. I can lean on her if I have to, and I will – the stupid little cow.'

I couldn't answer. I was pretty sure that Ilona hadn't said everything there was to say, but I didn't know; and something made me want to protect her. Loyalty between wives, perhaps? I laughed, and the sound was more bitter than I'd intended.

'What is it?'

'It's perfectly likely that Davey didn't tell her anything. He was like that with women. Look, I've got to think about it. I may be able to remember somebody from the old days. I'll try.'

'I'll have another long talk with her tomorrow.'

I warned him, 'She thinks that if she talks to you they'll come back again.'

'She's probably not wrong. Even so, I'll have to persuade her. She'll be safer in the end if we can tie this up.'

'I keep telling her that finding them is the only way.'

'Never a truer word. And?'

'Not convinced.'

'Unh.'

He walked silently beside me out of the building and up the street to the Volvo, withdrawn into his own thoughts. As I unlocked the car, he seemed to notice me again.

'I'm off duty in half an hour. Have you had anything to eat yet?'

I told him I was still waiting for the pizza. There was something else. 'If you do find out who the link is – the contact – will that mean you'll be able to arrest Campbell? You see, she really believes that if she talks to you, they'll kill her.'

'It depends. At the moment, all I could do is bring him in for questioning. He'd just laugh in my face, because there's not a scrap of evidence against him. Somebody's going to have to tell us the whole story and then go into the witness box. I don't see this being solved through external evidence – if there was any, we'd have found it before now. There's our funny bomb, of course, but that would tend to let Campbell off, if anything.'

I stared. 'Funny bomb?'

'Well, yes . . .'

'Explain?' I suggested.

'We've got the full forensics report at last. They studied pieces of the device that they found, and some of the components seemed odd. In the end it was sent to a lab in Germany, and they've identified some of the material as Russian. Apparently a lot of Moscow gangsters have taken to bombing their friends.'

I stared at him. '*Russian?*'

'Crime is international these days,' Paul observed darkly. 'With the IRA in suspension and the Libyans quiet, things are changing. Anyway, that's what they say.'

'And there's no connection with Campbell?'

Paul shrugged. 'Well, you wouldn't expect the big-shot to do his own dirty work.'

'Can't you guarantee Ilona anything?'

'We could keep her name off the record, if it came to that – unless it was essential for her to go into the witness box.'

Oh yes? Unless it 'came to that'? I began to understand Ilona's lack of enthusiasm for a deal that might give her nothing but trouble.

'Let's leave it until I report back and talk to people. About the pizza – we could manage a bit better, couldn't we? I know a nice, convenient place in Upper Street, not far from you. We could meet there as soon as I'm off. And then I can make sure you get home safely. You do need a bodyguard.'

I laughed at him, but without disagreeing. 'I'll check on Barnabas,' I said, and produced my mobile. Perhaps after all I could get used to technology. However, when I dialled I got the 'unavailable' tone. I switched off uncertainly.

'He's been having trouble with his line,' I said. 'The repair men were in the road, earlier, but it doesn't seem to have come back yet.'

Before I had stopped speaking, I felt a tide of uneasiness rising.

Paul saw it in my face. He pulled the phone out of my hand. 'I'll tell the station that I'm going to check on him and get them to phone in to the hospital and warn my constable that I've left. Let's not waste time. Look, my car is in the hospital grounds – and I'll get there faster than you could.'

20

Bug

'I find this increasingly ridiculous,' Barnabas observed gustily. 'Of course I'm all right! What should have happened to me?'

'Your telephone is dead!' I snapped. 'You're the one who's always complaining if *I'm* not on the end of the line whenever you decide to be nervous.'

He gestured helplessly. 'Perhaps we should calm down. Come in, both of you, I feel the need of a sherry.'

Paul and I entered my father's sitting room like the United States Cavalry arriving at full gallop into the middle of a Sunday school picnic. Barnabas began his usual act of trying to find three seats which, if not actually empty of papers at the moment, could at least be cleared without too much effort.

He said, 'And my phone is working now. The engineers fiddled about outside for a while . . .' He broke off long enough to revert to his old tutorial habits and pass out servings of amontillado. Paul inspected his nervously, giving me the impression that polytechnic students weren't normally given sherry by their tutors. 'One of the engineers came in and checked it when they'd finished.'

Paul put his glass down quietly on a pile of books. 'Checked in here?'

Barnabas's expression slowly became thoughtful. 'Yes. He said they were pretty sure that the trouble was outside the house, but they weren't absolutely certain.'

I made a guess. 'Perhaps we shouldn't be letting strangers into the house? Not just at the moment?'

Paul got to his feet and wandered over to the work table where the telephone balanced on top of the usual pile of books. I noticed then that the box that held the Ireland Collection was sitting on the desk chair and one of the volumes near the telephone looked familiar.

I said, 'What have you been doing?'

Barnabas winked. 'Looking at the books. Collating. Page by page. Looking at watermarks. Looking for anything that shouldn't be there, in short.'

'And the manuscripts?'

'More likely, so I was saving them for last.'

'*And you let a stranger into the place with that stuff sitting around?*' I hissed.

'Do you really think a stranger would notice anything?' Barnabas retorted; but his tone was apologetic.

I tried to be fair: to inspect the room with the eye of somebody who was not familiar with it. All right: the place did look like a cross between a jumble sale and a compost heap.

I opened my mouth, but Paul, following his own thoughts, was picking up the telephone. We watched him listen, hesitate, and put the receiver back.

'Where was this man working?'

'Outside. There is a box on the side of the house to the right of the stairs.'

'Wait here a minute.'

Paul left. Not being the kind of person who does as I'm told, I followed and found him crouching over the metal box where the telephone lines entered the building. There was an untidy tangle, but Paul, ignoring it, was nosing away at the metal box itself.

'He's been working at this, all right; I can see scratches where the cover's been unfastened.'

'Why are you worried about it?'

'Maybe I'm jumpy about anything out of the ordinary right now. I'm going to use my mobile and find out whether Telecom had their engineers here today. What's your father's number, again?'

I told him, backing away from the box. Not that I really thought it had been booby-trapped. I went back into my father's flat, and we made desultory conversation until Paul returned.

'Whoever he was, the phone company has no record of a problem here,' he reported when he reappeared at the door of the flat. 'They're sending one of their managers over as fast as they can. We'll know about this in ten minutes.'

When a car drew up outside, he vanished again. From the window I watched him intercept a man with a tool kit. Grant was showing his warrant card and explaining something. Then the two of them moved to the corner of the house, the tool box was opened, and I waited while the engineer did things. He pointed. He shook his head. Paul turned, saw me standing at the window, and grimaced. A minute later, he was back.

'The telephone's been tapped. He cut into the line and put in a little transmitter. That's what's giving you a slight echo on the line – there seems to be a bit of feedback.'

'Good heavens,' Barnabas said, looking interested. 'You've removed it?'

'In fact . . .'

I said loudly, 'In fact what?'

Paul looked at my father. 'It can be taken out quite easily if you'd like. Only . . .'

I was a little surprised by the sharp glance my father gave him. 'You'd rather not?' he asked.

Paul grinned at him. 'Unless you find it impossible to deal with, I'd like to leave it in place until we find out who's eavesdropping.'

'What do you mean?' I asked. 'My father depends on that phone . . .'

'What's involved?' Barnabas asked.

'The device is broadcasting to a receiver within about two hundred or two hundred and fifty metres from here. They'll be able to listen in on your conversations. Oh – and I should warn you, they'll be able to make out the numbers that you dial on outgoing calls.'

My father looked calm. 'I'm beyond the age when my phone calls deal with embarrassing matters. I need to be able to phone the doctor, of course, and Dido.' He looked at me severely. 'That is, provided she remembers what's going on and doesn't say anything silly.'

'I'm not likely to forget that we're being listened to,' I assured him grimly.

'Ye-e-es, but you'll have to try not to sound self-conscious,' Barnabas agreed annoyingly. 'I'd better not phone Pat – it would be best if they didn't get her number – but she can phone me and we'll bore any stranger rigid, I'm sure. As for any other . . . I can't think there'd be any harm in it, and obviously it gives us the advantage.'

'Yes: it will give us a chance to find where they are, and perhaps catch them,' Paul said briskly. 'I'll get rid of the engineer and phone the station. I'll ask them to put out a couple of men on foot. If they're in a van in one of these streets, we'll have them inside half an hour.'

'What if they're indoors?' I demanded.

'Harder. We'll have to try to locate any empty property that they might have got into. I'd better get on to the post office. Their delivery men have a habit of noticing when property is empty – and when somebody moves in.'

'Ask Mr Stanley,' said Barnabas.

'Who?'

'Upstairs.'

I said, 'Of course. Mr Stanley on the first floor always knows what's going on around here.'

'I will go and ask,' Barnabas said firmly. 'It will probably be much faster than talking to the postman. I'll tell him that you're a family friend looking for temporary accommodation in this vicinity. Is there anything I haven't thought of?'

Paul looked bemused. 'Yes, all right. That should do it.'

'Give me ten minutes.'

We listened to his footsteps slowly climbing the stairs and heard his knock. After a moment the upstairs door closed.

'We'll hear him coming back,' Paul said. He was right about that, and we were standing innocently on opposite sides of the sitting room when my father returned, flushed with success.

'Mr Stanley says that there's an empty flat on the first floor of the little block just down the hill, and For Sale boards out in front of two houses in the street behind us; also a Mrs Palmer, at number seventy-three, has recently sub-let her place for a couple of months while she is visiting a daughter in Australia.'

Paul looked amused. 'Do you reckon that's all?'

My father said that he thought it probably was.

I could see that Paul was anxious, and assured him that I was capable of getting myself back to the Volvo without his help.

'You don't have to put up with this,' I said to Barnabas when he had left. 'Though you probably deserve to suffer. Imagine, letting a stranger in like that when you spend half your time moaning about me being careless!'

'It's different.'

'How different?'

He said, 'Just different. Anyway, there's no harm done. They didn't come to hurt me, they came to get information by bugging my phone. I am perfectly safe from interference now that they think they'll be getting information through me. As long as that thing is transmitting, they'll be perfectly happy that they have both of us under their thumbs. It's not in their interests to take any steps against either of us. Now, that . . .' He broke off and seemed to be listening to a private suggestion. Eventually, he went on, 'So I shall phone you before bedtime and enquire whether you had a good day and you can tell me about it.'

It was so obviously different from what he had been going to say that I exploded: 'You're up to something!'

'I am,' he said with measured dignity, 'finishing a scholarly task. Until I've completed it to my satisfaction, I shan't be leaving the flat. By the by, Dido, we ought to arrange a code.' I stared at him. 'Something simple. If, for example, I phone and mention the name of Professor Tullett, that means that I am in immediate danger and want you to send the police. If I mention that I am thinking of going over to Dublin in a few weeks, that means that I have some news that I wish to communicate without it being overheard.'

'You could just mention Ireland,' I said sourly.

He said stiffly, 'Dublin, I think, will do.'

'Maybe they'll have caught them by tonight,' I sighed, 'and have you had your aspirin yet today?'

He glared. 'I have NOT forgotten it.'

I said, 'Well, take care,' and left.

The sky over the hill was red with sunset as I crossed the road. I'd half expected to see signs of police activity, but nothing was happening. The lights were beginning to come on in the windows of the Victorian villas, and a bus approached. I ran for the stop.

What I hadn't remembered was a piece of family history. If I'd thought of the stories Barnabas used to tell when I was little of how he'd worked in Signals Intelligence during the war, I might possibly have made an inspired guess. I'm not sure. Anyway, that was a long time ago, and I was absorbed in my own wars now.

21

Fair to Middling

Frankly, my attitude to book fairs is mixed; sheer torture alternates with a tinge of anxiety, the occasional dollop of greedy triumph, and quite a lot of boredom. To begin (and for that matter, end) with, there's the physical exhaustion of loading and transporting a large car full of heavy books and clattering folding book cases, and then heaving them on to a trolley, along pavements, and up and down stairs to get them into the exhibition rooms of the hotel off Russell Square where the monthly event is held.

In theory there are porters to help and often, with luck, in practice. I have even been known to bat my eyelashes.

You arrive at an ungodly hour on Sunday morning already feeling tired, and spend an hour 'setting up' – unpacking and shelving books while badly hindered by an unruly scrum of your fellow dealers digging for unnoticed and under-priced treasures, like hyperactive bargain hunters in the first hour of Liberty's sale. Then, having completed that stage and hopefully made enough to have got the cash flowing, you heave yourself into action and join the vultures around the filling shelves of later arrivals, looking in turn for some unconsidered trifle. All good fun, but a bit bruising.

At one o'clock the doors open and it's every man and woman for itself until the fair closes for the day. At two minutes past seven, we're all in the hotel bar manoeuvring over buying rounds of drinks and boasting or moaning – depending more on character than hard fact – about the day's business. For me, this time, it was the real business of the day.

At four minutes past the hour I took a breath right down into the abdomen and said clearly, to the dozen men and my old friend Veronica who were shuffling into a ragged circle of chairs around two tables convenient to the bar, 'I'm buying this one.' Into the little hush of curiosity that followed, I threw my planned announcement: 'I've sold the Ireland Collection at last. It's been on my hands for so long, I'd started to think of leaving it in my will. Never mind – I've packed it off now, thank God. What will you all have?'

'Irish collection of what?' a voice asked at my shoulder. 'Not that it matters, I'll have a Hine anyway, since you're offering.'

I smiled dazzlingly at Jeff, the cockney bookseller who hails confusingly from Swansea, and told him, 'Not "Irish", Ireland – William Henry,' in a voice that did its best to carry twenty yards to the far end of the room. I added a few tempting details and received the appropriate murmur of congratulations and spate of orders from a captive audience. I offered Jeff my silent and secret thanks for giving me the opening I'd needed. However, despite keeping my eyes and ears open, I couldn't detect more than friendly interest anywhere. Perhaps it was too much to hope for. However, the story would spread; with luck it would reach its target, and with a little more luck somebody would back off long enough for me to make my lie come true, The next day was Monday, the day I'd been promised an answer from the Constance Hance. Dear old Connie: just let her come up trumps please.

I paid over a fair percentage of my day's profits to the barman and led him and his heavy tray back to my table, believing that it was money well spent. In my optimism, I even joined the group for a noisy and lagerish Indian curry afterwards, with the result that it was past eleven o'clock by the time I got back to the flat.

Barnabas's inevitable message awaited on my answer machine: he was fine and getting some work done. It was too late to call him. I negotiated with the cat, washed my face, and fell into bed in a hopeful mood. Surely, surely the worst was over. If I had any dreams, they weren't the kind I wake up remembering.

Sometimes I think nobody goes to the second day of book fairs, especially not the exhibitors. By the middle of the afternoon I'd sold four books –

and two of those on behalf of absentee friends with stands near mine. The profit from my own two minor sales had already gone on a glass of white wine and a chicken sandwich at the pub down the road.

Returning at 2.40, I found that Alan Gates, one of my neighbours, had accepted a cheque for my Ackermann. The signature was unfamiliar to us both, but Alan said that he had seemed like a nice man. I shut my mouth, crossed my fingers and prayed. Then my deputy went off to a rendezvous, presumably in the hotel bar, and it was my turn. I settled dutifully on to the folding chair crammed between his stand and mine. The one customer in sight was a distant figure making his way along the side aisle from shelf to shelf, looking at everything and buying nothing. I speculated on the possibility that he was gradually transferring dozens of valuable little things into inside pockets of his mac, and sank into a kind of bored stupor. It was two hours before I could even think of starting to pack up, and until then I proposed to gather my strength. It had been raining gently when I came back from the pub. Getting my boxes and shelves home dry was going to be a struggle. I yawned and started wondering why I'd chosen to make my living in this unlikely fashion when I might still have been working in a lively and comfortable publisher's office in Manhattan. Or why I wasn't clever enough to have got myself happily married to a prosperous doctor, like Pat, with a nice, modern house and nothing to worry about except the school run. I was getting another bout of indigestion.

By ten past seven I was struggling with my overladen trolley halfway along the two hundred yards from the hotel door to the Volvo, parked as close as I could find space for it – which was as usual around two corners and down the mews – when my mobile began to trill. I stopped, draped myself over my load to shelter it from the drizzle, and switched on.

'Dido? What are you doing?'

'Hello, Barnabas. Listen, this isn't a good moment.'

'You sound breathless.'

I said, 'I am breathless. Is everything all right? I'm just loading. Can I call you back?'

'No need. I was hoping to see you this evening.'

I pricked up my ears and said carefully, 'All right, why don't we eat together.' I thought quickly. 'Can you hang on until I get home and unload, or are you too hungry to wait?'

'There's no rush.' His tone was reassuring: he had picked up my worry.

'I just wanted a chat. You know, I've been thinking of getting away for a few days now that spring is here.'

I stood upright, forgetting about the danger of rain on books, and waited.

'Yes, well, my book does seem to be progressing, but I want to have a look through the collection at Trinity College some time.'

I cleared my throat. 'You mean, Trinity College, Dublin?'

Barnabas replied mildly, 'They do have an excellent collection of early printed sources, and . . .'

We both seemed to be getting a bit too close to the mark. I interrupted, 'Look, I'm nearly finished here, so if you're all right, I'm going home. We can talk it over later, but I really think you'd better ask the doctor whether you're well enough to go off on your own.'

'You're right,' my father appeared to concede. 'I'll make an appointment tomorrow or the next day.'

'In the meantime,' I said quickly, suddenly aware of water running along strands of hair and trickling down my neck, 'I'll get there as soon as I can. We can talk about eating when I arrive, all right?'

Barnabas broke the connection, and I gritted my teeth and continued. For one reckless moment, I had considered dropping everything and rushing off to Crouch Hill, but the consequences of such irresponsible behaviour would be very time-consuming, and I abandoned the idea. Besides, I had to visit my answering machine. I groaned, grabbed the handle of the trolley, and heaved myself into motion.

It was just after eight when I double-parked outside the shop, staggered in with the first carton of books, dumped it inside the front door, remembered to disable the alarm, and panted into the office. The red light on the machine was blinking repeatedly, and I had to listen through three messages offering to sell me books that I didn't want before the American voice I was expecting began greetings, explanations, and finally apologies. There were new budgetary constraints this year. There were decisions to be made about The Way Forward. But unfortunately and regretfully they were obliged to pass on this one. Maybe in a few months' time. They hoped to receive my future catalogues.

I switched the machine off and stood for a moment in the gloom with my heart sinking into my stomach. Jilted by Constance Hance after so long . . .

But I decided to worry about it later; for the moment, Barnabas's call seemed more important. Mentally I straightened my shoulders and set about unloading the car and dumping everything inside the front door. I washed my hands and face at the office sink, reset the answering machine, locked up, and got back into the Volvo. I was halfway along Upper Street when I remembered forgetting to set the security alarm. Somehow it didn't seem to matter now. By 8.30 I'd parked and was ringing the bell.

Barnabas opened the door so promptly he'd obviously been watching at the window. I started to say, 'Are you all right?' but the look on his face stopped me. Something had happened, but not quite the triumph that I'd expected.

'Have you found something? Barnabas, the Constance Hance phoned: they don't want it . . .'

The thoughtful look deepened into an odd mixture of amusement and relief. 'Don't they, indeed. It's just as well.'

Exasperation. '*Barnabas . . . !*'

He hauled me into the flat and across to the desk. He had drawn the curtains. The reading light had been positioned to the right of the book, and I saw that he had brought the lamp from his bedside table and positioned it on the left. In the strong pool of even brightness, a calf-bound quarto lay open at the place my father had marked with a slip of paper.

I recognized the collection's Plutarch: North's translation of Plutarch's *Lives of the Noble Grecians and Romans*, the source of three or four of Shakespeare's plots. As a matter of fact, the recognition was instantaneous because this volume was the wreck of the collection as well as the biggest book in it, with its front cover detached, the back one missing, and the first four gatherings including the title page also missing presumed dead. The passing centuries had browned the pages and rotted the stitching so that the spine of the volume was dissolving, while dust and mould had given it the smell of the tomb. I'd nearly thrown this volume out several times, but Samuel Ireland's book plate on the inside of the flaking front cover had prevented me. This decay had once been a valuable 1579 copy, and it still added a kind of horrible authenticity to its companions in the collection. That thought, or a sort of historical fastidiousness, had prevented me, finally, from disposing of this disaster.

Oh, let's be honest: booksellers can never bear to throw anything old away.

Barnabas pointed. 'What do you see?'

'A disintegrating book,' I said promptly. 'I really wonder why I didn't chuck it.'

My father said quietly, 'Don't be silly.' He ran the tips of his fingers over what looked at first glance any other stained page.

The lower third of the left hand page was blank – had been left blank by the printer. Under the bottom line, if something made you look closely, marched a dozen lines of faded handwriting. The old ink had faded to sepia barely darker than the paper itself, illegible. It looked like verse. I peered at the ghostly markings. 'This is impossible, Barnabas. It's contemporary handwriting, isn't it? Sixteenth or early seventeenth century? What is it – notes on the text?'

My father's voice remained sober: 'It's easier with a magnifying glass. That is a short handwritten passage from *The Rape of Lucrece*, by William Shakespeare. The initials "W.S." stand at the bottom of the passage, if you look.' He pointed, his finger not quite touching the page. 'They appear to be consistent with one form of Shakespeare's signature. Also, the handwriting of the passage looks to me to be consistent with the initials. Observe the capital S here. In addition – though this seems almost a minor point in the circumstances – there are two slight variants of the poem as published in 1594. I can't as yet guess whether they are later revisions or an earlier form.'

Breathing was suddenly difficult. 'Is it real?'

'I don't know. For what it's worth, you'll recall that this is the volume with Samuel Ireland's book plate. It must have been in his own collection, and may have had nothing to do with his son's, um, work.'

There was one fact shrieking at me. Davey had found this. He hadn't told me, but he'd seen it, all right, and he'd known what it was. Or what it might be. Or maybe wasn't. I remembered to start breathing again.

'I can't believe it.'

My father shrugged slightly. 'I'm not a Shakespearean scholar, so I'll only say that it seems to be of the right period – unless, of course, it's a very high-class forgery. We'll have to show it to a specialist.'

'Davey would have assumed that it's real. Unless you think that *he* might have . . .'

'Done it himself?' Barnabas shook his head decidedly. 'I think not. As I say, I'm certain that it is *of the right period*. Well – more or less. Davey didn't have the knowledge to do this. And in answer to the next obvious question, I've looked at our letter, and at the photos of William Henry's so-called "Tudor" handwriting in the Grebanier book. William Henry's handwriting is, ah, illiterate. This is not his writing.'

'Davey wouldn't have cared,' I realized suddenly. 'He'd have told himself that it was good enough anyway to get him out of trouble. Perhaps even to get himself a lot of money.'

'Indeed.'

'Barnabas,' I said, 'what do you suppose this would be worth? If it really is, I mean. Genuine.'

We considered that question, staring at each other. From one point of view I knew the answer, working from the old principle that a book or manuscript, like any antique, is worth what a collector will pay. I touched the page with my clean fingertips because Shakespeare had also touched it once, perhaps. How much would you pay to touch this piece of paper? And to own it? The powdery roughness of the surface reminded me of dust.

'It's been worth a couple of deaths.'

'We must get rid of it,' Barnabas said promptly. 'It is much too dangerous to keep. The problem is that I don't quite know how. Perhaps the Constance Hance would take it after all, given the new circumstances? At a higher price, obviously.'

'Too rich for them,' I disagreed. 'I get the impression that they're going to spend a long time re-evaluating their purchase programme. What about a bank vault?'

'I thought of that. If nobody knew about it, that would be the best answer. But I don't have to say that unless you and I were to move into the vault with it . . .'

No, he didn't have to say. I snatched my hand away. 'Let's get out of here. Let's leave it and go. You can spend the night at my place. I don't want to be in the same room with it.'

Barnabas chuckled unexpectedly. He seemed a great deal more cheerful than I felt; no doubt the scholar in him was enthralled, I told myself sourly.

'In the short term,' he said, 'I couldn't agree more. I've been ready for dinner for the past two hours. We'll leave it here and go to Rocca's, shall we? Or somewhere comfortable. I'll even spend the night in George Street, if it will make you happy. And by tomorrow, in the light of day, we'll have thought what to do.'

'I'm going to phone Paul Grant for help. I'll do it from the car, after we've got well away from here. Come on.'

My father had closed the big book and was inserting it gently on to a top shelf full of old, leather-bound volumes, making the space for it by removing two of his own. To my feverish imagination, it sat there shrieking. I took a grip and admitted, coldly, that in fact the thing blended into my father's vast collection. He put the two displaced treasures on top of the mounds on his desk and we turned to go.

'I'll leave a light on,' Barnabas said. It was the only sign of nervousness he had betrayed.

As for myself, I couldn't get into the Volvo fast enough. If I'd owned a big illuminated sign reading 'It's in my father's flat: take it and go!', I swear that I'd have bolted it to the roof of the car and set it flashing.

'We'll drink a really nourishing bottle, I think,' Barnabas decided as I turned towards the Angel. 'A bottle of the Barolo. It's been a hard couple of days' work. Those lights are about to turn red, Dido.'

I braked in time.

22

Raiders

The telephone was ringing much, much too close to my ear. I listened to it dreamily. Eventually, I managed to remember that I'd made Barnabas sleep in my bed last night. Apparently I'd been so exhausted that exile in the sitting room hadn't kept me from happy unconsciousness. Anyway, I was lying wrapped in spare blankets on my own sofa.

I struggled up, reached the receiver, and pulled myself together long enough to make 'Ummm?' sound like a greeting.

'Dido, how are you this morning?'

The voice belonged to my father, who I'd assumed was still asleep in the other room. I took a grip.

'Where are you? I'm still asleep.'

'It's ten o'clock. Well, nearly. I've been back here for two hours. I tried not to disturb you when I left because you seemed tired.'

'Where are you?'

'At home, of course. I have work to do.' His voice had taken on a warning tone, which reminded me about the probable listener. The memory distracted me: damn it, what was Paul Grant up to, leaving Barnabas with a compromised phone for so long? My anger reminded me that I still hadn't been able to get through to him, either: more unfinished, and increasingly urgent, business,

'Um. Right.' I was thinking as quickly as I could, which was not top fast. 'All right. I mean, is everything all right? You don't need anything?'

159

'Of course I need something, Dido; that's why I'm phoning.'

I woke up. 'Go on.'

'I need to be taken shopping. I seem to have run out of food of all kinds. And stamps.'

I blinked, leaned on the sideboard, and thought about this. It was the first time in history that Barnabas had ever phoned me up and demanded to be taken shopping.

'In fact . . .' His tone suggested that he was considering. 'In fact, why don't you bring your young man with you? He could make himself useful carrying the potatoes.'

Paul Grant? Bring a policeman to carry potatoes? Alarm bells rang. 'Good idea,' I said heartily. 'I'll see if he's free. We can all have coffee together.'

'I'm out of coffee,' Barnabas replied patiently, 'but you have the right general idea. I'm awaiting a delivery at ten thirty, but I should be ready to leave by the time you get here.'

Delivery? I wondered whether this was some Barnabas code meant to confuse the listeners, but it hadn't been pre-arranged, and it was certainly confusing to me. At least it wasn't the coded call for help. I surrendered and rang off: I'd go and demand an explanation face to face.

My mobile rang two minutes later while I was in the bathroom. This time it was Paul.

I said, 'I thought you'd vanished. What's happening about Barnabas's telephone? Is it still tapped? We can't go on this way. Haven't you located them yet?'

'Never mind that.' His tone was peremptory; he seemed to be having difficulty keeping his temper. 'Listen, what the hell is your father up to?'

I said cautiously that so far as I knew, he was up to doing a little shopping, and that he had requested our joint assistance.

'I know.'

'You *what*?'

'We have a tap on his line from the exchange. It's all right, he knows about it.'

'He didn't tell me. Do you have a tap on mine too?'

Paul's voice was impatient. 'Of course not, or I'd have got your consent.'

'So you already know that he wants us both around there. I'll be leaving as fast as I can get out of the door. Are you going to meet me there?' I couldn't stop myself adding, 'I missed you this weekend.'

He said quickly, 'I missed you, too. Listen, I'm in the car on my way up to Crouch Hill. Or I mean I'm supposed to be. At the moment, I'm stuck in traffic. What I wanted to ask is whether you know about this pick-up?'

'Pick-up?'

'He phoned one of the big security companies about forty minutes ago. My man only just got around to listening to the tape, or I'd have been over there before now. He arranged for an armoured van to pick up a parcel at ten thirty, and he asked for two hundred thousand pounds' worth of insurance. Damn this traffic. Why did he use his phone? Did he forget the tap? What the hell is this all about?'

Feeling distinctly as though I'd been punched in the stomach, I said breathily, 'I know he didn't forget the tap, but I don't have time to talk. I'll see you at Crouch Hill. Can you get there quickly, please?'

'At the moment,' Paul's voice grated, 'I'm sitting in the usual jam just north of Highbury Corner. It's solid, and I can't even turn off. If you're coming up, take another route.'

I hung up on him and went to insert my unwashed body into yesterday's clothes. The jacket had picked up a prominent red wine stain on the sleeve and was probably not the outfit I would have chosen for a romantic rendezvous, but there was no time to do anything about it. I checked that the mobile was in my bag, grabbed my keys, and dashed. Forewarned, I took the Volvo in a great detour eastwards, because I didn't have the advantage of a flashing blue light or two-tone siren or anything.

Even so, I got there first.

Barnabas greeted me amiably at the door. I said, 'Barnabas!'

'What?'

'Have they been?'

'Who?'

I counted backwards from ten. 'The security firm. Has it gone?'

Barnabas regarded me benevolently. 'How did you know?'

'Paul phoned. The police heard every word you said. So did the other lot, of course. Why did you call from your own phone? You could at least have gone upstairs!'

Barnabas beamed me into his sitting room. 'They were all supposed to hear it. For goodness sake, Dido, stop puffing at me – you sound like Pat. Use your brain! I *particularly wanted* them to hear: your boy detective doesn't seem to be able to do anything, and I was becoming uneasy about sitting around wondering which of us was going to receive the next visit. Do shut up squeaking, Dido! I planned it all in the middle of the night when that blasted animal of yours decided to visit my pillow – I mean yours – and woke me up. It was only a matter of getting the security van here before they had time to do anything about it. I made the arrangements from a public phone on my way home, and I confirmed from here just before the van was actually due to arrive shut up Dido. Now they realize, I hope, that the book is out of our hands. With any luck, they may assume it's gone to America. We ought to be safe for the time being.'

'But,' I said and sat down uncomfortably on a chair which turned out to hold a slippery pile of newspapers. 'All right, where did you actually send it?'

Barnabas looked amused and a little smug. 'I told you, I'm not really qualified. The next step is to consult an expert. Mackenzie in Birmingham should be able to judge the holograph, but if he can't, then it will have to go on to the Folger in Washington. Either way, we can do with having it out of our hands. Satisfied?'

A familiar car was drawing up to the kerb in front of the house. I said hastily, 'What are we going to say?'

Barnabas sighed. 'A censored version of the truth, I should imagine. I've identified the valuable object. I've sent it off for verification. We are going to the supermarket and the post office. What else?'

Well, what else? . . . and yet I had the curious feeling that there was something else – if the two of them would just give me a moment to think.

I went to open the door, but the path was empty and Paul still sat inside his car. He beckoned. When I leaned down to the car window, I found him listening to his mobile with a kind of grim concentration, so I climbed into the passenger seat and waited. He switched off.

'Trouble?'

He didn't smile. 'We're getting reports that an armoured van has been hijacked on the Holloway Road. It's the firm your father phoned. I think we can assume that it's the same van. I've told our people to get straight into the empty flat where they've been monitoring your father's phone and arrest everybody there. We'll have to see what we pull in.'

I got my voice under control, more or less, and asked, 'You mean that you knew where they were? Why didn't you tell Barnabas? He's worried because he thought you weren't doing anything . . .'

'All right, so I hear! Your father got fed up waiting, and as a result it looks like we've lost a security van and two men. Why can't he mind his own business?'

I'd often felt the same way about Barnabas, but it wasn't down to Paul Grant to say it. On the other hand . . . 'What's happened to the security men? Are they all right?'

'We don't know, damn it! I haven't got the whole story, but it sounds as though they were followed from here and jumped at their next stop by armed men. Now they've vanished, along with the van. There's a radio tracer attached to the vehicle, of course, so we'll catch up with them, but . . . If they've been killed, I hope your father can square that with his conscience.'

'How did they manage it?' I asked humbly. 'They were awfully quick!' I didn't like the look in those brown eyes this morning.

'How? Well, why not?' His voice was stiff with anger. 'These people have resources, and they must have been on to the van by the time it left here. Is he in there? I want to know what he thinks he was up to!'

In the circumstances, I suppose, it was understandable, but I still felt like hurtling to Barnabas's defence. If Paul expected a respectable old man to anticipate the kind of violence that normal people only see on television screens, he was out of touch.

We got out of the car just in time to see my father coming down the front steps with a big nylon shopping bag in one hand. Perhaps he was counting on Grant to be easier to deal with in public, but I could almost touch that half-controlled fury beside me.

'Barnabas, they've got it!'

'What?' He came to a startled halt.

Paul growled, 'I don't know what kind of trick you were trying to pull, but the security van has just been hijacked, and we don't know yet whether the men are alive or dead.'

Barnabas frowned. 'Lord, I didn't realize it would be so easy! I assumed those security firms were safe. They're always standing around at the bank, looking military and keeping watch in helmets and what not . . .'

Paul twitched his shoulders impatiently. 'Let's go indoors while you tell me what all this is about.'

Barnabas looked mildly embarrassed and decidedly stubborn. 'I'm sorry, but I really can't. I have an appointment later this morning which I must keep, and a couple of minor errands which have to precede it.' He noticed the expression on our faces. 'I suggest that we stop wasting time. If we get into your car, Inspector, you can drive and I'll explain as we go. You can stay in touch with your people, and if you have to go somewhere in a hurry, we can get out at once and go on by taxi.'

I said, 'Barnabas, they GOT it!'

He frowned. 'Well, obviously they got the van, but they may not have found my parcel. There must be a lot of parcels, and they may not have had the time to search for it. Inspector, I really do assure you I didn't think for a moment that it would go this far.'

Grant controlled himself with a visible effort and ushered us both into his back seat, putting me in my place: member of the public. My mind turned uncontrollably to the memory of that bed on its scaffolding platform. I got hold of it and reminded it of the serious things that were going on.

He turned the key in the ignition, signalled, and pulled away from the kerb.

'If you head for the clock tower in Crouch End,' Barnabas suggested humbly, 'I'll be able to do everything I need to around there.'

'What,' Grant demanded very clearly, 'was this parcel worth two hundred thousand pounds?'

'A book,' Barnabas said simply. 'One of that collection of books which Dido was selling to Professor Warren – to his library, that is – for ten thousand pounds.'

Grant braked irritably behind a small van which seemed to be unable to decide whether or not it was turning right. 'Dido told me. You mean, you found the thing that everybody's been looking for?'

Barnabas leaned back in his seat and embarked on a lecture. He had finished the short version by the time we came to the crest of the hill. We ran gently down towards the lights at Crouch End while he expanded. Grant was suitably impressed by the idea of a genuine piece of Shakespeare manuscript, and curious about the financial implications.

'It's complicated,' Barnabas told him. 'Like an old master painting: it's valuable, very valuable, but you can't just sell it.'

Grant drove along a high road lined with illegally parked cars, edged to the right, and stopped on the double yellow lines just outside the post office. He turned his engine off and said, 'I'm not convinced.'

Barnabas mimed polite resignation. I said, 'Why?'

'Let's take the example you mentioned: a painting. Nowadays, a stolen painting is more or less worthless. The more famous it is – the more valuable – the more worthless it turns out to be. Remember "The Scream" a couple of years ago? Ugly Norwegian thing. There was lots of publicity, reproductions everywhere, including on the Internet, items on television, articles in the newspapers. That theft was supposed to have been political – a variation on terrorist hostage-taking – and they probably didn't intend to sell it anyway. But if they'd tried, it would have been dangerous – impossible. They got the painting back. The thing is, everybody knows about these things and they aren't going to buy something like that from a dodgy source. Your Shakespeare poetry may be worth something to you, but it's worthless to anybody else. Well . . . isn't it?'

Barnabas said something appropriate. I shut up. If Paul was right, it wiped out certain assumptions. In fact it seemed to put us back where we'd started.

Not quite. Because something had happened: the news that Barnabas was sending off a valuable parcel had resulted in immediate action. Somebody knew about the Shakespeare, all right: it was just that we still hadn't identified them.

'I am going to buy stamps,' Barnabas announced, and let himself out of the car.

'I'd better go with him.'

'All right.' It was still a growl, but the anger seemed to be softening. Perhaps we were going to be forgiven after all.

Paul stayed in the car to make calls. I rushed after Barnabas and joined him in the queue which was slowly inching its way towards the counter.

'He's right,' I mumbled.

Barnabas sighed grumpily. 'He's right in his own lights, but we still don't know enough about their intentions. Are you feeling all right? You're looking pale.'

I said, 'I'm feeling sick because I haven't even had coffee, much less breakfast, and we've lost a treasure worth a fortune. I'm fine.'

'Don't worry.' Barnabas patted my hand. 'It was insured. It cost a great deal, but I did insure it.'

'They won't pay up, you know. They'll demand evidence of its value, which we haven't got, and then they'll demand compensation for those men if they've been hurt. They'll sue you, and then they'll sue me for not keeping you under control.'

'You are indeed in a bad mood,' Barnabas said with unexpected mildness. 'Ah! At last!'

I wandered back towards the door and stood watching with half an eye while he engaged in negotiations with the woman behind the screen. I felt uneasy about Barnabas. I was sure he was up to something he wasn't letting on about, but a car horn blared in the street, interrupting my concentration. When I looked out, Paul's black Ford was pulling away from the kerb. I caught a wild wave of a hand before it vanished.

Something new had happened so quickly that he couldn't stop to explain.

At my shoulder, Barnabas was saying, 'Good! Now for one or two other little calls before . . .'

'Paul's just taken off. He was in a hurry.'

'I saw. They've probably found the van,' Barnabas said simply. 'It wasn't ever going to vanish, you know.'

'I hope those men are safe.'

'And so do I, of course. I never really thought . . .'

'I know. What's next – supermarket?'

'Not exactly,' Barnabas said. 'Actually, that will have to wait.'

Knowing my father, I narrowed my eyes at him and said, 'What's up? Come to think of it, why did you want Paul Grant in the first place, and why are you looking so happy that he's gone?'

Barnabas took hold of my elbow and steered me briskly out of the building and towards the clock tower. 'I wanted his company to be sure of getting away from the house safely. Let's just say I'd become uneasy. It was all beginning to feel . . . you know, as though something was about to happen.'

Oh yes? 'And why did you want to get rid of him? Is it this important appointment you mentioned?'

'Precisely. You said you're hungry?'

'Absolutely sick with hunger,' I sighed, not exaggerating.

'We'll go and have coffee and Danish pastries. There's a quarter of an hour to spare.'

'Before what?'

'Before the next stage of our investigations,' he said pompously. '*Do come along!*'

23

Heritage

Physically restored by an almond Danish, two cups of cappuccino, and some hard talking, I stood in the street watching Barnabas's taxi disappear southward.

He'd got rid of me. Not only that, but he'd done it by sending me on an errand I didn't like.

Of course it was perfectly true that somebody had to approach Dan Colbert at Heritage Books, find out whether Davey had been lying about a Japanese customer, and pump him for the buyer's name – if he existed. For preference, without warning him that he was being pumped. And certainly without letting him develop the slightest suspicion that I'd been lying when I announced the sale to the Constance Hance. Dan was a gossip, and if he ever guessed the truth, all my scheming at the book fair would have been in vain.

If I'd had my wits about me, I'd have done the pumping days ago instead of rushing around like a headless chicken all this time. Why don't I have a logical mind?

Unfortunately Barnabas does have a logical mind. He had pointed out that, of all possible pumpers, I was the logical choice, a point he'd been putting to me pretty forcibly over coffee. The problem was that my qualifications consisted largely of Dan Colbert's tendency to lay hands on me. I had no wish to play Mata Hari, so I knew that I would have to be unusually fast-moving if I were not to emerge from my visit rumpled in body and temper.

I would even have preferred another little talk with Ilona Mitchell, which might have been just as profitable. I was beginning to know how her mind worked. Confront her with the truth, and she'd confirm it in a sideways, well-maybe fashion. I'd even got as far as phoning the hospital on my way to the bus stop, which was how I learned that she had discharged herself the previous afternoon. I wondered whether Paul knew. We seemed to be having a communication problem.

There was one more thing bothering me as I climbed aboard a bus in a less-than-angelic temper: Barnabas had some plan of his own which had involved getting rid of me. He hadn't even pretended otherwise. By the time I'd got to Bloomsbury, I was not in a pretty mood.

Colbert's shop was situated in one of the narrow streets just south of the British Museum. Its window, as I was impressed to see when I arrived on the doorstep, held nothing but a black vase with white carnations, and a tasteful display of extravagant French art bindings arranged on the mahogany shelving which at once obscured the interior of the shop and promised treasures within. I paused for an elaborate acting out of what I hoped would look like sudden interest in rococo gilt. My mood was not improved when I happened to notice the CLOSED sign and realized that the performance had been unnecessary. My watch said that it was half past twelve – two hours after the sign promised a shop open for business. Presumably Colbert required additional recovery time on a post-book fair Tuesday morning. Don't we all! I kicked the door furtively and retreated to a dingy café across the street.

Despite the formica-with-plastic-flowers decor, the Italian staff made excellent coffee. I was so encouraged that I ordered a plate of mushroom risotto and settled in at a window table to admire the view and wait.

The shop invited admiration. Or did I really mean envy? The position, the phoney leaded windows, the door with its mouldings – all spoke of a reputable prosperity. Not for Colbert the worry about thinning stocks, dubious second-rate libraries in Banbury, or the empty spaces in a prints cabinet. He'd even got himself a new shop sign since I'd been there last: a shiny, self-congratulatory board with gilt Gothic letters on a midnight-blue background proclaiming in a self-confident way that this magnificent place was COLBERT'S HERITAGE BOOKS. If I could afford a shop like that . . .

I whispered it to myself: Colbert's Heritage.

He was, of course, English – as far as I'd ever heard. He was Daniel

Colbert, and he always pronounced it 'Coal-burt'. But originally it was a French name, all right.

Oh, Ilona, why couldn't you just bloody *tell* me?

Just after 1.30, when I'd finished off the delicious risotto without even noticing it, the plump figure of Dan Colbert (Coal-burt, Cole-bare – the name, and therefore his very identity, had become unfamiliar) strolled into sight from the direction of Tottenham Court Road. He was not hurrying. He looked pale and preoccupied, and I chalked up a mental plus for guessing a hangover. He too stopped outside the window and stared at the display. It didn't seem to give him as much pleasure as it would me, if I'd owned it. I watched him unlock the door, stand hesitating on the threshold for what seemed like minutes, and then drift inside.

Finishing my second coffee, I allowed him another ten minutes to settle in so that it wouldn't appear that my arrival was anything but accidental.

Nevertheless, as I stepped through the doorway I thought that a shadow crossed his face and lingered just long enough to be noticed: as though I was the last person he either expected or hoped to see. It threw me off balance. I paused without meaning to and gave him the chance to recover himself and bustle forward.

'Dido! Poppet!' I received an embrace and a peck that hit my ear. 'How nice? On a shopping expedition, I hope? Anything specific?'

I assumed an air of businesslike propriety. 'Just stock-hunting. One or two sections seem to be getting a little thin, and since I was down this way . . .'

Colbert made a visible effort to grin amiably. 'My pleasure, of course, though it's rather a mess downstairs. I haven't had time to unpack from the fair.'

I allowed a sympathetic smile to play over my face. 'Still, mustn't complain, must we? Anyway, I've seen what you had at the fair, so that doesn't bother me a bit, I'll start up here and just carry on.'

If it had made any sense, I would have said that the proposal struck him with horror. For some reason he didn't want me anywhere near him. It was so contrary to Colbert's normal flirtation that I was afraid I might let him see my surprise. I smiled most sweetly. I thought his hangover deepened.

'I have to go out in a minute . . . Sotheby's. Sale.'

If it hadn't all been so odd, I'd have enjoyed seeing him squirm. But I'd have preferred to have known the reason. I gritted my teeth mentally, checked to make sure that my intentionally inane smile hadn't cracked, and got down to business, because whatever the reason, he was certainly off balance. This was my chance to push.

'I'll just have a look around until you need to leave, shall I?' It didn't sound like my voice at all. 'You know, I have some American money coming in, and it does seem to be the time to restock.' So there.

I stepped swiftly towards the nearest rank of illustrated natural history books, dug into a pocket for my notebook and pencil, and reached for the first volume that met my eye in order to establish my serious intentions. Colbert hesitated, murmured unintelligibly, and retreated to the large desk in the corner of the room, from which he always issued invoices and watched for shoplifters. I pretended to immerse myself in the task of finding something to buy.

'Are you sure there isn't something in particular . . . ?' he asked after a few minutes.

'Just for stock,' I replied pleasantly. Time to strike now. 'Our last catalogue went rather well, and we're a bit low. You know.'

'Oh.' There was a silence that somehow promised something more. I waited, almost unaware of the volume I was pretending to collate. Surely he had to take the opening I'd given him? I replaced the book, considered, and pulled out a Bewick. A lorry passed in the street, rattling the window. I risked a covert glance out of the corner of my eye. Colbert appeared to be examining the grain of his desk top.

'Yes,' I sighed. 'We've had a couple of big orders, and my stock looks a bit thin. I need to pick up a few things for the June book fair. You know the kind of thing. This Bewick is nice, but not quite . . .' I hesitated and moved slowly down the rows of shelves, inspecting spines. Colbert shuffled his papers.

Next step . . .? I said, obviously absent-mindedly: 'Isn't it awful about Job Warren?'

A handful of papers slid from the desk on to the floor. Colbert precipitated himself after them, vanishing behind the desk in a way that would ordinarily have been comic. 'Yes.' The voice was muffled by his efforts. 'London is becoming abominably violent.'

I sighed. 'Yes, isn't it.' Be careful now. 'We were devastated. Apart from the fact that he was such a good customer, he was a friend. You know, he'd just bought the Ireland Collection from us, and he was coming round for dinner, to discuss provenance and things – you know – the very night he was killed . . . Oh!' I straightened up and replaced another random

170

book on its shelf. 'What a strange coincidence. I've just remembered Davey said you were interested in it too!'

There was another pause which lasted so long that I finally spoke into it myself: 'But of course, Professor Warren had got it for the Constance Hance before I knew you were keen.' I listened to the silence and worked out the next move. 'Did you see him, by any chance, this time?'

'No! Alas. He would have come, of course.'

'Yes, I remember this was one of his regular stops. Well, we've both lost a good customer. Now that he's dead, I suppose I'll have to explain about the provenance to his successor.' I picked another book at random and was lost in contemplation of its engraved title page. Go on, then!

'Provenance? There isn't a question about that, is there?'

I kept my eyes on the page. 'M-mmn.' I suddenly discovered that I was enjoying myself.

'Well, do tell. Can I help?'

'Oh, I'm sure we can satisfy the library. There's no question about title, and of course the origin of the stuff is perfectly clear. Didn't Davey say you had an enquiry about it? Some regular customer? Anyone I know?'

'No, oh no. Just a businessman, not a collector.'

I raised my eyebrows and gave him my full attention. 'Not a collector? Then why on earth was he interested in buying it?'

Colbert's hands fumbled. 'It's a little complicated. He . . . Mr . . . It was somebody who was introduced by one of my export customers. He wanted something for a Japanese business associate, a present, a sweetener, I suspect. The details I do not know, of course. I happened to think of the Ireland Collection. Just the right thing for Japan, you know – very English, quirky, old, expensive . . . but with the strong yen, something of a bargain. Can't think why you never offered it to me, my poppet. I could have shifted it to Japan months ago.' He cleared his throat. 'You haven't a problem with it, have you?'

I turned back to the bookshelves. 'Oh, no. Just that Professor Warren died before he'd come to us. You know how he always paid by cheque at the end of his visit. Still, I'm sure that the Constance Hance will be all right. The collection has probably reached them by now. I'll have to write them a long letter about provenance, of course, but . . .' Now for the hook. ' . . . I'm sure they'll keep it.' I picked up a gleaming, calf-bound quarto which might have contained a collection of Superman comics, for all I would have noticed. I considered it. 'I'm sorry I didn't think about offering it to you, though. I know you have a lot of foreign customers. Look, if by any remote chance something does go wrong – because of Job Warren's death, I mean – I'll get back to you. You could put me in touch with your businessman. There'd be the usual in it for you, of course.'

I was proposing the kind of mutual deal than we often make. Booksellers often pass on customers we can't deal with ourselves, and consider it only polite to be offered anything from a drink to a couple of hundred pounds in recognition of the favour. So I was taken aback when Colbert burst out, 'I don't think it would do.' He noticed my surprise. 'In fact, I'm sure they won't be interested any more.'

I raised an eyebrow. 'Really? Why?'

'No, he . . . I've found him something else. Dickens. In parts.'

I sighed and turned away, digesting the news that Colbert's client was now out of the Ireland market. Well, of course, there could be a perfectly simple reason for that, but if he was lying, there seemed to be no way I could tell. For the moment my inventive powers had failed. Paul Grant, of course, might have better luck, or greater influence. The thought cheered me up. At least I'd established that there *had* indeed been somebody interested in the Ireland, and if Colbert had his own business reasons for not wanting to give me a name, the police could certainly get it.

I almost started to leave, then realized that it would be a mistake. If I went now, Colbert might be left with the impression that this conversation had been significant, and I didn't want a lecture on minding my own business.

I said, placing a bright Baskerville Milton with a dazzling title page on the edge of Colbert's desk as my justification, 'I'll have this. And I'll just pop downstairs to see whether there's anything else.'

The basement saleroom was approached by a flight of stairs at one side of the shop. It was where Colbert kept most of his less valuable volumes, since it was less under his eye and therefore more vulnerable to customers with large inside pockets. I was surprised – and maybe worse than surprised – to find him stumbling downstairs after me. I had a momentary vision of him chasing me breathlessly among the book cases, but he hesitated halfway, apparently caught between following me and needing to watch the shop. He crouched slightly, bringing his angle of vision down below the stairhead, and stopped. I heaved a sigh of relief and became absorbed in a shelf of nineteenth-century three-volume novels, trying to ignore his awkward stance.

I might have been frightened, except that – as far as I could see from furtive glances out of the corner of my eye – he was looking as uneasy as I felt. What the hell was going on?

I heard the shop door open and close. Somebody asked a question. Colbert hesitated, glanced briefly in my direction, and bobbed back up. I could hear a muffled conversation.

What was wrong with the man? Or was there something in this basement room that was wrong? There seemed to be nothing very different to the last time I'd been here. A door that I knew led into Colbert's little store and packing room stood slightly ajar. I listened for a second to slow footsteps creaking overhead and the murmur of voices, then slipped across to peek into a windowless little cupboard. I switched on the overhead light, suppressing a moment's anxiety about burglar alarms and booby traps. At one side, the usual rolls of padded plastic wrap and brown paper hung on rollers from the wall. Colbert's packing table itself contained small piles of books, and a couple of wall shelves held the usual dusty scattering of packing tape, cardboard, and padded envelopes. It was just like my own place.

Puzzled, I checked the empty stairhead again and slid towards the table. The books were orders for posting with an invoice protruding from each. Could the thing that I was not supposed to see be an invoice in the name of Colbert's mysterious and valuable business customer? I tiptoed round the table, peering at the slips, but they all seemed to have the names of libraries on them. Ironically, one large order consisting of a double pile of calf-bound volumes with a few plastic-enveloped broadsheets perched on top was invoiced in Colbert's affected italic to the Constance Hance. I skimmed the rest and found nothing helpful.

The inaudible conversation droned on over my head as I returned to the outer room, and examined it helplessly.

All right, I was missing something.

Was he just worried that I'd stumble across some stolen book on one of the shelves? From time to time I'd heard whispers that Heritage Books was not above buying a valuable volume for much less than the normal price, no questions asked. Was it possible that he'd actually lifted something from my stand during the book fair? I could have been too preoccupied yesterday to notice something missing. But why would he have put such a thing out on the open shelves for anyone who wandered in to see?

When I heard the shop door closing, I picked up a Trollope and advanced on the stairs.

Colbert met me, saying, 'I'm sorry to chuck you out, my love, but I must be off . . .' just as I began, 'I'll take this and the Milton . . .'

I couldn't have brought myself to stay longer anyway.

I wrote out a cheque, accepted my parcel, and allowed myself to be hurried into the street. I'd taken one deep lungful of exhaust fumes and moved about five steps towards New Oxford Street when Colbert emerged, locked the door, and scuttered off in the opposite direction. He managed to escape without having to notice me.

When he was safely out of sight I dug out my mobile, tried Barnabas's phone, and gave up when it had rung a dozen times. It wasn't really surprising that he hadn't got back, but I did want to find out what he'd been up to, so I said, 'Bugger' in a frustrated tone that came out loudly enough to draw surprised glances from a group of four middle-aged American tourists heading towards the British Museum. I hailed a passing cab. When I'd given the driver Barnabas's address, I leaned back and tried to relax because it had been a busy day already, and there was quite a lot of it left.

A kind of twitching uneasiness, a mental itch, kept me tense. As the cab turned into Southampton Row and headed towards King's Cross, that uneasiness grew. My arrival had made Colbert so nervous that he'd revealed his feelings almost honestly, and . . .

Yes, I'd missed something.

I'd actually paid the driver, given him an unnecessarily large tip out of sheer absent-mindedness, and climbed halfway up Barnabas's front steps, before I knew what it was.

Colbert said he had not seen Professor Warren this visit. Yet on his packing table, where I'd never have seen it if I hadn't been nosing around, there sat a big pile of books addressed to the Constance Hance.

When Job went through one of his favourite bookshops, there was always a huge pile of his purchases for the bookseller to ship. I thought about it. Of course, I could have found an order from a catalogue, but if Colbert had issued a catalogue in the past four months, I certainly hadn't seen a copy. Besides, Professor Warren wouldn't have ordered books to be sent unseen if he was just about to arrive in London. He would have phoned Colbert, the way he had me, and asked him to keep things to one side.

And there wouldn't have been an invoice yet – not until he'd examined the books and decided to take them.

Job Warren had gone to Colbert's shop and Colbert had lied about it and there had been no possible reason to lie about it, no reason at all.

I found myself inside Barnabas's flat without any memory of opening his door. Because there was a reason for the lie – the only possible reason. Colbert would only have lied because he didn't want anybody to know that he had seen Professor Warren. And the only possible reason for that was that he knew something about the murder.

Someone would have to ask him about that, wouldn't they?

But not me.

24

Indigestion

'Not so mysterious,' Barnabas said soberly. He had returned just before me, and we were sitting at his kitchen table sharing a pot of tea. 'I was doing exactly the same as you. You mentioned that you'd had an enquiry from Quaritch about the collection. I took a taxi down there, found Allen Ferrars – from whom I was buying books when you were still in the nursery – and asked him about it.'

'And?'

'He hadn't dealt with it himself, but he found the client's card.'

'For goodness sake, Barnabas, tell me!'

'The customer was a Mr M. Campbell. It meant nothing to him, or to me for that matter.' He looked at me carefully. 'You've heard the name.'

I had. Oh yes. My chain of villains was complete, and it fitted too well to be much of a surprise. While I was wondering what to do about it, I asked automatically, 'Was there an address?'

'12A Wilding Road.'

'*What!*'

'That's correct, he gave them Davey's address. It doesn't help much, except to confirm . . .'

I said, 'Yes. Oh, hell, Barnabas, why doesn't Paul Grant phone?'

'I suppose your mobile phone is switched on this time?'

I was saved the bother of replying by the trilling coming from inside my shoulder bag. When I'd disentangled the machine from a nest of crumpled tissues and bus tickets, I said, 'Hello, Paul. What's happened?'

'Hello, Dido.' He sounded less edgy than when I'd seen him last. 'We've found it. It was dumped in among the lock-ups on a council estate in Tottenham. It was reported by a couple of schoolkids walking their bull terrier. And the men were inside – shaken, but all right.'

I mouthed the words, 'All right' at Barnabas, who was trying to listen. He nodded and relaxed.

'You didn't by any chance find the book?'

'No. They went through everything, but the driver says they were looking for something specific. They grabbed a few bags, and your father's parcel is certainly missing. They shifted to a car that was waiting there; they were long gone by the time we'd arrived.'

'What about the ones who were listening to my father's telephone?'

'We'd spotted them in the empty flat just up the road, and we sent two cars in to pick them up the moment we got the news about the security van. We missed them by a few minutes. They just left everything and scarpered, probably when their mates let them know they'd got the van.'

I excused myself and summarized the story for Barnabas, who remained remarkably stoical for a man who has just lost a national treasure.

'What happens now?' I demanded.

'Looking for witnesses, trying to get a line on the car they were using . . .'

'Tell him,' Barnabas commanded.

His voice was loud enough to carry, and Paul said, warily, I thought, 'Tell me what?'

I said, 'Marty Campbell, I'm afraid,' and explained.

'You're sure about all this?'

I said, 'No, I'm not sure about anything. But I had a very strong impression. It can't hurt to get the name of Dan Colbert's customer at least. Maybe it's all perfectly innocent.'

'Maybe it isn't.'

I agreed. Because if I were a suspicious kind of person, I might think I knew why Dan's customer was no longer interested in the Ireland Collection. You can't purchase something you've already stolen.

Paul asked, 'What's Quaritch? Are they all right?'

Barnabas, beside me, looked shocked. I explained: 'More than all right. Respectable and aristocratic. Like Harrods.'

Paul seemed to snarl, 'I'll check. It all has to be checked out. Colbert first, though. He won't be at the shop, so where does he live?'

I said I thought somewhere in south London.

'All right, I'll see what I can find. I'll be waiting at the shop in the morning if we can't get to him tonight.'

'He'll give you the name? He'll tell you if it's Campbell?'

'Oh yes,' Grant said shortly. 'And of course it's bloody well Campbell.'

'Will you tell me what he says?'

'Where will you be this evening?'

I said that I wanted to wash my hair.

'Then I'll ring in about an hour, an hour and a half. Or drop by.'

I thought, Promises, promises, and poured another cup of tea. My father seemed preoccupied. I assumed that he was immersed in the problem of how to persuade an insurance company to pay up, if worse came to worst. Good luck to him, I thought cynically. As for me, I just didn't believe it would happen. Any of it.

Some time after midnight I sat in the living room, damp around the edges and wrapped in my green terry bathrobe. Comforting. It was as quiet outside as London ever gets, though the traffic never really stops. Down in the street a car door slammed. It was quiet enough to hear the footsteps, and when my doorbell rasped I was already halfway to the window. Paul Grant's wedge-shaped face looked up at me when I leaned out.

'I brought this.' He held something up toward me like a peace offering, and after a moment I recognized my own telephone and laughed. 'Is it too late?'

I shook my head vigorously and went down to let him in, feeling the little bubble of excitement explode under my breastbone. We kissed behind the closed door.

'I thought you weren't coming.'

'Sorry. I've only just got away from my desk. DIs don't arrange work, you know – we just do it.'

I got hold of myself. 'You must be coining it with the overtime rates.'

His eyes closed for a moment. 'I think we got paid overtime, once upon a time, if I can remember three or four reorganizations ago. I save on food.'

'Can I . . . ?'

'I wouldn't mind a sandwich.'

By a kind of miracle I had both ham and acceptably fresh bread. There was even a slightly dry scrape of Dijon mustard. We sat in the kitchen eating ham sandwiches and drinking Scotch under the yellow eye of Mr Spock who was doing his statue act on top of the fridge.

'Tell me, then – has anything turned up?'

Paul shrugged. 'We traced your elusive colleague to an address in Kingston-upon-Thames, but he wasn't there. I've also been phoning round trying to find out where Marty Campbell is living at the moment. Somebody thought he might have a flat in the Barbican. I'll try to check in the morning. We spent a couple of hours taking the men who were in the van through our photos, but they don't admit to recognizing any of the people who jumped them.'

'What's next?'

'I'll catch Colbert at his shop as soon as he gets there tomorrow. I mean today. A thousand to one he'll tell us that his customer was Marty Campbell. The question is whether he can give us an address.'

'He may not be willing to,' I warned him, thinking again of all the blanks, all the questions that needed to be asked about Colbert's behaviour.

'I know. The other thing is to get a forensic team into that flat on Crouch Hill. They left the place in a rush, and they must have forgotten something. We should at least get fingerprints, and I'll be surprised if they aren't on record.'

I asked the question that had given me such anxiety for the past few hours. 'Is my father safe now, do you think?'

Paul looked at me seriously. 'I think you can assume that you're both safe enough. They've got what they wanted, and there's no reason for them to come back. How is your father taking it?'

'All right,' I said. 'Quite cheerful. He was trying to get rid of the thing, you know, and he has – not quite the way he intended, but at least it's gone. I don't believe we'll ever get it back.'

Barnabas had been very casual about the loss. I told myself he was being courageous, and that it was the best thing for him, in his health, to take it like that. But it left me feeling that there was something I didn't understand. Apparently he had persuaded himself there was something unreal about the whole episode. Almost as though the Shakespeare autograph had been just one of Davey's fictions. What seemed to console him was that he had made a copy facsimile of the writing, so that the variant version of the poem had not been lost. When I'd remarked, perhaps slightly heatedly, that it didn't seem to me to be much of a substitute for the real Shakespearean touch, and that it certainly wasn't worth the same money, he'd given me a lecture on the inflated values of antiques, and a moral sermon which came down more or less to the point that we ourselves had never had any special moral rights to the holograph. All very philosophical, no doubt, but we both knew that the people who had got the Plutarch were killers with a lot less right, either legal or moral, than we had. In fact, the whole thing made me mad.

'It is a terribly small, fragile thing, but we might be lucky,' Paul said hesitantly. It didn't sound as though he thought so.

'At least nobody else was killed.'

He echoed, 'At least nobody else was killed.' The sandwiches were finished. 'Dido?'

'Yes,' I said, 'I'd love you to stay.'

We slept and woke and slept again. When I woke for the last time it was because there was a bell warbling and a startled movement from beside me as Paul woke and delved under the pillows for his mobile phone. I lay on my back, eyes slitted against the daylight, watching him.

'Grant.'

He listened to a lengthy speech, but at the end of the first sentence he was rolling out of the bed. I retrieved the duvet and hid under it, paying attention. He had started to gather his clothes with one hand, still listening. After a long time, he said, 'Stay there and keep an eye on the place. I'll pick up the warrant. What time is it? It'll be ready by now. Say half an hour.'

He switched off and began to dress.

'What is it?'

He looked at me for the first time, bent over, and kissed my forehead. 'That was my man down in Bloomsbury. He says some old girl turned up with a key just after he arrived, and opened up.'

I considered. 'That's Mrs Wigginton, I expect. She's part-time. Doesn't know anything about books, but helps out weekends and when Colbert is away: takes money, writes invoices, and wraps parcels.'

'Wigginton? Right. Then he turned up a quarter of an hour later. Spoke to her, opened the post, fussed around a bit. Looked jumpy, my sergeant said, as though he was waiting for something. There was a phone call, which seemed to make him very anxious.'

I said, 'Your man seems to have seen a lot. Where on earth was he?'

'Coffee shop across the road, having his breakfast, with binoculars.'

'Oh,' I said. 'I know it.'

'There was an argument of sorts. Then he made a phone call himself, even shorter but a bigger argument. Then he had a word with Mrs Whatsit and left in a hurry.'

'Where to?'

'She said he told her that he was going to be out all day, and that she should open up tomorrow morning too, unless she heard from him.'

I propped myself up against the pillows. 'Is your man following him?'

'Following? No, of course not. What we need just now is to have a close look at the shop, especially his paperwork, customer lists, anything that might tell us how he's involved with Campbell – assuming that he is. I prefer talking to awkward witnesses after I have some kind of facts under my belt: it makes life easier. For me, I mean. Last night I arranged to get a warrant to search the place, just in case I needed it. I told them I was expecting to find evidence relating to Professor Warren's murder. I'll go and get on with it now.'

He kissed me again, struggled crookedly into his jacket, and flung open the bedroom door, tripping over the waiting cat as he headed toward the stairs.

I roused myself to yell, 'Phone me! Let me know what you find!'

A half-audible reassurance drifted up, interrupted by the slamming of the front door. Mr Spock arrived on my bed. He had spent the night in tactful exile – the tact had been mine – and was not in a good temper. Neither was I. Apparently being a policeman's partner consisted largely of being dropped abruptly at the wrong moment.

After a while I told myself that staying in bed wouldn't help, and set about the business of the morning. I had my own shop to open up and the rest of my life to get on with, and there was something about the past hours which had left me uneasy and restless.

Dido, that was a nice night.

Of course it was.

That was sex. You ought to get more of it.

You don't say!

You're feeling wonderful this morning.

I think I'm feeling tired this morning.

Don't whinge. The man is lovely. You're getting old.

Yes, lovely.

182

What's wrong with you?

Nothing's wrong with me. I don't know what's bugging me, all right?

Yes you do.

It's the morning after, that's all. Piss off.

I bathed, dressed, stroked and fed Spock apologetically, listened to the news from Bosnia, drank coffee, and finally tucked my restored telephone under my arm and trudged down to the shop. It wasn't until I was unlocking the door that I remembered about the stack of book cartons and folding shelves which was blocking the right-hand aisle. I still hadn't unpacked from the weekend fair.

Just for one fleeting moment I thought of backing out and running away to sea. Instead, for no very good reason except perhaps the lack of any credible alternative, I left the CLOSED sign up for the time being and began reshelving the books.

I worked quickly. If I was going to open up for lunchtime business, the aisle had to be cleared. I made my mind a blank and turned into a machine. It was not quite eleven when I finally shelved the last quarto and manoeuvred a tottering pile of empty cardboard boxes through the door and into the office. The last touch was to plug in the phone, and I stepped back then and ran my eyes over a shop which looked normal for the first time in a month. Just at that moment, normality seemed wonderful.

Time for a coffee before I opened for business? I assured myself that there was and went out, locking the door behind me without bothering to set the alarm. Another sign of normalcy. In celebration I decided that there was time to make a pot of real coffee, and I put the water on to boil, ground the beans, and opened a window a little wider. The late April sun poured on to my flat roof, and I stood for a moment to watch Mr Spock basking in its warmth, flattened and luxurious. The kettle began its first tentative hum before the water boiled. I wandered out into the sitting room yawning. And saw the red light blinking on the answering machine.

Paul? Damn it, he might at least have tried the downstairs phone and had a quick word, even if he hadn't found anything at Heritage. Didn't the man understand that I'd be waiting to hear?

I rewound the tape, gradually realizing that it was an unusually long message, and started it playing.

And the voice after all was my father's.

25

Twist

The message needed two hearings, and still it made no sense.

Dido? Good morning. Will you listen to this carefully, please, and do EXACTLY what I ask you. It's eight o'clock. I'm waiting for the post to arrive. It will contain the Plutarch. I'll explain later. As soon as it arrives, I am going to take it to show to somebody. I discussed this with Allen Ferrars yesterday, and he agrees that this is best in the short term, although the book will probably have to go over to the Folger if first impressions are that it's authentic. Clear so far, I trust? Now, I want you to come over here at about ten thirty.

I looked at my wristwatch. I was late.

Assuming everything goes to plan, I won't be here. Just let yourself in and have a look around. I'll leave you a note. I expect, knowing you, that you'll probably want to join me.

I probably would, at that. *Or was he in fact asking me to follow? Barnabas? What are you up to?*

From some kind of obscure feeling that I'd better preserve the message, I left the machine switched off and rang the station. After the usual three-minute wait, somebody informed me that DI Grant had left. I tried his

185

mobile without any result. Stopping long enough to peer at my bloodshot eyes in the bathroom mirror and reflect that I was incubating a headache and another bout of indigestion, I flung aspirin, Alka-Seltzer and my hairbrush into my bag, grabbed keys and mobile, and ran. I gave a moment's thrill to a van driver by rushing across the road to the Volvo without looking both ways first. Taking the experience to heart, I set off towards Crouch Hill at a more sober pace. I was fifty minutes late by the time I drew up to the kerb outside my father's house.

The mobile rang. I slammed the car door and leaned on the garden wall. 'Yes?'

'Hi.' This time it was Paul. 'Sorry I didn't get back to you, but something has come up. Your father isn't answering his phone, so you'll have to help me if you can.'

Confusion. 'What?'

'Your father said Professor Warren always carried a briefcase around with him.'

I straightened up. 'You've found it?'

'An old-fashioned brown leather case, with a big computer print-out of book titles headed "Graduate Research Library" – ring a bell?'

I felt sick. 'That's his. Where did it turn up?'

'In the shop. Tucked away in a dark corner under a table in the office . . . Hello?'

'I'm still here,' I said hastily through the buzzing in my ears. 'I . . . I must have almost stumbled over it. I'm glad that I didn't see it.'

'You're right – it was best not to touch it.'

That was not what I'd meant.

'We're doing a hard search now. If he was killed here we'll find something – a spot of blood, a hair – there's always something. I think it must have happened here, because it's the obvious explanation for the briefcase.'

'Why wouldn't they get rid of it?'

'I don't think they noticed it. It was pushed well back out of sight.'

I leaned even harder on the Volvo. 'Do you mean that *Colbert* killed him?'

'We'll have to ask him. But if he didn't, then he damned well knows who did.'

After a moment, the only thing I could think to say was, 'This is horrible.'

'Yes. Look . . . I'll keep you informed.'

I said thank you. Then I switched off. Afterwards, I remembered that originally it was I who had phoned him, and that there had been a reason for it, but I felt too sick to ring back. I didn't even want to think about DI Grant, Heritage Books, or murder: finding out what Barnabas was up to was about as much as I could manage just now. I breathed deeply until I knew that I'd make it the few steps to the flat, and let myself in with my set of keys.

Of course, he wasn't there.

The message had said to look around. A padded envelope lay opened on the desk, with a Recorded Delivery label on it; it was addressed to Barnabas in his own handwriting, and it was big enough for the Plutarch, so I had no doubt what it had held. I held it up to the window for a closer look. The faint postmark said it had been mailed in Crouch End the day before.

After a moment, I stopped laughing long enough to work out what he'd done.

The famous stolen parcel had been a decoy: one of his own seventeenth-century books probably – he owned quite a few – or maybe even another one from the Ireland Collection, perhaps one with Samuel's book plate temptingly displayed in it. Either would have been enough to fool the hijackers, if not an expert.

The old stories popped into my head, the ones my father used to tell Pat and me about his intelligence work during the war. When you cracked an enemy code, you had to make sure they didn't find out, so that you could both intercept their plans and feed them false information in return. You had to be tactful, because if they suspected the truth you lost your advantage, and maybe they twisted things around and fed you the false information instead, and led you to disaster.

Barnabas had worked in Signals Intelligence during the war. He'd really enjoyed himself. He would never forget the old tactics.

So he had used his telephone as a channel of communications with the enemy. So long as they didn't know he knew about them, he could feed them anything. He told them that the Shakespeare autograph was leaving our possession, and they'd believed it and hijacked the security van. With their attention distracted, my crafty old father had calmly inveigled Paul Grant and me into escorting the real thing to the post office, where I had unknowingly watched him post it back to himself for safety. No wonder he had been so unworried by the theft.

The trouble was, as I seemed to recall, the need for secrecy meant you could never be certain who was misleading whom. Also, you could never do anything that might tell the enemy you were on to them. We were so busy making sure the Germans didn't realize we'd cracked their code – Enigma, it was called – that when we learned they planned to bomb Coventry we couldn't do anything about evacuating the city. Because then of course they would have changed it. I seemed to recall that a lot of civilians had been allowed to die because of that. They claimed that it was justified because it meant we won the war.

Maybe, this time, it would work. So, Barnabas: what did you do next?

He was taking the real book to show it to somebody. Not Allen Ferrars, obviously. It had to be somebody much bigger than that: a scholar, an authority on Shakespeare so eminent that his word would be credible even in this incredible situation. Was I supposed to guess?

No – I was supposed to find a note. I examined the desk. The papers had been put away; nothing there was of special interest. The box that held the remainder of the Ireland Collection seemed the other obvious place, but there was no note inside. If anything was in the kitchen, it had been put out of sight, which seemed unreasonable. The bathroom proved equally tidy and unhelpful.

In the middle of Barnabas's neatly made bed sat his old yellow leather suitcase with an envelope centred on the lid. I tore it open, fumbled with the sheet of paper inside, and unfolded a long paragraph of Barnabas's cramped handwriting.

My dear . . .
By this time you will have realized that I'm not coming back there today. While the coast is clear, I'm taking it up to Oxford to ask Tullett . . .

I sat down with a bounce on the edge of the double bed.

. . . ask Tullett to have a look at it. There is no one else whose judgment I'd trust in these overly dramatic circumstances. I mean about Shakespearean material, of course; he was and remains hopeless with the earlier stuff. If he reckons it is authentic, then the next step as you know will be to send it straight over to Washington.

Or take it, perhaps? I am catching the next train, and suspect that you'd insist on following me, so will you save me the trouble and bring along the little case? I shall probably have to stay up overnight. You'll know where I'm staying, of course, and if you decide that you can't make it up there, perhaps you'd just give a ring and leave a message so I shan't be worried, and I shall be back some time tomorrow. Be careful.   B.

Suppressing my natural impulse to throw his note and his overnight case across the room, I redialled Paul's mobile. For once, he answered before I could fret.

I said, 'Listen to this one,' and told him. Even read him the whole message.

There was one of those things which are traditionally described as 'an eloquent silence'.

'I'd better go after him,' I said quickly. 'He shouldn't be left carting that . . . that thing about on his own.'

'I suppose so.' Paul sounded cold. 'When you catch him, I wish you'd section him. Or maybe send him off to Washington out of my way. Why Washington? Is he going to take over the White House?'

I started to explain about the Folger Library, but he broke in.

'Don't you realize it's possible that Colbert is following him?'

I hadn't. Damn it! 'It has to be a coincidence. Doesn't it? His absence?'

'No. Well . . . possibly, but no. I'm thinking about the phone call that Colbert received. Who could have told him, at nine in the morning, that your father was packing a suitcase to go away?'

I said loudly, 'Nobody. Could they?'

'Well . . . I suppose, theoretically, they might have had someone watching his flat because they'd discovered that they hadn't got the real thing and were wondering whether he still had it. When he went out carrying a parcel . . .'

' . . . or a briefcase . . .'

' . . . they would have followed him. There'd be no problem, at Paddington, finding out where he was going. Presumably Colbert was told to go with him, or after him at the very least.'

My indigestion kicked into action. 'Colbert? Last night, when he wasn't at home, he must have gone to check the book they stole. He would almost certainly have worked out that it was wrong – valueless. He had the whole night to examine it.' If it had been me, I couldn't have waited an hour to see all that fame, all that money . . . 'Paul, I'm going straight to Oxford.'

'I don't suppose you'd listen to reason?'

I told him that this didn't seem the moment to start doing that.

'All right. I'll meet you in Oxford. Where will I find you?'

'I'll be looking for him. There are only two places he'd think of staying: his old college – Queen's, in the High Street, in one of the guest rooms – or the Randolph Hotel if Queen's is full.'

'I'll leave as soon as I can get hold of a police car. I can make better time in that. Look for a message at the hotel reception, or with the college. And I'll ring through to Oxford CID as I go and warn them to expect trouble.'

'I wish you were coming with me,' I said, and switched off, because there was nothing to be done about that.

I stopped to swallow two aspirins and, for good measure, brushed my hair in preparation for the fray. It was just after noon as I pulled away from the kerb, and I calculated that Barnabas must have arrived by now wherever he was going. At least the traffic shouldn't be too heavy at this time of day, and barring road works I might get into central Oxford in ninety minutes. I headed the Volvo towards the Westway and the M40 to see just how far my luck could be pushed.

26

Going In

Once past the heavy traffic heading towards the M25, I allowed myself to start thinking again about Barnabas, carrying the perilous Plutarch and accompanied by thugs.

It wasn't real thinking. Worrying – that's the correct description.

I put my foot down until the Volvo slowed to a crawl on the long rise up to High Wycombe, reminding me that I still hadn't arranged the car's overdue service; but over the crest of the Chilterns, the rest of the trip was quick.

I'd decided to take the A40 into the city. It meant a long drive through built-up areas, but would take me straight past Queen's and might save a minute or two in the end – if things worked out that way. Once past the shops, and the red light at the Headington crossroads, I made satisfactory time until the cars creeping down St Clement's forced me into second gear.

I used my mobile to phone as I drove. On my third attempt, I'd persuaded somebody to answer the phone in the porter's lodge at Queen's. No, madam, we have not seen Professor Hoare today and I do not believe that he has booked in to stay. Oh yes, madam, I would certainly recognize the professor, as I have worked here for seventeen years. Of course I will be glad to give the professor a message. I suppressed temptation and merely said I would try again later.

At Christ Church, Professor Tullett's base, another voice with identical intonations informed me that Professor Tullett was not there, and not expected, and that the speaker would of course be glad to give the professor a message if he did return unexpectedly . . .

My problem was imagining what message would cover the situation. '*If my father turns up, please take his book away from him, tie him up so that he can't hurt himself, and throw the book out the window*'? I opted for tact and left instead the simple statement that I was just arriving in Oxford to meet my father who was, I believed, intending to visit Professor Tullett, and I would ring back in an hour. Even as I did so, the Volvo was progressing at last over Magdalen Bridge and into the old city.

I turned into Longwall and surrendered myself to the peculiar system of filters and diversions with which Oxford struggles to pour twentieth-century traffic through its mediaeval core. After a quarter-hour's crawl around the Parks, and a couple of painful turns, I abandoned the car in St Giles, hoisted my father's overnight bag out of the passenger seat, and began to trudge towards the Martyr's Memorial.

Now – that felt appropriate.

My goal, however, was the Randolph Hotel on the corner of Beaumont Street – a yellow-brick pile built in the style that I always think of as Victorian-Baronial. When we used to live in Oxford, my father bought me an elegant tea there at the end of every school term. I suspected that his real intention had always been to treat himself to the Randolph tonight, and hang the expense.

The main door was flung open in front of my nose by a porter in a black suit whose manner suggested that he believed me to be at least a lady, and probably a marchioness. He was, obviously, a skilled worker. I sailed in trying to look like an absolute duchess, and stopped.

The lobby swirled with tourists, and the clothes and voices around me were mostly American. I'd hoped to find Paul Grant lurking there with a little fighting circle of plain-clothes detectives, but if any police were in attendance, they were keeping a very low profile. There was certainly no sign of Paul among the armchairs, mirrors, flowers and bodies.

A second porter, seeing me with Barnabas's ancient case, jumped to the obvious conclusion, snatched it from my hand, and swept me over to the Gothic-style reception desk. An equally smooth thin man behind it gave an impression of a courtly bow and wondered whether he could help me.

I repeated my story: 'I'm here to meet my father. If Professor Hoare has booked in already . . .'

The impression of a bow froze, and I caught a speculative look that told me I'd come to the right place.

'May I ask who is enquiring?'

I told him that I was the one who was doing the enquiring, and was puzzled for a moment to see him consult a scrap of paper on the desk. Curiosity gave way to sheer bewilderment when I craned my neck and caught a glimpse of my own face – a photo, taken at the wedding reception, of me cutting the cake and simpering sideways at Davey's profile. Barnabas must have found it in his billfold. It goes without saying that I hadn't seen or thought of that image for a very long time.

But I was being identified.

Evidently I resembled myself. The bow turned into a knowing beam, and the thin man grew confidential. 'Professor Hoare is resting in his room, room 108. He asked me to let you have the second key.' It was produced and pushed across the desk. 'He has booked you into room 219. I also have a note for you. The porter will take you up now, if you are ready.' Another key was produced and handed to the porter, and an envelope to me. 'There's no need to sign the register. Your father has taken care of everything.'

Booked in, was I? I'd walked into somebody else's scenario, but swallowed a protest and trotted after the swift-moving porter and my father's case. I hoped Barnabas was intending to pay, because I seriously doubted that I could afford the Randolph this month. On the whole, working booksellers can't, though I had stayed once when the Association had negotiated special room rates for a book fair at the hotel. (Even the Randolph makes some concessions to modern life.) I turned to face forward just as the lift doors were closing.

I looked back towards the main entrance just in time to see Marty Campbell step in from the street. He was about fifteen feet away, and looking in another direction, but I ducked. I had an impression that he was not alone. They probably hadn't noticed me.

By the time the lift had reached the second floor, I had the beginnings of a plan. The first thing was to get rid of the porter. I pressed forward on his heels, and we arrived slightly breathlessly at 219. He unlocked the room and made a valiant attempt to usher me inside – I got a quick impression of cream paint, dark carpet and cream-coloured furniture – and demonstrate the light switches and other such pleasures, so I pressed too much money into his hand and more or less bundled him out. Then I flung myself on the bedside telephone and dialled 108. I was expecting anything, but all that happened was that Barnabas's voice said, 'Hello?'

'I'm here. In my room. I'm coming down to you now. Listen, Marty Campbell just came into the lobby . . .'

My father's voice became fussy and precise. 'Have you actually read the order?'

My eye fell on the unopened envelope. Did he mean that? 'No,' I said.

'I thought not. Room service. I would prefer to have Earl Grey, assuming that you haven't run out. Can you bring it in about fifteen minutes, please?'

For a moment I was confused. Then I realized that 'Room service' hadn't been spoken to me, but to somebody who was with him, somebody demanding an explanation for the phone call.

I found that I could still speak. 'Are you in danger?'

'No, not at all.' If anything, he sounded amused. 'And I would prefer lemon with that tea.'

Right. 'I'll read your note first. Can I ring back then?'

'Not really.'

'I'll phone the police.'

'That won't be necessary, thank you.'

The telephone clicked and went dead. I turned cold. Or maybe I'd gone cold a few minutes earlier.

I ripped open the hotel envelope. There was no form of address this time, and the words straggled with the writer's hastiness.

Dan Colbert was at the station. Must have followed me. He pretended he was surprised. Tried to get rid of him by doing some telephoning, but he wouldn't leave. Dropped me off by taxi, so will presumably be back shortly. I can and will deal with this. Don't worry – they have no reason to do me any harm, rather the reverse. It's important that you stay in your room with the door locked. Hang on to my bag until I contact you, and make no attempt to bring it to my room. Stay in your room.

The last line had been underscored so violently that his pen had pierced the paper.

I would have thought it through if I'd had the time, but time had just run out.

194

An Oxford phone book sat in the bottom of the bedside stand. I found the number of the police station, dialled, remembered that I would need an outside line, dialled again, and asked for the CID in a voice so urgently authoritative that I was put through at once.

'DI Morrow.' It was a woman's voice.

'My name is Dido Hoare. Have you been contacted by DI Grant from Islington, London?'

The voice became urgent. 'Miss Hoare, I know who you are. Inspector Grant has just left here with two of our men. They're going to the Randolph Hotel. There was a message from the hotel desk to say that one of their guests, your father I think, had asked for assistance. Where are you?'

I gave her my room number. 'If they're on their way, then I'll go down to the lobby to meet them,' I said.

She was speaking when I hung up, but I couldn't help it: I needed to know what was going on, and it looked as though nobody except Barnabas himself would have answers. I pounded a fist against my knee. Think!

Barnabas had been delivered to the hotel by Dan Colbert, who'd then gone to get Campbell. They'd known about my father's movements. Colbert must have followed him on to the train. Presumably he'd let Campbell know where they were heading, and had been instructed to stick to him until Campbell arrived. My Volvo wasn't the only car to go blazing up the motorway that day.

But my father had seen what was happening, and taken steps to keep me out of the way, before Colbert could bring in reinforcements. Barnabas had also managed to call for help. Why on earth hadn't he just left the hotel while he had the chance?

Leaving that practical question to one side, I opened my door far enough to look out. The only person in sight was a maid who was harmlessly wheeling a trolley towards the end of the corridor, so I slipped outside and made sure that the lock caught behind me.

Wait a minute: think. There was a reason why he hadn't fled: he *intended* to talk to them. He was using the book as bait and making sure that both Colbert and Campbell would be caught in the act of trying to steal it. He must have believed he could provide Paul Grant with some kind of evidence against them. It would be just like my father to decide that this was the only way to get rid of our problem; it matched everything else he'd done through all this crazy business.

Instead of going along to the lifts, which they might be watching, I found some service stairs through a door at the far end of the hallway. It was two double flights to the ground floor, and I flung myself down them, hanging on to the rail, and burst into a carpeted corridor which turned at a right angle towards the lobby. I trotted past a bar, ran into a bunch of the Americans who apologized vaguely, and hesitated near the lifts. The lobby was not very big, and it was getting crowded. I searched again among the gathering bodies for a familiar tall figure, and wondered what to do about the fact that nobody appeared to know anything about the drama on the first floor. It all looked so normal that I groaned with sheer helplessness.

A hand gripped my arm bruisingly from behind and I was pulled backward into a little alcove with a public telephone.

'Paul! Oh, thank God. Barnabas . . .'

'All right, I know.'

'But you *don't*,' I stammered. 'Marty Campbell got here ten minutes ago. Probably Colbert is here too, though I didn't see him. I know that they're in my father's room, because he spoke to somebody when I rang him there, and he couldn't talk to me.'

Paul shook his head impatiently. 'I know. Colbert, Campbell and two of Campbell's thugs are in there with your father. One of the local detectives got into staff uniform and let himself in with a couple of clean towels. Your father is all right. No, *listen*! He's talking to them. I'd warned our constable to be sure that your father didn't seem distressed. He couldn't stay, of course, but he said your father looked fine and they all seemed perfectly friendly.'

'Well, why don't you go in and arrest them?' I howled.

Grant put a hand over my mouth. 'Because Campbell's men are usually armed, if you must know, and we aren't – yet. Anyway, I don't want to risk a shooting here. There are too many people around, not to mention Barnabas. We're watching the lifts and the stairs, and waiting for more units. We'll have the hotel sealed off in ten minutes. When it's secure, I'll phone up to the room and talk to Campbell. If a pro like Campbell knows he's boxed in, he'll be sensible.'

'Paul, can I point out to you that if they have guns, they also have a hostage? What makes you think they'll give up?'

'They'll give up because it won't pay them to do anything else.' He had gone vocationally deaf.

'They've already killed two people! And you think they'll just blush and say, "Sorry"?'

Paul flushed. 'I don't have time to talk criminal psychology with you, I'm trying to get a job done and keep Barnabas safe. Listen, I want you to go back to your room and stay there. I'll call you when it's all over. We'll argue about it then.'

He pulled me forward to the lift, watched while I got in, and punched the button for my floor before pulling back. I didn't say, My father has a bad heart, he's an old man, I know he's going to be killed now by his heart if not by one of their damned bullets. I turned as the doors were closing, and caught a glimpse of his face, preoccupied, just waiting to make sure that I did as I was told.

When the lift stopped and the doors opened, I pressed the button for the first floor. That corridor was deserted and silent except for the noises drifting up the staircase from the reception desk. If there had been any sign of the police it might have been different, but I crossed the dark red carpet without stopping to think. Everything felt unreal.

The door of room 108 was closed and I couldn't hear anything through the thickness of the wood. It was too risky to use the key, so I rapped on it sharply before my nerve went. 'Barnabas, it's Dido! Can you let me in?'

The ensuing silence seemed so long that I started to wonder whether they had killed him already and gone. I stepped back. But the door opened then and Colbert stood back to let me walk inside.

27

Supping with the Devil

I heard the door close behind me, but I was too busy checking the room to worry about it. Paul had been right: Marty Campbell was watching me with an expression that revealed absolutely nothing. Colbert, behind me, was muttering some kind of protest. Barnabas looked up from an armchair beside the coffee table. His face betrayed exasperation. That left two strangers, one sitting beside Campbell and one lounging against the wall – I put them down as Campbell's minders. Barnabas and I were rather outnumbered.

'Dido! For just once in your life, you might have . . . Well, never mind. I should have known.'

'Are you all right?' I asked humbly. But I could see that, for some incomprehensible reason, he was. Certainly he was quite calm. Unlike me.

I opened my mouth and realized that I didn't have anything to say.

'Would you sit down, Miss Hoare?' That was Campbell, upright on the chair by the desk which he'd turned around to face the room. He was wearing an Armani suit; his black shoes gleamed and his white hair could have come straight from the hotel barber shop.

'Dan, give Miss Hoare your chair. You can squat on the bed.'

All right, if we were being polite . . . 'It's scarcely worth it,' I said. 'I've come to take my father down to the lobby before things get out of hand. I don't care what you people do about it, but I really think that you ought to leave the hotel quickly.'

Campbell smiled slightly. 'You've called the police?'

I said grimly, 'I didn't have to. Barnabas, will you come?'

'Not for one minute, please.'

It was a new voice, heavily accented: something from the eastern edges of Europe but overlaid with American. One of Campbell's thugs. I looked at the bear-like man who was overflowing the second armchair, and revised the judgment. Not one of Campbell's thugs.

He was a middle-aged man with a square, heavily lined face and bright blue eyes under a thatch of spiky iron-grey hair, badly cut. He sat quietly, powerfully relaxed, his broad workman's hands lying easily on the arms of his chair and his short legs stretched out comfortably.

A thug, but not Marty's.

Barnabas said, 'This is Mr Grigor Bakatin, a Russian gentleman. He is the one who wants to purchase our Shakespeare autograph. Mr Bakatin, my daughter Dido.'

I was registering the word 'purchase' as the broad face shifted suddenly into a grimace that was obviously meant to express friendliness. It didn't fool anybody. Bakatin heaved himself to his feet, grabbed my right hand so quickly that I hadn't the chance to flinch, and bowed astonishingly over it. The hand that had shot out to take mine was topped by a gold Cartier wristwatch, as I couldn't help noticing.

'Miss Hoare, I am delighted making your acquaintance. Please to take my chair. We can talk.'

'Sit down, Dido,' said Barnabas grimly.

I sat in a kind of dream in which sheer terror struggled with curiosity. 'What's happening?'

'We're negotiating,' Barnabas said outrageously. I took a wobbly breath. Right: he was trying to string them along until help arrived. I was in favour of that strategy. Barnabas explained chattily, 'As I understand it, Mr Campbell owes Mr Bakatin for something . . . a business deal.' My father's voice skated lightly over the phrase, declining to make any judgments. No matter how carefully I looked, his face was as calm and expressionless as Campbell's. I suppressed a squeak of sheer panic. 'Mr Campbell has offered to arrange the purchase of our, um, Shakespeare item on Mr Bakatin's behalf.'

Keep them talking . . . . 'What about the Japanese customer?' I asked.

'A figment of somebody's imagination,' Barnabas said drily. 'It's good to get these confusions cleared up so that we all know where we stand.'

I said, 'What do you mean, "purchase"?'

Bakatin broke into a slow, confident grin. 'I am buyink. Or to speak more precisely, Mr Campbell is buyink on my behalf. Shakespeare . . . we Russians love your Shakespeare. He was English with a Russian soul. It is my great privilege to own a poem written by the hand of a great spirit. The professor has explained everything about this, how it was discovered by a great lover of Shakespeare two hundred years ago, how it was lost . . . It is a romantic story. I will take the book, but I will send photographs to the professor, X-rays, everything he needs, and he will publish about the poem in his academic publications. It will be my privilege.'

'It will also guarantee that the document is genuine and that you have a proper title to it – just in case you were ever to wish to sell it for its full value,' Barnabas added in the careful tones of somebody who has been saying the same thing over and over in the hope that everybody will understand his full meaning.

I began to grasp what was going on and opened my mouth in outrage. And closed it again because I suddenly saw that the big man was sincere about one thing: whatever he was, he really loved our Shakespeare.

Barnabas was watching me closely, but it was Campbell who spoke, shaking his head slightly as though his scalp itched. 'It will make Mr Bakatin very happy.' He looked at me with the first flicker of an expression which I couldn't quite identify. And wasn't sure that I wanted to. 'Your father is right – I owe him.'

I said, 'I guess you must owe him a lot. Mr Bakatin, if you don't mind my asking – who are you? You speak very good English. It sounds as though you've lived in the United States?'

Bakatin looked at me with a kind of instinctive rage that changed, in a flicker, into unlikely laughter. 'I am business man now. The new Russia. Before I was KGB, and yes, you are right, I was for some years at the Washington Embassy.'

I thought, So this is the new world. Businessman, Mafia, secret service thug, and lover of Shakespeare . . .

Barnabas said, 'Dido, would you mind getting the book and bringing it here.'

I mimed bewilderment.

Bakatin misunderstood. He leaned over me and grasped my hand earnestly, looking into my eyes. 'You will get your money. Two million dollars. You may have either dollars or Deutschmarks, only tell me. You will get the money, on my honour, cash.'

From beyond the man's bulk, Barnabas said, 'I believe you. Either of those currencies will be perfectly acceptable. Dido . . .'

'*Barnabas . . .*'

'The Plutarch is in the little case you brought with you.'

I staggered mentally and told myself not even to think about what might have happened. And then I heard a voice that sounded like mine say quietly, 'There is just one little matter that all of you are forgetting, and that's two men being dead, and one of them was Davey, who was a fool and never really hurt anybody, and one of them was Job Warren, who was a lovely old man . . .' The sentence ended in a gasp as I heard what I'd been babbling and went cold and stopped. And found myself crying for Davey, for Job Warren, for me.

Behind a curtain of tears, Barnabas was springing up and rushing forward; but the big Russian arrived before him. I was swept up into the bear's grasp, and there was a kind of roaring whisper: 'Of course, of course, you must cry, but not now.'

Barnabas cut through: 'Dido! Go now!'

Bakatin let go. The ghost of a much quieter American-Russian whisper said, 'It is all right. You will find out.' I thought, a moment later, that I must have imagined it.

'Go now, Dido.' That was Barnabas again.

'I can't leave you here with them!'

'Don't be ridiculous. What's going to happen to me?'

Campbell was beginning to seethe with frustration. It wasn't a happy sight. 'Is the thing in your room? Colbert, you'd better go with Miss Hoare and get it. Don't hang about, there's no time left.'

He nodded at the fourth man in the room, the one who'd been lounging against the bathroom door frame. I saw him palm a mobile phone and begin to mutter into it.

No time . . . that was my danger and also my advantage. I kicked my paralysed brain into action. I'd stopped crying for the moment, but my face was wet.

'All right, Barnabas, I'll do it, Listen, Dan comes with me to get the book, but the rest of you leave this room when we do. My father must be left alone. As soon as he locks the door behind us, then I'll go with Colbert and give him the book. It's up to you how you get it out of the hotel.'

Colbert – the least of evils, I was thinking. I had despised Dan Colbert for a long time.

There was a universal hesitation.

I screamed, 'There's no time for anything else! Don't you know that there are police in the hotel already?'

Campbell said, 'Do it! You know where we'll be. Miss Hoare, you do understand that if you do anything stupid you'll both hear from me, don't you!' His face was almost as white as his hair.

I didn't bother to answer. The five of us tumbled out of the room into the corridor which was still miraculously deserted. I wondered distractedly whether the police had cleared it, whether they were lurking just out of sight, whether momentarily there would be a burst of gunfire and I would be dead. I wondered whether it would hurt. I caught a last glimpse of Barnabas's anxious face and said, 'Close the door. Don't worry, I'll give them the book. It's a deal, all right?'

I turned away and heard the door slam behind me and the chain rattling into its socket. Campbell, Bakatin and their minder turned to the right, and I deduced that I wasn't the only one using the service stairs that night. Whether they had found some way out there, past the police, I neither knew nor cared.

Colbert grabbed my wrist and tried to pull me towards the lift. His hand was cold with sweat, and his face distorted in a grin of hatred, fear, rage. The face of Job Warren's killer. I kicked, and he let out a shriek as my heel connected with his shin. The sound had the effect of snapping me into a kind of fearless excitement. I snarled at him, 'Keep your hands off me and come on. Don't hang about. If you want the book, you have about one minute to get it and get away. Do you understand?'

For a moment I thought he had gone mad. He was grinding his teeth and fumbling in a coat pocket. I thought, icily, *He has a knife* . . . And then I realized what I should have seen before: Colbert wanted me dead, me and Barnabas both, because our story meant the end of Dan Colbert the antiquarian book dealer, the end of Heritage Books. A life for a life . . .

My voice came from a long way off, saying, 'If you don't want Marty Campbell to skin you alive, you'd better come and get that book.'

It was the most effective thing I could have said. Colbert blinked and regained control; his hand came into sight, empty. I was safe until I put the Shakespeare autograph into his hand. I turned my back on him, the way you do with a mad dog who will attack you for looking at him, and trotted to the lift doors to punch the button. The indicator, which said that the lift was on the ground floor, did not move.

'Stairs,' Colbert said behind me in a kind of strangled groan. We flung ourselves up them, past two middle-aged women who had given up on the lift and were wandering down to tea. On the second floor a porter was wheeling a luggage trolley away. I hissed at Colbert, and we marched briskly and, I hoped, inconspicuously in the other direction. I slid my key into the lock and flung the door wide because I expected to find the room packed with policemen. It should have been, but it wasn't.

The case was on the luggage rack where the porter had left it.

I whirled on Colbert. 'Stay at the door! Keep watch up and down the corridor – you don't want the police creeping up and cornering you here.' And I don't want you any closer to me than absolutely necessary.

Colbert agonized, but hung back in the doorway and followed my instructions, nearly dislocating his neck in the attempt to watch me and the lift doors at the same time.

Barnabas's case was unlocked. My heart thumped with horror: it had been left unguarded here for however long the business had taken – it felt like hours. I scrabbled among the striped pyjamas and clean underwear and touched a hard, rectangular object wrapped closely in a bath towel. Yanking it out, unwrapping the towel, I held up the old quarto in its disintegrating leather binding. Now what? Not stopping to think, I opened the quarto at the familiar page. In the light from the overhead lamp you could just make out faded sepia scratchings. I carried it open to the door.

'Look, this is it: this page. You see?' I thrust it open into Colbert's hands, and watched his gaze slide from my face to the dim writing. Then I hit him in the stomach with both fists. Off balance, he gasped and staggered backwards.

I slammed the door. Leaned against it. Reminded myself not to faint until I could get the chain on. There was no air in the room, so I let myself slide down the slippery surface of the heavy, sheltering mahogany until I was on the carpet, leaning against the wall.

The telephone on the bedside table began to ring.

28

Roundabouts

We were in no state to patronize the dining room, so room service had provided not merely Barnabas's long-delayed pot of Earl Grey tea, but a great silver salver mounded with assorted triangular sandwiches of smoked salmon and rare roast beef, as well as champagne, flutes and an ice bucket.

Barnabas sat upright in one of the big stuffed armchairs with the food spread on the coffee table in front of him. Even after everything that had happened, he seemed to be full of a triumphant energy. I slumped in the second armchair and swore I would never worry about his health again.

Paul faced us from the upright chair which had recently held Marty Campbell. He was both cheerful and preoccupied; his mobile phone was positioned on the table beside him.

We were on our second bottle of Krug. Barnabas had insisted. I'd calculated the cost of this snack, added it to the rate for my bedroom and this rather overwhelming be-fireplaced room in which Barnabas was ensconced, and considered protesting. On second thoughts, what did it matter? A couple of bottles of Krug weren't likely to make much difference to our financial ruin. I thought I began to understand the attitude of the jet-set ne'er-do-well who goes bankrupt in luxury: you would simply and rationally decide that you might just as well enjoy yourself before the bank sent in its bailiffs.

The champagne was making me drunk. 'It's the bubbles,' I remarked to nobody in particular.

The room telephone rang. Paul snatched at it, listened without comment, and hung up.

'For you?' asked Barnabas in a mild rebuke.

'Hospital. He's dead. They did what they could, but the car had gone right over him.'

My stomach lurched, and then I thought about it and realized that there was a despicable part of me that was relieved.

'What about the others?'

'There's no sign of the car.'

Barnabas said innocently, 'It was quite surprising, the way they got away.'

It had all been in the planning. A car had been waiting in the entrance to the hotel garage, the one that most people never think about because there is never enough space for you to park there. Campbell had left a driver sitting in a new Rolls-Royce, a car that had apparently looked too grand to be suspicious. Having received its passengers – Paul said they had doubled through the service door to the bar and out on to a fire escape over the ballroom – the car had emerged from the gateway, turned sedately to the left, and vanished without haste in a direction that would take it to the railway station, the by-pass, or anywhere else in the northern hemisphere.

Immediately after its departure, one of the porters saw the injured man lying where it had been parked. As Paul said, the car had been driven over Colbert. Though not, it seemed, over the Plutarch, of which there was no sign. Well, just as Colbert needed to get rid of Barnabas and me, so I suspected that Campbell was happy to rid himself of Dan. You couldn't see him having any further need for an antiquarian bookseller.

The staff had raised the alarm, police had converged – it had taken a little too long for the ambulance to get the few hundred yards from the Radcliffe Infirmary through the evening traffic in St Giles, but it probably hadn't mattered much in the end.

Even now, hours later, I kept remembering that treacherous, consoling, bear-like embrace and the whispered reassurance. I shivered, and finished my drink. It doesn't do to have any illusions about people like Bakatin: and no, Colbert's death wasn't my fault. NO! But I kept wondering whether I had accidentally negotiated it as a part of the deal.

I wasn't going to mourn him, but this was something else that would visit my dreams.

I held out my glass for a top-up.

'Did you say something?' I was aware of Paul staring at me speculatively.

Maybe I'd forgotten to tell him about Bakatin's whisper. Maybe I'd heard it wrong. What did it matter anyway? I said, 'I guess Colbert actually did kill Professor Warren.'

Paul shrugged and selected another sandwich. 'When your librarian turned up in his shop, he must have thought his luck was in. It was his chance to make sure that the Shakespeare stayed within reach. He may have attacked him on impulse, in a panic – and phoned Campbell. It sounds from your description of his behaviour as though he wouldn't have minded a throat-cutting – we'll be looking hard at the knife we found in his pocket, by the way. But he would have needed help getting the body out of the shop. They've found some prints on that big table in the basement of his shop: one of Campbell's people was certainly there recently, and I don't suppose he's a collector. Of course, Campbell and your Russian friend were bound to help him out, since they still needed him to identify the thing that Davey had been trying to sell them. But after today, they wouldn't risk having Colbert around any more. He was only their technical expert, and he was redundant as well as unreliable.'

Barnabas frowned. 'Unreliable?'

'Colbert would certainly have wound up telling us all about who ordered Davey's death. I know that type. He was no longer of any use to them, and Campbell would know we'd probably be able to pressure him into testifying against the rest of them. Amateurs are always dangerous.'

I didn't miss the glance he threw my way, and I didn't like the way he was labouring the point. Though when I had time to consider my behaviour that night, I'd probably be consumed with horror.

Barnabas said, 'That Russian may be difficult to catch.'

Paul laughed. He sounded bitter. 'Russian mafia. He's probably out of the country already, and if he is, we're all going to get a slap. He's not a nice man.'

Barnabas and I stared, and Barnabas asked the obvious question: 'You know about him?'

'My Superintendent got on to Interpol as soon as I gave them the name. Everybody knows him. He runs the Moscow office of an organization responsible for about half the drugs trade between Western Europe and South-east Asia.'

'Oh! So that's . . .'

Paul looked at me. 'What?'

I was thinking it through. 'Campbell said, "I owe him". There was some drugs shipment that went wrong, wasn't there . . . Perhaps Davey got involved. Perhaps he made a mistake. So he owed Campbell, and Campbell owed Bakatin . . .'

'If we'd caught them,' Grant said angrily, 'we'd be able to ask. But – well, we've told Heathrow to watch for the Russian, but I don't suppose it will do any good. He's probably crossing the channel already, heading for Brussels.'

'What about computers?' Barnabas demanded. Maybe he was drunk too. 'What about the marvels of modern science? They'll catch him at some border. A character. I almost liked him.'

'You,' I said, 'were positively cosying up to him. I still don't see what you were trying to do.'

Through the haze of tiredness and alcohol, I saw Barnabas watching me. He smiled a little. 'I was getting rid of them, of course. Forever. In the only way that seemed to me to be likely to be permanent.'

'But they've got it!'

Barnabas sighed. 'I'm well aware of the fact. Don't you understand? My whole scheme was to let them get it in circumstances that would make them think they'd won and would give them no motive whatsoever for harming anybody else. In fact, I was able to persuade Bakatin that not only was he getting a bargain, but his satisfaction depended on you and me remaining alive and cooperative.'

'But Barnabas!'

'What have they got?'

I said stubbornly, 'They've got . . . I don't know, perhaps a tremendous piece of English literary history. Shakespeare's personal copy of the book that gave him the plots of three or four plays. Shakespeare's own work, his handwriting . . .'

Barnabas sipped his champagne. I waited.

'Yes, they may. But shall I tell you what Allen Ferrars actually said to me? He said, "Nobody will authenticate that. Ever. It's fascinating, but there is no possible way of knowing whether the thing is what it seems to be. There is not enough authentic handwriting for a comparison, as you well know. You might perhaps manage to prove that the inscription is of the right period, give or take a few decades, but no modern scholar can ever be certain that Shakespeare wrote it himself, and no one in their right mind would risk their reputation on it. You will have to sell it to somebody who likes mysteries. If you want to know the truth, I suspect the work of a copyist, or even another forger – not William Henry Ireland, but someone twenty years before him. I would offer ten thousand for it, probably, if it passed closer examination."

'I realized he was right.' Barnabas got into his oratorical stride. 'In this mean tail-end of the twentieth century, when academics spend their working hours writing out departmental business plans and worrying whether they'll get their short-term contracts renewed – thank God I got out of it when I did – no one in his right mind would risk the ridicule of being found wrong about something like this.'

'Why were you so sure they wouldn't harm either of you?' Paul asked suddenly. I looked at him, but he had his eyes fixed stubbornly on the sandwich tray.

'When I explained to Mr Bakatin that he needed to have a document describing the provenance of the Plutarch, and that he needed me to give it to him and to be prepared to back up the story in public, he understood the point immediately. He may love Shakespeare, but I'm sure that he also loves the idea of owning something monumentally valuable. I used the analogy of the stolen painting, and he took the point. He may have personal experience of such things: he said something that made me wonder. That, of course, was why I calculated that it would be best to deal with him: he wouldn't dream of risking his only guarantee of the value of the manuscript.'

Barnabas amazes me.

'Will you really do a provenance?'

'And will they deliver the money?' Barnabas countered. He didn't fool me. There was a reckless gleam in his eye.

'How much is he supposed to be paying?' Paul asked soberly.

Barnabas said, 'Two million dollars.'

Paul laughed. He at least seemed to have no illusions about the Russian's promise.

'He was very convincing,' I heard myself say; 'he seemed to mean it.'

'Two million roubles, maybe.'

I wondered how close two million devalued roubles would be to ten thousand pounds.

'For a genuine piece of Shakespeare, of course, it wouldn't be enough,'

Barnabas sighed. 'I wonder whether I shouldn't have held out for more?'

'Who would buy it? Honestly, I mean – not like tonight.'

'The Americans, probably. It would go to auction, of course. I imagine that the Folger would bid for it, and no doubt an export licence would be refused, there would be a national appeal, and so forth. That is, of course, assuming that people did accept the thing for what it appears to be. Ultimately some library would buy it and keep it in the dark, in a locked, temperature-controlled, humidity-controlled case. If you were in Washington, or London, or wherever, and you had the right credentials, you could go and have a look at it.'

I could see Paul considering this.

Barnabas expanded. 'It's like a religious relic. Well . . . I wonder.'

We looked at each other, with the question hanging in the air between us.

Paul said, 'I'd better get off. It's late. Are you driving back to London in the morning? I'll be tidying things up and trying to square my Super tomorrow, unless I have to fly off to pick up some prisoners somewhere. Will you come and talk to me – officially – the day after? For the record.'

I looked at Paul. Barnabas looked at us both, cleared his throat, and said, 'I'm just going to the bathroom to wash my hands, if you'll excuse me.'

When he had shut himself in, I said, 'You could stay. Barnabas seems to have booked me into a double room.'

Paul was looking at the tray. 'I can't tonight. Look, there's something I've been shying off saying, but you probably knew that I'm married. It's been finished for a few months now. That's why I'm staying at my friend's place. But tomorrow is my daughter's birthday, and I said I'd get over to the house first thing in the morning with Gina's present.'

Why wasn't I surprised? I asked carefully, 'How old is your daughter?'

'Four.'

'I hope she has a happy birthday.' I hesitated, because this was delicate for us both. 'Are you thinking of trying to get back together?'

He reached for the Krug and divided the last of it between our glasses. 'I don't think so. Sometimes it's all right and sometimes it's impossible. I don't know what's going to happen.'

No, I thought, nobody ever does.

A little while after he'd left, Barnabas emerged and sent me off early to bed as though I were still a child.

29

And Swings

I was in the middle of writing a guarantee card number on the back of a cheque when the phone rang. Smiling professionally at my customer, I ignored it until I had returned his card and handed over the 1824 quarto edition of *British Poets*. My credit card bill had just arrived, and it had left me in no doubt that I was going to have to concentrate on selling books for a while.

Besides, it went on ringing until I got there and picked it up.

'Dido?' Barnabas's voice interrupted my greetings. I could hear panic. 'Can you come? Or maybe I should phone the police. Or the Army. I think they do it.'

I groaned. 'Hello. Stay there. I was just closing anyway.'

I didn't stop to set the alarm – it seemed less essential these days – but trotted straight to the Volvo, shouting, 'Get out of it!' to the dog I found inspecting a wheel. Highbury Corner was not, of course, clear. Sometimes I think that Highbury may defeat me – drive me away from London, or possibly England. Sometimes I dream of never seeing that roundabout again.

Barnabas met me at the door. There were two hectic red spots on his cheeks which I didn't like the look of. I said, 'Sit down. Calm down. What is it?'

'I am perfectly all right,' he lied.

'Have you taken your aspirin?'

'I took my aspirin last night. I shall take my aspirin again tonight. I think it's a bomb.'

For the first time in three weeks I felt that familiar thump of panic. 'Where? What's happened?'

'I'll show you,' he said, and towed me towards the bathroom, where he stood blocking the doorway. I peered around him. The bathtub was filled with water, and in the water was a parcel that looked like an overgrown shoe box wrapped in brown paper.

I gaped. 'Why would it be a bomb?'

'The doorbell rang, and when I went out that was sitting on the top step. It isn't stamped – it was delivered by hand. I must admit that I thought of Davey.' He hesitated. 'I begin to feel a little foolish. I may have panicked.'

'It must be safe now, anyway,' I said. I leaned over the tub and touched the box gingerly. It sat firmly on the bottom of the tub. Barnabas removed the plug and we contemplated the parcel as the water oozed out, tinged with the pale blue of running ink. His name and address were faded but still visible.

'Perhaps we ought to have a look before we phone for help,' he conceded.

I said drily, 'I think we should. Knowing our luck, it's probably a couple of valuable books that somebody wants to sell us.'

Barnabas grimaced and lifted the heavy, dripping parcel into the hand basin. The wrapping paper was soggy and fell away in lumps from a disintegrating cardboard box that claimed to hold jars of sun-dried tomatoes. Barnabas delicately lifted away a sodden lid.

He had been soaking tightly packed bundles of American bank notes.

After a very long moment Barnabas said, 'Ah. What a lot there is. They can't be real.'

I dug out one bundle. The paper band around it fell away, and I was left with a sodden, compacted handful of what seemed to be one-hundred-dollar bills. I peeled the top one away gingerly. The face of George Washington stared at me in a friendly kind of way beside small letters that assured me that this note was legal tender for all debts, public and private. I turned it over cautiously to the picture of Independence Hall. The thought struck me that these things would buy me quite a lot of independence. I couldn't explain to Barnabas why I was laughing.

Having lived and shopped in the States for several years, I was pretty familiar with the currency – though not necessarily with the higher denominations – and this looked and felt all right. Closely examined, the engraving was clean and sharp. The serial number of the note in my hand was different from the next one in the pile. They weren't even consecutive; apparently someone had kindly ensured that we were presented with used notes.

'Believe it or not,' I sighed, 'I think they're genuine. In fact, I'm sure they are. Oh, Barnabas . . .'

'If they are,' my father said hastily, 'the paper won't dissolve, the ink won't run. Perhaps you could dry them with the iron? Or . . . if we dry them flat they'll be quite all right. I don't think I've ever seen quite so much cash in one place at one time.'

He extracted a soggy note from the top of one bundle and smoothed it experimentally on to the bathroom mirror, where it stuck. 'There. It will loosen and fall off of its own accord as it dries.'

'You can fit two on to each tile in the room,' I suggested brightly. 'There's enough here to cover the walls. Art students do that kind of thing – they're called "installations".' I was probably a little hysterical.

Barnabas seemed amused. 'Bakatin, of course. We already knew that he believes in paying his debts.' That was too close to the thought of Dan Colbert's death. Barnabas coughed. 'Not just like this, of course; I assumed there'd be a postal order or something appropriately anonymous in an envelope with a first-class Russian stamp. Though I can see the attractions of the cash economy. No doubt he will write to me from Russia to ask for his authentic provenance. I shall compose an authoritative document, with footnotes and a bibliography, and you will pay some person with a computer to lay it out beautifully with typographical ornamentation and print it on parchment with a laser thing. It's the least we can do. Good Lord, I wonder how much there is?'

'Two million dollars?' I suggested. I pushed down the impulse to start laughing again at the impossibility, but I couldn't stop my hands shaking. When we had finished counting up and plastering on, I consulted the exchange rates in the newspaper. I'd been right. Well, actually it was close to two thousand dollars over. Maybe he was contributing to the bank's commission charges. We were richer by something like £1,282,052.

I didn't believe it yet, so we went to drink a pot of tea at the kitchen table, from where we could watch the bathroom door.

'I think,' he said after a long silence, 'that we should keep this money. You have sold a book – that's all.'

213

'It's dirty money,' I said. 'Drugs money. Blood money.'

Barnabas said mildly, 'I believe that most money is, taking the arms trade, Third World debt, oil pollution and factory farming into account. Of course, the tax bill will be horrendous. Well, if you want to give it all away, I shan't object. Do you want to donate it to charity, then?'

I closed my mouth and considered that question. I examined my poverty, Barnabas's state of health, the attitude of my invisible letter-writing bank manager, and the moral state of our culture. Also my own state, moral and physical. I even – to blow my own trumpet – briefly recalled Ilona Mitchell's current homelessness. It isn't so difficult to adjust to certain kinds of possibility. To a utilitarian approach. I'm not proud of it.

This was as good a time as any.

I said, 'Actually, Barnabas, I'm pregnant, and I've decided to keep the baby, so no, I don't want to give it away. Not all of it, anyway. What I want is to be a *rich* single parent.'

Barnabas had dropped his cup, which duly smashed. Tea splashed over our feet. After a while, sitting amid the wreckage, he said, 'I'm glad. I think. Dido, do you mind if I ask . . . Has he gone back to his wife?'

I'd told him about Paul. He hadn't spoken about it again until now.

'I presume he has. I'll probably be seeing him some time, because I understand that it's an off-again-on-again thing. That's what he told me. He can't get rid of the marriage and he can't keep it together.'

'You wouldn't marry him?'

I laughed. I wouldn't marry him. Paul Grant was quite definitely desirable, but I had no plans that seriously included him. Not at the moment. I said, 'I think you're going to have to be the man in her life. Or his.'

He looked at me closely. 'I suppose it *is* Paul's?'

I hesitated – though not from any doubt, because Paul was a responsible kind of person and we had always used protection. Besides, the dates weren't quite right. It wasn't a question of the fact, but of how I was intending to deal with it. Oh well. Head-on, as usual.

I said, 'I guess now that I've told you, I'd better phone Sally. I have a horrible feeling that she's always wanted to be a grandmother.'

Barnabas said, 'Good grief!'

In the silence, I heard the first drying bank notes fall off the tiles, rustling to the bathroom floor like autumn leaves.